PRIME FORCE

PRIME FORCE

Bob Langley

This first world edition published in Great Britain 1995 by
SEVERN HOUSE PUBLISHERS LTD of
9–15 High Street, Sutton, Surrey SM1 1DF.
First published in the USA 1995 by
SEVERN HOUSE PUBLISHERS INC of
425 Park Avenue, New York, NY 10022.

British Library Cataloguing in Publication Data
Langley, Bob
  Prime Force
  I. Title
  823.914 [F]

  ISBN 0-7278-4781-3

Typeset by Hewer Text Composition Services, Edinburgh.
Printed and bound in Great Britain by
Hartnolls Ltd, Bodmin, Cornwall.

TOMORROW

Berenger's palms felt sweaty as he strode along the corridor. Tension gathered in his stomach, sending tremors through his angular frame. The sensations surprised him for he was not a man who frightened easily. Among his colleagues he was known as "Mister Ice", an appendage he found both flattering and amusing, but it was hard to maintain an unflappable image on an occasion such as this.

Berenger was a member of the elite band of US Secret Service agents whose job it was to protect public figures from assassination. His protege tonight was the future candidate for the Vice-Presidency, Senator Arnold Huxley, who was about to be interviewed on the TV talk show *Prime Force*. For Berenger, the job was largely routine; he was accustomed to escorting dignitaries from all over the world and Senator Huxley, despite his controversial image, was not considered a serious risk. Berenger's real interest – though it embarrassed him to admit it – lay in the prospect, about to be realised, of meeting the show's charismatic host, Caroline Force. In barely eighteen months, the young Englishwoman's fearless, no-nonsense interviewing style had taken the country by storm. *Time* magazine had labelled her the most trusted woman in America and *Prime Force* was reputed to be the nation's top "talking heads" show.

Berenger did not consider himself an impressionable man; he was seldom awed by the people assigned to his care, but he had to admit that it was rare to encounter such beauty and intelligence in a single package. Men admired

Caroline Force for her looks, women admired her for her poise, journalists admired her for her insight.

His mouth felt dry as he paused outside her door. It was, he noticed, a perfectly ordinary door with little to distinguish it from the dozen or so others lining both sides of the passageway, except of course for her name printed in small, scarcely definable letters, and a cartoon sketch of a barracuda which some joker had stuck beneath it. He straightened his necktie before knocking.

"Please come in." Berenger recognized the familiar English accent.

The room was smaller than he'd expected, its cramped confines accentuated by a row of metal filing cabinets which took up almost a third of the floor space. Caroline Force was seated at her desk with two male associates. She was a tall girl, her figure slender but rounded in all the right places, and though her face was delicately sculpted, the eyes held a hint of tenacity that was difficult to ignore. They were green eyes, not lime green or emerald green but chameleon-like, ebbing and changing with the shifting influences of light and shade. Berenger thought she looked even more devastating off-screen that she did in front of the cameras.

"Can I help you?"

The voice, clipped, perfectly modulated, sent a tremor through his diaphragm. He cleared his throat. "Jake Berenger, Miss Force, US Secret Service. I'm head of the security contingent today. I just wanted to let you know that I'm around."

"That's kind of you, Mr Berenger. It's reassuring to hear that Senator Huxley's safety is in professional hands."

"Yes, ma'am."

He glanced at the two men seated in front of her desk. They did not look like executive types. Had he been asked to speculate on their professions, he would have labelled them Marines or Special Forces. They had muscular builds and tanned, aggressive faces. They stared at him coolly, their eyes neither friendly nor hostile.

He turned back to Caroline, his cheeks beginning to

flush. He felt embarrassed by what he was going to say but something inside him was urging him on. "I'd like you to know how much I enjoy your show, Miss Force. Usually, I don't go for that kind of stuff. I stick to sports most of the time, but the way you put those politicians in their places, I think you're the best thing we got on TV today."

"How kind of you, Mr Berenger. Thank you for telling me so."

She rose to her feet, glancing at her two associates. She looked tense, Berenger thought, and (was he imagining things?) strangely imploring. Years of police work had made him sensitive to the subtle messages of the human body. Caroline Force was frightened; he knew it as surely as he knew his own name.

One of the men with her gently took her arm. "I think we'd better be getting down to the studio, Miss Force. The Senator should be arriving at any moment now."

A veil came over her eyes and she held out her hand. "Thank you for calling, Mr Berenger. If I need anything, I'll certainly contact you."

"That's what I'm here for, ma'am."

He was thoughtful as he watched her set off along the corridor, accompanied by her muscular associates. Something about the encounter troubled him. Outwardly, Caroline Force exuded the calmness and serenity for which she was famous, but he had the feeling that inwardly her emotions were being thrown into a turmoil. What the hell, he thought, millions of viewers would be watching *Prime Force* tonight. She wouldn't be human if she didn't feel a little uptight. TV stars got nervous, same as everybody else. Berenger went back to work.

The Senator's party arrived at eight-thirty precisely. Huxley was escorted first to the make-up department, then to the studio floor. Berenger had deployed most of his men around the entrance area but he had two on the roof and a further twelve scattered throughout the station's interior. He was as confident as he could be that no one could penetrate his security cordon.

5

The *Prime Force* signature tune echoed faintly in his ears as he made his final rounds. When he reached the Hospitality Room, he found to his surprise that the door was locked. He knew members of the Senator's entourage were watching the show on the TV set inside, and he frowned in puzzlement. "Everything okay in there?"

Silence.

He tried the handle again, his sense of uneasiness deepening. There was no sound from the room's interior. He tapped lightly on the door. "This is Jake Berenger, US Secret Service."

Something moved on the ground at his feet and his senses chilled as he saw blood oozing beneath the door to form a macabre starburst around his Italian leather shoes. For a moment he stood quite still, scarcely daring to breathe, then he snatched the two-way radio transmitter from his pocket and bellowed into the microphone: "Code Red, Code Red. All agents in Section 14 proceed at once to the Hospitality Room. This is an Operation Immediate. Repeat – this is an Operation Immediate."

Clawing his Walther from its leather holster, he stepped back and drove his foot savagely against the door. It sprang open with a splintering crash and Berenger dropped to a crouch with both arms extended in the classic firing position. There was blood everywhere, forming a sticky shroud that covered carpets and sofas alike. Scattered around the floor lay the bullet-ridden corpses of four men, their faces frozen into the glassy rigidity of death. The monitor set cast a blueish sheen across the macabre spectacle, diffusing its horror to some extent. The bodies looked crumpled, their dignity diminished by the grotesque alignment of limbs and torsos; they might have been bundles of bloodsoaked clothing left behind by some capricious tornado.

Berenger jumped as a shot echoed along the corridor, amplified by the TV microphones. He spun on his heel and tore along the passageway, sucking desperately at the air. The whitewashed walls seemed to close in on either side, holding him like a vice. He had almost reached the

Prime Force studio when a man appeared in front of him, dragging a woman by the wrist. Berenger recognized Caroline Force. She was struggling desperately to free herself from her captor's grasp.

He knew he had no time to get off a perfect shot. The intruder was armed with a .38 mm pistol fitted with a metal silencer and was already raising it in Berenger's direction. Berenger fired by instinct, feeling the Walther kick against his palm, but his shot went wide and his spirits sank as he realised the intruder had his weapon already in alignment. He saw twin spurts of flame and for no reason he could clearly explain found himself sprawled on the floor with a burning sensation lancing his upper thigh. He touched his hand to it and his fingers came away wet with blood. Footsteps clattered as his associates came charging toward him along the corridor.

"He's gone up the stairway," Berenger croaked, and they scrambled off in the gunman's wake.

SS Agent Berenger knew he wasn't seriously hurt, but what he didn't know, couldn't even begin to speculate as he lay bleeding on the corridor floor, was that the incident in which he had just played such a painful role would not only lead to the greatest scandal in television history but in a more oblique sense, though it seems incredible in retrospect, threaten the peace and stability of the United States.

YESTERDAY

Chapter One

The TV station seemed strangely sombre in the dour English morning; at some time long ago, it had served as a warehouse for foreign barges coming upriver and the stubby remains of the pulley systems could still be seen jutting from the building's roof.

Caroline Force paused to examine her reflection in a store window. She looked good, she decided, better than she had a right to considering the way she was feeling. A terrible uneasiness had gathered in her stomach and her legs felt like India rubber. She had never appeared on television before and she had no idea of how she would respond.

She crossed the street, moving with a fluid grace that caused a group of passing sailors to gaze after her admiringly. In the TV lobby, the receptionist checked her name from a list on the counter in front of her. "Who was the researcher who contacted you, Miss Force?"

"Myriam Maddox," Caroline said.

"Please take a seat. Miss Maddox will be along in a moment."

Caroline settled herself on the sofa, breathing deeply to steady her nerves. She scarcely knew what she was doing here. They had called her that morning at the advertising agency for which she worked. Would she be prepared to discuss the subject of motor-neurone disease on the *Minute-By-Minute* programme tonight? They understood that her father was a sufferer. And she'd agreed, that was the crazy thing. In fact, she'd scarcely even hesitated. But now she was beginning to regret her impetuousness for with thousands, possibly millions of people watching, she felt sure she would close up like a clam.

She saw a dark-haired girl approaching her from the lobby rear, dressed in a floppy jumper. "Hi, I'm Myriam Maddox. We spoke on the telephone."

Caroline rose to her feet. "Hope I'm not late."

"Don't worry, we've oceans of time before we go on the air."

The girl led Caroline along a network of passageways which looked oddly delapitated as if the building was falling to bits. "Ever been on television before?" she asked, glancing over her shoulder.

"Never. I'm scared out of my wits, if you want the truth."

"Don't be, it's a piece of cake. However . . ." She looked at her wristwatch. "We've got a bit of a flap on tonight. One of our items has bombed and the producer's panicking. Do you mind if we pop into the news office while I check on the state of play?"

"You're the driver," Caroline said.

The newsroom reminded her of a primeval cave. The L-shaped chamber was completely deserted, and the blinds had been drawn to shut out the sun. Mugs of half-drunk coffee cluttered the desktops and the floor was littered with crumpled newspapers. Pinned to the wall was a portrait of the British prime minister on which someone had drawn a luxuriant moustache.

Myriam Maddox was slightly embarrassed. "Sorry about the mess. It's part of television ethics to operate in a state of perpetual confusion."

"Where *is* everybody?" Caroline could scarcely believe the office was preparing for a live transmission.

"Good question." Myriam looked worried. "Do me a favour, will you, and hang on here while I find out what's happening? I'll only be a minute or two."

Caroline sank into a chair as Myriam hurried from the room.

NWTV's new programme controller, Rachel Bartlett, slim, elegant, thirty-six years old, gazed across her desk at

12

the middle-aged producer seated uncomfortably in front of her. Noel McCarty had taken off his jacket and in the pale light of the April evening, his rumpled shirt was soaked with sweat. He looked, Rachel thought, like a man who had gone past his prime, anxious, edgy, tense as a coiled spring. She felt little sympathy.

"*Minute-By-Minute* is a disgrace," she told him. "You've got the lowest ratings of any programme this station puts out and when we ran an audience research poll last month, more than half the people questioned didn't even realize you were on the air."

"Come on Rachel, that's hogwash and you know it. On Thursday, we picked up a thirty-two per-cent viewing share. Pretty good going for a local current affairs show."

"The only reason you got that share was because the BBC was putting out a parliamentary broadcast at the time. For God's sake Noel, we should be licking the opposition into a cocked hat every night of the week. *Minute-By-Minute*'s coming apart at the seams. It's soggy, it's dull, it's colourless. We've got to make the viewers feel that if they miss just a single edition, something important will be lost from their day. We need to sharpen the editorial content, brush up the presentation techniques, create a distinctive tone of voice. I want journalists who can think on their feet, who don't rely on rehashed items dredged out of the local newspapers – people who can produce a programme with style and flair."

"Give me more money and I'll pick up some hired guns from London," McCarty said.

"I haven't got the money, and you know it. Any changes we make will have to be done on the current budget but there *are* going to be changes, I promise you that."

Noel McCarty sighed. Ever since Rachel Bartlett's arrival, his life had been subjected to a constant barrage of upheaval. Rachel had cut her teeth at ITN, becoming the youngest subeditor in the company's history, and six weeks earlier she'd taken command at NWTV with the

13

self-declared aim of revolutionizing the station's output. From the outset, she had done her damndest to make her presence felt, and there was scarcely a person in the building from the cleaning woman upwards who didn't realize there was a new hand at the production helm.

Not that McCarty disliked Rachel. On the contrary, with her angular cheekbones and inherent sense of poise, he found her an alluring woman. Had he been about ten years younger, he might have gone for her in a really big way, though he had a hunch that the new programme controller was too absorbed in her job to show any true interest in the opposite sex.

"These news scripts," Rachel said, picking up a sheaf of papers from her desk, "they're disgraceful."

"How's that?"

"They're badly written, for a start. The sentences are too tight, too controlled. They've been turned out by journalists who are more accustomed to writing for the printed page. They've got to learn that the human ear can't absorb this kind of guff. Our role is to make the viewers sit up and take notice, not put them to sleep."

Still clutching the news scripts, she rose to her feet and strode from the room, her high heels clicking resolutely. She knew McCarty resented her interference but she was determined that, whatever happened, he would either go along with the changes or be swept out with the rest of debris.

She found the *Minute-By-Minute* office deserted except for a girl with reddish-gold hair who was seated alone at a desk in the corner. Rachel strode toward her and dropped the bulletin into her lap. "I want these scripts redone," she ordered.

The girl blinked. "Excuse me?"

"We're supposed to be inspiring the viewers not boring them to death. Rewrite the lot from start to finish and bring them along to my office at the end of the corridor. And remember we're on the air at eight."

Caroline watched with amusement as Rachel stormed back the way she had come. The lady, whoever she was, had clearly mistaken her for a member of the NWTV staff. She picked up the bulletin and thumbed through it, smiling curiously. It was easy to see where the problem lay. Though the items were skilfully constructed, the sentences were too rigid and constrained. To the human eye, they looked erudite and clever but much of their meaning would be lost amid the cadences of the newsreader's delivery.

She thought for a moment, then swivelled a sheet of paper into the platen of the nearest typewriter and began revamping the individual items, trying to give the words more fluidity and rhythm. When she had finished, the scripts seemed markedly improved. She took them along to Rachel who was seated in her office, talking to a fleshy-faced man in shirtsleeves.

"That was quick," Rachel said, glancing up as Caroline entered.

"Well, most of the donkey work had already been done."

Caroline suppressed her merriment as Rachel slipped on her spectacles and began to read. The man sat staring at her in puzzlement.

After a moment, Rachel said: "Now why couldn't you have written it like this in the first place?"

"Because nobody asked me to."

Rachel turned to the man with a sigh. "See what I mean, Noel? What we need is clearer direction. Your staff have to understand what's expected of them."

"This young lady isn't a member of my staff," the man protested. "I've never seen her before in my life."

Caroline smiled. "He's right. I only happened to be in the newsroom by accident. I'm a guest on the *Minute-By-Minute* programme tonight."

"Are you telling me that you rewrote this bulletin without any previous experience?"

"Well, the difficult part had already been done. It was mainly a question of giving the thing a little more tempo."

"What are you, a journalist?"

15

"Not in the accepted sense. I work for a publicity agency, writing advertising copy. I also write after-dinner speeches for visiting celebrities."

"Why didn't you tell me you weren't employed here?"

Caroline's eyes twinkled with amusement. She seemed to find the situation hilarious. "Maybe I was hoping you would offer me a job."

Rachel sat in front of her television set and watched Caroline describing in graphic detail the horrors of her father's illness. Something about her triggered a chord in Rachel's senses. She carried an air that was impossible to define. Her words were articulate and intelligent, her face mesmeric and compelling. She seemed to know instinctively when to push forward and when to hold back.

Rachel pursed her lips as the lens switched from a mid-shot to a close-up. The camera liked her, that was apparent. When it lingered on her features, the effect on the screen was riveting. Her eyes, clear as crystal, gripped the viewer's attention. Never in her life had Rachel seen such a powerful television presence.

She called her secretary from the outer office. "What d'you make of this girl?"

The secretary examined the TV set curiously. "She's quite a looker."

"Never mind her looks. What about personality?"

"Powerful. You'd notice her anywhere."

"My impression exactly."

"You're not thinking of hiring her, Miss Bartlett?"

"Why not? She needs a job and I need someone who can give this programme a shot in the arm."

"But she looks so young."

"Youth is exactly what we need. Young attitudes, young ideas."

"We also need experience," the secretary said.

"Experience, we can give her. Right now, my instincts tell me that we'd be idiots not to make use of her."

She pushed the button on her intercom machine.

16

"Noel," she said, "can you pop into my office for a moment?"

Noel McCarty sounded incredulous. "We're in the middle of transmission, for Chrissake."

"I realize that. Please hurry before the end credits start rolling."

When McCarty arrived, the interviewer was bringing Caroline's item to a close. Rachel waved at the TV screen. "What did you think of her?"

"The Force girl? Put her points well, I thought."

"She'd be perfect for *Minute-By-Minute*."

"You can't be serious?"

"I was never more serious in my life."

"She's an amateur, for Pete's sake. Okay, she looks confident, I'll admit, but she's untried and inexperienced. You can't make a decision like this on the basis of one studio interview."

"I've been making decisions like this all my life, and so far I haven't made a wrong one yet. Caroline Force has something money can't buy, and all the experience in the world can't buy it either. She's a natural. She doesn't have to lift a finger and she comes through that screen like a sledgehammer. She looks good, she expresses herself well and she's down-to-earth. My bet is, the viewers will take her straight to their hearts. Besides, you saw the way she rewrote those news scripts. She's an instinctive communicator."

"Rachel, you're out of your mind."

"If you're right you'll be getting my job in six months' time, but until that happens I want you to take her on."

"What as, for Chrissake?"

"Let her read the local news. She'll be a damn sight better than that milksop you're using at the moment."

"Supposing she makes a mess of it?"

"Speaking personally, I don't think she will, but put her on an initial four-week contract, just to be on the safe side." Rachel's lips twisted into a crooked smile as she added: "I always believe in hedging my bets."

* * *

17

Caroline came out of the TV station and paused for a moment, staring into the darkened street. She could scarcely believe the events of the past few hours. She had walked in as a programme guest and was walking out a professional presenter. It seemed a miracle.

She found a phone booth on the corner and slipped a coin into the slot. After a moment, a voice said: "Cresthaven Hospital, Sister Jenkins speaking."

"Will you put me through to the motor-neurone ward, please?"

There was a brief pause, then a second voice came on the line, a man this time. Caroline recognized Doctor Harris. She said: "Doctor, it's Caroline Force."

Harris's voice softened immediately. "Hello, Caroline. We watched you on TV tonight. I thought you were terrific."

"That's kind of you, doctor."

"If you felt nervous, you certainly didn't show it. Anyone would think you'd been doing it for years."

Her cheeks flushed. "Is my father still awake?"

A note of seriousness entered the doctor's voice. "He's resting at the moment, Caroline. Under sedation."

"Has something happened?" She felt a cold pall of dread.

"Another fall, I'm afraid. Nothing serious, but he lost his balance on his way to the TV room. However, he's a resilient fellow, so please don't worry. We expect him to pull out of it in a day or two. However . . ." The doctor hesitated. "The problem with your father is that he refuses to accept the constrictions of his disease. He insists on doing things which are really beyond him. I want you to be aware, Caroline, that his condition is steadily deteriorating. He may live another year, possibly two at the outside, but by that time he'll be a living vegetable, his brain unable to control his body."

Caroline's eyes moistened with tears. "Is he in pain, doctor?"

"Not as you and I understand that term. His pain comes from frustration. Mentally, he's as sharp as a razor but he

18

knows that he's coming apart at the seams and for a man like your father that's a terrible thing to accept. I suppose yours is the hardest role to bear. You have to stand by and watch someone you love disintegrating from the inside out. However, you have your whole life in front of you so try to concentrate your energy on that. You can see your father at the weekend. I'm sure he'll be delighted to hear how well you did on the interview tonight."

"Thank you, doctor. You're very kind."

She stepped from the phone booth, shivering a little in the chill. From the river, she heard the muffled wail of a ship's siren. Caroline's father had raised her single-handedly after her mother died, determined that whatever happened, she would not be destined for a life of mediocrity. Nightly after school, he had supplemented her daytime studies with lessons of his own making, teaching her how to rationalise, how to present her arguments in a cogent, persuasive manner, instilling within her the heady aspirations which he himself had never been able to realise. She loved him passionately, and the idea of a universe in which he no longer existed filled her with desolation. Amid the harsher simplicities of life, she thought, the world of television didn't seem real at all.

The skies above Los Angeles were stormy and grey, darkening rapidly with the first onset of evening. Dulcie Chantresse heard the footsteps as she turned into the empty street. They were not particularly loud but something in their resonance, a kind of hollow ringing sound made her pause for a moment and catch her breath. Several of the housefronts were ramshackle and distorted, creating a curious nightmarish effect. Far off, so far it seemed barely an echo inside her head, thunder rolled across the heavens. Her sense of isolation was almost overwhelming.

The footsteps started again, closer this time, their ominous rhythm matching the beating of Dulcie's heart. A tremor of fear passed through her body. There were no lights in the surrounding windows, no sign of people ahead. She stopped for a moment, listening intently. The only sound was her terrified breathing. It rose and fell in a seesaw rhythm, forming a vapour around her lips and nostrils. The sky was growing darker by the minute and somehow the pools of desultory light cast by the battered street lamps imbued the block with an air of insidious menace.

She began to walk again, her movements jerky and erratic, her body shaking beneath the tight-fitting skirt she wore. When the footsteps restarted they seemed so loud, so unbelievably close that for one wild moment she thought they were clattering inside her head. She saw a metal stairway framing the housefronts and with a strangled cry ran toward it, mounting the steps two at a time. She had almost reached the landing when a figure emerged from the darkness and stepped directly into her path. Its features were humanoid but any resemblance to conventional normality seemed purely accidental for its head was grossly misshapen, the brow forming a bizarre bulge that almost obscured the eye sockets. The nose was barely recognizable for at some time long ago it had been squashed flat against the skull, and the skin carried a waxen pallor that reminded Dulcie of a rotting corpse. Only the eyes seemed alive. They blazed like coals amid the icy devastation of the face.

The figure raised one taloned hand toward her, ripping the front of her blouse from throat to waist. Her naked breasts shimmered in the lamplight as the creature gathered her into a macabre embrace. She sucked in her breath and poured all the energy she could muster into one last despairing scream . . .

"Cut."

Thirty feet away, the director rose from his chair, snapping his fingers. "End board it."

"*Nympho Bloodsuckers,*" a second voice intoned. "Slate Twenty-Four, Take Sixteen."

Dulcie tugged the blouse across her naked breasts as the actor who had been attacking her stepped back and tore at his rubber mask. The studio lights came on, revealing

20

the street to be nothing more than a clapboard facade. Beyond the circle of light, cameras glided like animated robots.

The director walked into the glare, rubbing his hands vigorously as if trying to infuse them with warmth. "All right, my darlings, that is a wrap," he announced. "Back on Monday for the coven scene. Have a nice weekend, and take it easy on the booze. This may be a vampire picture, but let's leave the bloodshot eyes to the make-up department, shall we?"

In the dressing room, Dulcie stepped under the shower, letting the water soothe her tired muscles. It had been an exhausting week. She hated these low budget movies where everything had to be done on a shoestring; there was no room for manoeuvre, no time to prepare or rehearse. Her pulses quickened as she thought of the weekend ahead. She was spending it with Danny Le Hir, a handsome young Californian she had met at a Hollywood party. He was lean and athletic, and despite the difference in their ages (Dulcie was nearly forty, at least ten years older) he made her feel like a shy young girl again. He had proved a sensitive lover, not like some of the men she'd met; he cared about her feelings and when they went to bed together, he aroused her senses like a musician tuning a delicate instrument. She was flushed with anticipation as she pulled on her things and hurried out to the parking lot.

She saw Danny seated at the wheel of his open-topped Porsche. "Hi," he said cheerily.

"Sorry I'm late. We had to retake the last scene sixteen times."

"That's okay, I know what a bitch filming can be."

He tossed her suitcase into the trunk and headed out of town, joining the long line of traffic making for the high sierra. It had been Danny's idea to get away for the weekend and Dulcie had readily agreed. She was not a country girl at heart, but the prospect appealed to her senses; they could fantasise a little, pretend they were a happily married couple.

21

Danny seemed in good spirits. He chatted happily as they left the highway, climbing into the network of mountain roads. After a while, the only traffic they saw was a solitary ranger's truck heading in the opposite direction. Mountains towered around them, their snowcapped summits etched against the sky. Dulcie saw a river running pearl-grey in the sunlight, dropping into a breathtaking cascade.

"Oh, look," she said, sucking in her breath at the sight of such beauty.

Smiling, Danny brought the Porsche to a halt and took off his sunglasses. She never got tired of seeing Danny smile. He did it so artlessly, so unreservedly that it was impossible not to respond. "How about getting our feet wet?"

She followed him down a narrow path slanting between the pines. The grade wasn't steep but the track was covered with loose stones which clattered beneath their feet. At the river's edge, Danny squatted on a boulder to pull off his shoes. He stepped into the icy shallows, rolling his eyes in a parody of discomfort. Dulcie joined him, squealing as the chilly liquid sloshed around her naked ankles. They moved into the centre of the stream, the current rising above their knees. "Isn't this wonderful?" Dulcie cried.

Laughing gaily, she turned to look at him but when she saw his face the laughter froze on her lips for his eyes were hard and his mouth a thin, bloodless line.

"Danny, what's wrong?"

"I'm sorry, Dulcie."

He seemed distressed; there was a hint of moisture on his cheeks and a tiny nerve had begun to throb on his left temple. He seized her by the shoulders, tilting her backwards, and she gasped as her spine hit the icy stream-bed. She tried to wriggle into a sitting position but he pushed her down until the water closed above her head. Eyes bulging in disbelief, she saw his head outlined above her. Her first reaction was that he was playing some kind of game, but when she felt the power in his arms she was seized by a paroxysm of terror. She tore at his wrists but his muscular body held her stubbornly in position. She had to be imagining this, it didn't make sense. Danny would release her at any moment. He would lift her out of the water and carry her, laughing, to the river bank.

She felt her ribcage straining as she struggled to hold her breath, then her chest exploded in a flurry of bubbles and water flooded relentlessly into her lungs. Crazed with fear and bewilderment, she heard a roaring sound in her ears as her limbs went into a strange, unwilling dance and she kicked out her life in a last despairing struggle.

It was early morning when Danny Le Hir cruised into Palm Springs. He had driven all night, following the coastal route through Santa Barbara before cutting inland along Interstate 10. Now his muscles felt stiff and his eyes smarted with exhaustion.

There was a sprinkling of snow over the San Jacinto summits but despite the beauty of the desert morning, Danny was filled with a sense of despondency. He had liked Dulcie Chantresse, he reflected. She'd been a lovely human being and she hadn't deserved to die so cruelly. But whatever his personal feelings, he'd known where his duty lay. His duty was immutable and all-embracing. He was like a soldier in that respect.

The house stood on a rocky promontory overlooking Rancho Mirage. It had been built in the style of a Spanish hacienda with sloping red roofs, whitewashed archways and an elevated lawn jutting out from the mountain spur.

Armed security guards waved him through the entrance gate and he cruised slowly up the twisting drive, watching the building taking shape in front of him. It was clearly a millionaire's house, but even Danny after nineteen years of living here was unable to say with any real certainty how much his guardian was worth. Some people claimed the General was the fourteenth richest man in America and Danny was ready to believe it for not once during his short and eventful life had he been deprived of the slightest luxury.

A fleet of limousines stood parked on the cindered fore-court, their chauffeurs lounging in the sunlight. As Danny pulled to a halt, he saw Gendun, General Thirkeld's Vietnamese manservant, walking toward him carrying an iced daquiri on a silver tray. Gendun was small and exquisitely formed with olive green eyes. He was fifty-six years old, but because of his unblemished skin looked little more than thirty.

He bowed his head as Danny took the drink. "You look tired," he said.

Danny ignored the remark, nodding at the limousines. "Conference still in progress?"

"It should be breaking up at any moment now. The General would like you to lunch with him if you are not too exhausted."

"Tell the General I'll be fine as soon as I've bathed and changed."

Danny drained the drink and went up to his room. He stripped off his clothes and shaved in front of the bathroom mirror. Then he turned on the shower and soaked himself for ten or fifteen minutes. He felt better after he had towelled himself dry. At twenty-nine, he carried barely an ounce of surplus flesh and his muscles were strong and supple beneath the skin. His hair was trimmed short, his cheeks tanned and agreeably planed.

He heard voices from the patio as he finished dressing and walked onto his balcony, lighting a small cheroot. Below, the conference was breaking up and the delegates were making their way to their respective vehicles. They were nondescript men of varying age groups, but they all had one thing in common – they looked well fed and expensively dressed. Several noticed Danny standing on the balcony and waved in welcome.

Danny saw the General pushing himself along in his wheelchair. He was a heavy-set man with a barrel chest and strong, muscular arms. Even seated, he exuded a magnetism that seemed to flood the entire patio. His head was square, with cropped white hair which emphasized his pugnacious features. He was smiling as he chatted to one of the council members and Danny, standing on his balcony, looked down at him fondly. He remembered the first time he had ever seen Walter Thirkeld smile. He had been in his second year at the Baton Rouge orphanage when he had been summoned to the principal's office; there he had found the General, resplendent in his army uniform.

"You know who I am, boy?" Thirkeld had demanded, sizing Danny up with the air of a man evaluating a good horse.

"No, sir," Danny had answered politely.

"I am – was – your father's commanding officer. You know who your father was, don't you?"

"Yes, sir."

"A proud and brave American. It was your father, Corporal Randolph Le Hir who saved my life on the Mekong River. He died to protect me, Daniel. He threw himself on the grenade that was meant for me." The General patted his wheelchair ruefully. "Oh, I didn't escape the encounter unscathed. A piece of the shrapnel lodged in my spine and left me paralysed from the waist down, but it's only my limbs which are ravaged, boy. I still have a lion's heart, and that heart tells me that I owe your father the greatest debt one man can owe another. I have come here today to settle the account."

The principal spoke from behind his desk. "General Thirkeld would like to adopt you, Daniel."

Danny examined the visitor more intently. For almost two years he had dreamed of someone rescuing him from the dreary austerity of orphanage life. Could this crippled, charismatic soldier be his knight in shining armour?

"I plan to raise you along with my two sons, Wayne and Stephen," the General said. "I'll see that you have the finest education money can buy, but I am an old-fashioned man and I believe in old-fashioned values. I expect – demand – three things: truth, loyalty and determination. I'll drive you every inch of the way. Foul up anywhere along the line and you'll be back in this orphanage as fast as your feet can carry you. Apply yourself diligently, however, show me that beneath that youthful exterior you've got grit and backbone, and I promise you a life that'll be the envy of every boy in America. How does that sound?"

Danny considered for a moment. The visitor's square jaw suggested tenacity and toughness but there was something in his eyes that appealed to Danny's senses. He smiled cheekily. "Sounds like a pretty good deal to me, General."

That had been nineteen years ago, and throughout that time the General had been his constant mentor and companion. A deep affection had developed between the two men that was every bit as fervent as the love of a natural father and son.

General Thirkeld noticed Danny standing on the balcony and motioned him to come downstairs. Still smoking his cheroot, Danny made his way to the patio where the last of the council members were setting off in their limousines. He watched the line of vehicles picking a tortuous route down the steep winding exit drive.

Sunlight picked out General Thirkeld's spiky hair as he examined Danny shrewdly. "How'd things go?"

Danny drew hard on his cheroot. Below, the last of the cavalcade was passing through the security gate. "All taken care of."

General Thirkeld patted his hand, his features creasing in sympathy. "I know how you feel, son. If I could have spared you the pain I'd have done it like a shot, but the woman had to be silenced, there was no other way."

"I'm proud to be of service, General."

General Thirkeld took out a thick cigar and bit off the end, spitting it into a clump of blue thurnbergia. Danny watched him as he lit the tip. "It's always the good men who do the most harm in this world. Know who said that?"

"Henry Adams said it, General."

"Correct. But what would have been Henry Adam's reaction, I wonder, if he could have witnessed what is happening to our proud nation today? When I was a

26

young man, to describe yourself as an American was to declare a faith. We'd just licked the deadliest military force in history and we had at our disposal the most destructive weapon ever devised by man. It was our role – our Godgiven duty – to spread democracy throughout the world but in the happy proverbial phrase, we crapped out, Danny. When I see what our country's become, I want to hang my head in shame. The old values are being shot down in flames by spineless bellyachers who nibble at our most sacred institutions. We've let ourselves grow soft from the inside out. Mankind craves order just as he craves identity and purpose. That's why we need the Movement, Danny, because the Movement is our conscience. And that's why what you did last night, repugnant though it may seem to you now, was an essential part of the fight to make our country great again."

Danny was silent for a moment, then he whispered softly: "You always know just the right thing to say, General."

Thirkeld watched the limousines vanish into the traffic flow along Palm Canyon Drive. Seated in the wheelchair, he looked almost Churchillian. "You've been a good son to me, Danny. I couldn't be more proud if you were my own flesh and blood. My own boys, Wayne and Stephen – it pains me to say this but they've proved a bitter disappointment to me. Stevie may be a successful lawyer but he's turned his back on everything we believe in. I steered him through law school and he repays my generosity by defending the very dropouts who are dragging this nation into the gutter."

"He loves you, General," Danny said gently. "He has a different way of looking at things, that's all."

"He's a damn fool is what he is. His mother would turn in her grave if she could see him now. As for Wayne . . ." Thirkeld shook his head despairingly. "God knows, I tried to whip some sense into the boy but he fooled me at every turn. Only you, Danny, turned out the way I planned. You are my true offspring, my strong right arm."

27

Danny felt his throat seize up. He said thickly: "I owe you everything, General."

"We owe each other, Danny. We depend upon each other and that's good because it breeds loyalty and trust, two things sadly lacking in this miserable old world. But together, we are going to save our country from disintegration. With the Movement's help, we'll create a society we can be justly proud of. We'll use television because today it's television, not religion, that is the opiate of the people. All that's missing is the catalyst to cement it all together."

Danny's eyes prickled. Nothing moved him so deeply as listening to the General's rhetoric. He motioned at the desert in front. "Your catalyst's out there somewhere, General, and one way or another, I'm going to find it."

Chapter Two

Caroline started work on Monday, November 3rd. A secretary escorted her to the *Minute-By-Minute* news office which, in contrast to the last time she had visited it, now seethed with life and activity. Computers hummed, typewriters rattled and to add to the bedlam, a row of TV monitors stretching the full width of the room blared out programmes from four different channels.

The morning began with the daily production meeting, a confusing mixture of meaningless patois which left Caroline completely baffled, then the senior producer introduced her to each of her new colleagues in turn. Several, she noticed, treated her with barely concealed disdain. It was clear they felt she had gained her job through some kind of trickery. Most hostile of all was the programme's anchor man, Edgar Stewart. Stewart had once been elegant and urbane before years of indulgent living had left their mark on his chubby features; now middle-aged, he exuded a slightly decaying air as if his body was beginning to crumble from the inside out. His cheeks were covered with tiny blue veins and his hair had been dyed with some indeterminate substance which made it look slightly orange in places. Three times voted Northern TV Personality of the Year, Stewart was famous for his impish grin. There was, however, no sign of his celebrated charm as he shook Caroline's hand and examined her coolly. "Nice going. Studio guest to newsreader in a single bound. You must be quite an operator. Like the idea of being on television, do you?"

"I'll find out tonight when we get on the air."

"As a matter of interest, how did you swing it? Rachel Bartlett's said to be no pushover."

"Luck, I think."

He laughed unpleasantly. "You'll need plenty of that if you're planning to survive in this business. We have a pretty high mortality rate."

Stewart's enmity surprised her. She hadn't expected it from a man whose name was a household word. She was an intruder here, she realised, an interloper, and her feeling of nervousness abruptly increased. She dreaded the thought of going on the air that evening.

For almost an hour, she sat watching the morning melee with an air of mildly controlled hysteria. The noise was deafening. Everyone seemed to be acting a part, as if the most cardinal sin in the handbook was to display equanimity or reserve. The stream of profanity was unrelenting.

Just before noon, Noel McCarty, the programme editor, dropped a pile of news scripts on her desk. "You made a big impression on our programme controller the other day so let's see how you manage with this little lot."

Grateful at having something to do at last, Caroline slipped a sheet into her typewriter and worked steadily until one o'clock when a shadow fell across her typewriter. She looked up to see a young man standing there. He was medium sized and sturdily built with tousled black hair and a slightly pugnacious though pleasant face. He looked like a student or an aspiring artist. "How's it going?" he asked.

It was the first friendly remark Caroline had heard all morning and she smiled at him in gratitude. "Bit bewildering. Is it always so extreme?"

"Wait till transmission time approaches. Then it's like countdown at Cape Canaveral."

He held out his hand. "Hi, I'm Jake Lenehan. I cover sports. They won't let me on the screen because of my appearance so I write the bilge the other blokes spout." He paused, his dark eyes twinkling. "Listen, you plan to work all lunchtime or are you coming down to the pub?

That's where most of us recharge our batteries for the debacle ahead."

"Think it'll be alright? Leaving the office without permission?"

"This isn't Devil's Island, for Pete's sake. Come on, grab your coat."

The pub was packed with television people and Jake had to elbow his way to the bar and bellow at the top of his voice to make himself heard. He paid for the drinks and nodded toward the furthermost corner where they found a table mercifully removed from the din.

"Is it always this noisy?" she asked.

"Only at lunchtimes. If it wasn't for the TV station, the place would probably go out of business."

Caroline glanced at the customers thronging the counter; they were babbling and gesticulating like creatures possessed. "They're a little overwhelming," she remarked.

"They're playing a part. They believe that working in television makes them some kind of chosen species. Like the Israelites in the Bible, except that for them God isn't in the sky – he's hiding behind a camera lens."

"And you're different, I suppose?" she said with a smile.

"Damn right. I draw a line between work and play. It does wonders for the equilibrium."

"But not for the initiative."

"Hey, don't get the wrong idea. I'm as ambitious as the next sod. In fact, I've got my eye on the BBC or ITN. I'll be good too if they'll give me half a chance, but getting in cold's like climbing Everest single-handed. You need somebody in the know."

Caroline didn't miss the implication. She'd sensed it all morning, that faint distancing among her colleagues. She looked down at her glass. "I was lucky, I suppose."

"Well, let's just say that lightning hit your spot. Rachel Bartlett wants to spring-clean the station's output and you're part of her face-lift."

"Is that good or bad?"

"Good in one sense, bad in another. She has a vested

interest in watching you make the grade so she'll do her damndest to help you succeed. On the other hand . . ." He shrugged. "There are a lot of people who'd give their eyeteeth to see her take a tumble. They'll be praying that you screw up tonight."

"I have a feeling their prayers are going to be answered."

He laughed. "Don't worry, you'll be okay. Just stay loose and try to relax."

But Caroline couldn't relax. The uncertainly she felt at the prospect of going on the air was developing into near-hysteria. Rehearsals started in the early afternoon and something about the hollow resonance of the studio sent her into a mindless panic. Voices echoed and reverberated, as if she was sitting in the centre of some vast mausoleum. Electricians tinkered with the overhead lamps, sound engineers toyed with the microphones, and among this confusion the floor manager listened to instructions being beamed into his headset from the control room above.

After a while, Caroline was asked to read through her news bulletin. On the floor manager's cue, she began to speak, summoning as much confidence as she could. She was halfway through when he waved her to a halt. "You can't read the news as if you're holding a conversation at the local disco. It's not a shopping list, for God's sake. You've got to put some emphasis into your words, give the thing pace and rhythm. Let's try again, from the beginning."

Caroline concentrated on injecting authority into her tone, accentuating key words and phrases. Halfway through, the floor manager motioned toward the camera and she saw that the teleprompter had swung into operation, mirroring the script across the front of the lens. She made the switch with barely a pause, gratified to find that the words flitted by at exactly the right talking speed. When she had finished, the floor manager said: "That was much better. If we run out of time before transmission, keep it like that and everything should be fine."

The rehearsals continued in a disjointed manner, ending

finally with a thirty-minute pre-programme break while the cameras went into electronic line-up. By this time, Caroline's tension was almost at breaking point. She felt sure the minute she got on the air, her throat would dry up like a sponge.

At five minutes to transmission, somebody slipped a receiver into her ear so that she could hear the director in the control box above. The duty news editor appeared to make his final alterations. "How're you feeling?"

"Like a piece of jelly."

"Don't worry, it's the ones who get overconfident who come a cropper. Just remember, no newsreader died on television yet."

"There's always a first time," she told him dryly.

The last few minutes were agonizing. She kept glancing at the clock, trying to quell the queasiness in her stomach. Edgar Stewart took his place in the anchor chair and with a show of casual unconcern began joking with the cameraman.

"Thirty seconds to transmission!" the floor manager shouted. "Quiet in the studio!"

Caroline clenched her teeth, pushing her knees together. The final countdown began: "Five . . . four . . . three . . . two . . . one . . ."

As if in a dream, she heard music playing over the opening credits. The floor manager cued Stewart and with his familiar impish grin, he launched into his opening address. "Good evening . . ."

Caroline heard his voice droning in her ears but all she could think of was the sobering realisation that in a matter of seconds she would be beaming into millions of homes where every move she made could be coldly and clinically dissected.

". . . all that's to come," Edgar Stewart intoned, "but first the news from Caroline Force."

A voice echoed in her ear, "Cue Caroline," and she saw a red light flash on the camera in front of her. Words floated up on the teleprompter and an icy hand clutched her heart as she started to speak. "The Prime

Minister today outlined plans to boost northern industry. In an upbeat message to local government delegates in London, he revealed that a recent CBI survey showed a surge in manufacturing demand which pointed to steadily increasing growth, particularly in the north . . ."

Suddenly, a voice bellowed in her earpiece. "Got a train to catch? Slow down, for Chrissake. You're gabbling."

Caroline tried to modify her pace, injecting colour and tone into her delivery. Her words sounded disembodied, as if she was listening to them from a very great distance. Never in her life had she felt so completely alone. Though the studio was crowded with people, she knew that for the next few minutes at least she would have to rely entirely on her own resources. Soon, however, she found herself beginning to relax as the stories blended one into the other. It seemed almost an anti-climax when she reached the final page and her newscast came to an end.

In the Hospitality Room afterwards, several people congratulated her and Noel McCarty, the programme editor, ruffled her hair as if they had been friends for years. "You lost your cherry, sunshine," he said with a grin.

Through the numbness permeating her body, she was filled with a sense of elation and relief.

The morning after Caroline's debut, she was summoned to the programme controller's office. Rachel Bartlett was speaking on the telephone as she entered, and she waved Caroline to a chair. Something in her manner made Caroline feel uneasy. Rachel looked not deprecating, but not particularly approving either. When she had finished speaking, she said: "How did it go last night?"

"Okay," Caroline answered.

"I made a recording so you could take a look at yourself."

She switched on the monitor next to her desk and the previous evening's transmission flashed onto the screen. Caroline squirmed in embarrassment as she watched her performance. She had prided herself on getting through the ordeal with at least a moderate degree of panache but seeing the playback in the cold light of day, she was dismayed by the crudeness of her delivery. Every fault, every weakness seemed awesomely pronounced.

Rachel switched off the set and swivelled in her chair, examining her closely. "What did you think?"

She shrugged. "I thought it would be better."

Rachel said: "Newsreading sounds simple enough but doing it well is a practised art. You're getting a number of things wrong and it's showing. First and foremost, you're staring too hard at the camera and it's making you look glassy-eyed. Learn to glance down at your script once in a while. Not only does it break the tension but it helps to give you more authority. And don't follow the teleprompter with your eyes. I know you're reading the words off a screen but when you let your gaze flit from side to side, it makes you seem furtive and shifty. Watch for the key light. Always be conscious that leaning back casts shadows across your features. Fix your position and stay there."

Caroline blushed. Rachel's cool appraisal was like having a glass of water tossed into her face.

"You're slow on the camera changes," Rachel continued. "It's crucial that you know which lens you're speaking to. Several times you were a fractional second late, which looks to the viewers as if you're not on the ball."

"I'm sorry."

"Don't be sorry. Get it right. For the few minutes you're on the air, you have to be conscious of the minutest detail. You have a tendency to speed up when you're feeling tense. Don't. Not only does it obscure your words but it tells people you're nervous and that's the one sin they'll never forgive. No matter how scared you are inside, you must appear – outwardly at least – to be in complete control." She paused for a moment, then her eyes lit up and her face broke into a dazzling smile. "Otherwise, you did just fine."

Caroline took Rachel's advice to heart and went to work at polishing up her delivery. Within a week, the improvement was tangible. Not only did she sound relaxed but she gave the appearance of having been doing the job for years. Once, when a piece of newsfilm snapped in the gate, she carried on with the newscast as if nothing had happened, her poise impeccable, her timing perfect. It was clear to everyone that despite her inexperience, Caroline Force had come to stay.

At the end of the month, Caroline picked up her father from the hospital where he lived and drove him into town for a celebratory dinner. Despite his condition, Michael Force was still able to walk with crutches. He was exuberant at Caroline's success. "If only your mother could see you now," he said as they seated themselves at the candlelit table. "She'd be so proud."

"There's nothing to be proud of, Daddy. I'm reading words off a teleprompter, that's all. It's hardly what you'd call a stunning achievement."

"Listen to me, my girl. I've told you till I'm blue in the face, it isn't the job you do, it's the way that you do it. I never in my life saw anyone so much at home in front of a camera."

"You're a little biased, Father," she told him with a smile.

Despite the disease ravaging his body, Michael Force was still a handsome man. His body was trim, his features sensitive and intelligent. He had spent his life in local government until the first developing symptoms of paralysis had forced him, unwillingly, to brace himself for a future of infirmity and dependence. Now, Caroline knew, he was hoping to find fulfilment through her, a prospect she found both troubling and disturbing.

"I may know nothing about television, Caroline, but I do know talent when I see it and you've got more of that in your little finger than all your colleagues put together. Believe me, you're going right to the top."

"You're expecting too much, Daddy. You don't know what it's like in there. Most of the people I work with feel I haven't paid my dues."

"Forget the people you work with. You're national

36

material, Caroline. That's why you've got to get off the newsreading.

"You're not an actress, you don't need scripts to make you shine. You've got something special, something in here . . ." He pressed his fingertips against his chest. "Tell them you want to try interviewing."

"They'll never buy it."

"How can you be sure until you ask?"

"Because interviewing's a specialised art. I'm only a beginner, for God's sake."

"What difference does that make?"

He paused, examining her shrewdly in the candlelight. There was a strange look in his eyes, one she didn't know how to decipher. "There are four kinds of people in this world, Caroline, and the secret of success lies in indentifying your rightful category."

"What does that mean?"

He smiled, warming to his subject. "Well, first there are the super-rich, most of whom are bored out of their wits. They do drugs, gamble and have affairs in an effort to relieve their boredom. At the other end of the scale are the desperately poor. They too do drugs and have affairs, but that's to take their minds off how miserable they're feeling. In between lies the great wedge of 'middle' people. They subscribe to standards they have neither the wit nor temerity to question."

"And the fourth category?" Caroline said.

"Ah . . ." Her father's face beamed. "They are the gypsies, the chosen few. They belong to no identifiable strata of society and they move up or down according to circumstance. They never abide by rules laid down by other people." His eyes shone with an elusive humour. "*You* are a gypsy, Caroline. You'll go your own way, no matter what. So never again let me hear you say that you can't do something because of your colleagues' disapproval."

A shadow fell across their table and a woman stood smiling down at them. She was middle-aged with elaborately coiffured hair. "Miss Force? It *is* Miss Force, isn't it? From the *Minute-By-Minute* programme?"

"Yes, it is," Caroline said.

"I knew I was right. I recognized you the moment you walked in. I said to my friend; that's the girl who reads the TV news."

The lady placed a piece of paper on the table. "Will you please give me your autograph? The ladies at the department store where I work think you're the best thing on television. If those TV bosses had any sense, they'd offer you a show of your own."

"You're very kind."

Embarrassed, Caroline scribbled her name on the slip of paper, and her father chuckled as the lady returned to her table. "What did I tell you?" he whispered softly. "You are on your way, Caroline."

Michael Force was right. Caroline *was* on her way. In the weeks which followed, she honed her performance to the finest degree. Her style became measured and authoritative and she exuded a crisp, straight-to-the-point manner which viewers respected and atuned to. Soon, she was the most recognizable figure on *Minute-By-Minute* and though Edgar Stewart remained popular as the show's anchor, it was Caroline's vivacity which the audience remembered most of all. At the end of the year, she was voted the most promising newcomer in northern television.

Caroline, however, was not content with simply refining her role. Encouraged by her father, she set out to learn as much as she could about the way a TV studio worked. She talked to the electricians, discovering how and why they placed their lamps at certain angles. She questioned the sound engineers about the advantages and limitations of their various microphones. She stood in the director's box and watched how he composed his shots.

This single-minded absorption was not, of course, lost upon her colleagues. Edgar Stewart in particular regarded Caroline as a serious threat to his survival and began making derogatory comments about her which, happily, no one in the newsroom took seriously. Stewart's carping was accepted for what it was, the bitterness of a middle-aged man afraid of losing a lucrative livelihood.

Stewart, however, did not confine his campaign to straightforward backbiting. He frequently tried to distract Caroline's concentration whilst they were on the air. He would wait until she was being counted into a news item then toss her a question from the adjoining desk. Once, he even fashioned a paper aeroplane out of his programme script and floated it into her face while she was reading an important commentary.

These petty manoeuvres had little effect upon Caroline however, and she reported each week to the programme controller's office where Rachel Bartlett analysed her work and offered criticism. Rachel was delighted with her protegee's improvement. "You've done splendidly," she said. "Anyone would think you'd been reading the news for years. You're cool and relaxed, and your camera presence is remarkable. I'm extending your contract for another year."

Caroline hesitated. She was grateful to Rachel for her support, but she knew too that her father was right. She couldn't go on being a newsreader all her life. Sooner or later, she had to diversify. "Why don't you give me a shot at interviewing?"

Rachel examined her coolly. "Why should I?"

"Because I think I'd be good at it."

"You've only been in the business for five minutes. What makes you think you can match someone like Ewan Collis?"

Ewan Collis was *Minute-By-Minute*'s star interviewer. He was noted for his cool, meticulous approach. Caroline said: "I've been studying Ewan's technique. He's good, he's really good, but I think with time I can be good too."

"Live interviewing's a damn sight harder than it looks. Ewan learned his trade the hard way, doorstepping politicians and doing vox-pops in the street with a hand-basher and stick-mike."

"And it shows," Caroline acknowledged. "Ewan's terrific, he really is. But you need somebody who can put the questions from a woman's angle."

Rachel said: "Don't try to run before you can walk. You're good at what you do, damned good, but live interviewing's a difficult art. I've stuck my neck out once for you already. I have no intention of doing so again."

Caroline was disappointed by Rachel's refusal but she was determined not to let the matter drop. One evening, she approached Ewan Collis as he was leaving the studio.

"Fancy a drink, Ewan?"

"Now that's an interesting idea," he said. "Got something special in mind?"

"Brain-picking. I can't stay a newsreader for the rest of my life. I want to learn about interviewing."

Collis laughed out loud. "For God's sake Caroline, take this business seriously and it'll crucify you. The best advice I can offer is to loosen up and remember that you're not piloting a Boeing 707."

"I'm buying," she said pointedly and he reached for his coat with a mischievous grin.

"You just uttered the magic words."

Collis was a wiry little man with heavy-lidded eyes and a sleepy expression. In the pub, he sat toying with his glass. "I honestly don't know how I can help you. Basically, interviewing's a matter of instinct."

"Hogwash. I've been watching you for months. You play your guests like fish on a line."

"Experience comes into it too, I suppose."

"Come on, Ewan, give me a few pointers."

"Well, just remember this is only an opinion. Don't take it as gospel."

She waited impatiently for him to begin. "Bear in mind that an interview's like a story," he said at last. "It needs a beginning, a middle and an end. You can't tackle a subject from fifty directions at once. The viewer has to be taken through the ingredients step by step. Now that's pretty easy when you're prerecording – you can edit afterwards

40

and shape the thing to your own satisfaction – but in a live studio, it's a different matter. There, you have to offer something to get something back. If the interviewee thinks he's carrying the transmission single-handed, he'll panic and close up like a clam. You have to put him at his ease, let him see that you can fill in the awkward bits when he finds his vocal chords drying."

"What about the questions?" Caroline said.

"Never think in terms of questions. Only answers. Concentrate on the answers and the questions will form themselves. Never go into a live interview without knowing exactly what you want your respondent to say. Sometimes, of course, you'll get a chance to meet him beforehand and when you do, talk about mundane things and study the way he looks and moves. Watch for the body signals which show when he's under stress and tuck them into your head. When you're on the air, you have to control him like an unruly horse. The one thing no one will ever forgive is allowing your guest to take command."

"You make it sound like a military campaign."

"As far as you're concerned, a military campaign is exactly what it is. Even in a friendly debate, you have to be the focal point. Lose that focus and you lose your backside, understand?"

"How about structure?"

"Work it out beforehand, just like a newspaper column. Timing's important. You have a certain amount of information to play with and you need to unveil it in chronological order. You've got to pace the thing, make sure that you're not serving up the meat course before the coffee and dessert. You'll find, when you get going, that your brain separates into different compartments. One section listens to what your guest is saying and picks up instructions from the director's box, another watches the camera movements and concentrates on speeding up or slowing down according to the passage of time."

"Sounds a pretty tall order," Caroline said.

"You'll get the hang of it. But remember, the people on the receiving end have one major advantage – their

41

survival doesn't depend on the quality of their performance. Yours does. Politicians use television as a weapon. They train for it the way a fighter trains. They have their own schools and their own media advisers. They'll crush you if they get half a chance. No matter what line you take, a politician will try to steer the discussion to his own advantage and you have to be ready for that. Keep your mind fluid and your wits alert. Make sure they answer your questions and never let them off the hook. They're there to serve the public and sometimes you're the only person who can hold them to account." He paused and looked at her quizzically. "Is it making sense, any of this?"

"Sense, yes. But I'll be an old woman before they give me a chance to try it out for myself."

"Thank God for that," he said with a grin. "I thought you were about to take over my job."

Rachel Bartlett sat in her apartment watching Caroline winding up the evening's programme with a summary of the day's headlines. She was a natural communicator, Rachel thought, a professional to her fingertips. She made her colleagues seem colourless by comparison. Was it right to stand in Caroline's way? After all, she couldn't remain a newsreader for ever. She had talent, real talent. It was raw, a little on the primitive side, but what she needed most was a chance to stretch herself. Shouldn't she, Rachel Bartlett, be the one to give her that chance?

Rachel was thoughtful as she switched off the TV set. Her decision to take Caroline on had been an involuntary impulse, a spur-of-the-moment thing. If she'd been wrong, her enemies would have crucified her in the NWTV boardroom. But Caroline hadn't failed. She'd succeeded beyond Rachel's wildest dreams. Maybe she deserved a little something in return.

Rachel had no illusions about the true nature of her predicament. It was instilled into her like a secret affliction. She liked the girl so why not admit it? That golden-red hair, those delicate features. It had nothing to do with professional ethics.

Rachel couldn't help the way she had been born. Even at school, she had realized that she was not like the other girls. Boys held little interest for her. Her instincts, her emotions were slanted in different directions. At the age of thirteen, she had fallen in love with the school hockey coach, a young woman of twenty-six. Fortunately, Rachel's obsession had materialised in nothing more sinister than a series of violent mood changes but when, two years later, she'd been caught naked in the showers with a pubescent classmate, she had been summarily expelled.

During the ensuing years, Rachel had tried to focus her attentions on a more acceptable level, embarking on a series of heterosexual love affairs which had brought her neither fulfilment nor happiness; in the end, bitter and disillusioned, she had decided to devote herself to her work.

She had managed it admirably too; already, she was programme controller of a company which had grossed fourteen million in its last annual profit and this year she had been promised a seat on the management board. Everything had been going swimmingly until Caroline Force had made her appearance. Caroline was driving her crazy but should she be penalised for Rachel's weakness? Rachel couldn't base her decisions on the activities of her hormones. The girl had a powerful television presence. Was it right to stifle such talent?

Rachel sighed as she walked into the kitchen and switched on her microwave. It was a bewildering dilemma, whichever way she looked at it.

Chapter Three

It was almost three o'clock when Noel McCarty strode into the newsroom and called his special assistant, Sam Herries, into his private office. Anchor man Edgar Stewart, realising something was up, listened through the clapboard panelling. He heard McCarty say: "Rachel wants Caroline to have a crack at interviewing. She thinks the girl's being wasted in the newsreader's chair."

An icy coldness settled in Stewart's stomach. It seemed incredible that Caroline, after barely eighteen months, should be moving into the domain normally occupied by Ewan Collis and himself. Edgar Stewart lived his life in a state of perpetual dread. Since the girl's arrival he had tried hard to mend his ways. He had cut down on his drinking habits, but her impact on the programme had been so vibrant and dramatic that he'd ended up hitting the bottle more heavily than ever. He hated her with the unbridled passion of a man who sensed the end of a lucrative and fulfilling career.

He came to a swift decision. Clearly Caroline had to be stopped. He was fighting for his very existence. She was too talented to be ignored. He leaned forward and examined the running order. There were three interviews scheduled for the studio that evening; two had been allocated to Ewan Collis and one, the Chancellor of the Exchequer, to Stewart himself. Stewart knew the Chancellor was a mercurial character with a reputation for making mincemeat out of TV interviewers. He was arrogant, bombastic and brilliantly withering.

Stewart sat for a moment, thinking hard, then he loosened his necktie and walked into the editor's office, mopping his cheeks with a handkerchief. The two men looked at him with surprise. "Something wrong, Ed?"

"I feel lousy," Stewart complained.

"You don't look awfully good," Herries admitted, examining Stewart worriedly.

"It's the flu, I think. My youngest brought it home from school and it's been running through the family like a dose of salts."

"Got a temperature?" McCarty asked.

"Hell, I feel as if I've been run over by a ten-ton truck. My joints are aching and I'm starting to see double." Stewart tried to sound apologetic. "I don't suppose you could manage without me, just for tonight?"

McCarty glanced at Herries. "Think Ewan can handle the anchor spot? Edgar ought to be in bed, the state he's in."

"Well, we'll have to sort out the interviews. Collis can't handle all three."

"I'll give one to Caroline."

"The Chancellor's a tricky customer, Noel. He'll need delicate handling. Ewan can't do it and hold the programme together as well. It's too big a strain."

McCarty saw what he was getting at. He rubbed his cheek reflectively, studying the running order. "What the hell," he said at last, "*we* didn't put Caroline in the hot seat. If anything goes wrong, it'll be Rachel Bartlett's arse in a sling, not ours."

Edgar Stewart watched the exchange in silence, his heartbeat quickening. The two editors had taken the bait, hook, line and sinker. He tried to inject a note of sympathy into his voice. "Maybe I can help Caroline with the structuring."

"Forget it, Ed," McCarty said. "If you're sick, I don't want you spreading those flu germs around my staff. Go home and sweat it out. And don't come back until you're bright-eyed and bushy-tailed, understand?"

Stewart glanced at Caroline as he headed toward the newsroom door. Let's see you wriggle out of this one, you high-flying bitch, he thought. He was humming softly to himself as he made his way downstairs.

*   *   *

45

Caroline sat in the studio chair, waiting nervously for the interview to begin. She had never felt so frightened in her life. Reading the news was one thing – all it required was a little coolness and nerve – but taking on the Chancellor of the Exchequer was like climbing into a lion's den armed with nothing more than an ordinary catapult.

The Chancellor himself, clearly bored by the proceedings, was examining his fingernails as Ewan Collis's voice droned from the anchor desk. He had a politician's instinct for determining who was important and who wasn't, and it was clear that he considered Caroline scarcely worth acknowledging.

A terrible coldness settled in her stomach. She couldn't have asked for a more terrifying debut; she knew the Chancellor would pull every trick in the book to throw her off-balance and she jumped as the director's voice echoed in her earpiece. "Coming to you in twenty seconds."

She heard Collis launch into his introduction and steeled herself for the encounter ahead. The Chancellor, cool as a cucumber, leaned back in his chair, gazing at some indeterminate point on the ceiling.

"Cue Caroline," the director's voice intoned, and she cleared her throat, her stomach quivering. "Mr Chancellor . . ."

Her first question had been carefully chosen. It was designed to halt the Chancellor in his tracks. He countered it with scarcely a pause and threw it back in her face, signed, sealed and delivered. Dear God, she thought. He'd scarcely hesitated, that was the maddening thing. His brain, honed by innumerable debates in the House of Commons, was trained to retaliate instinctively. Bad start. She tried again, hoping to pin him on a different tack, but he turned her question back on itself and wrapped it up in a neat little package. Damn the man. He was sharper than a scythe blade and faster than quicksilver.

She listened miserably to the timings in her earpiece, ticking off the seconds and minutes. She knew that she was horribly outmatched. He talked with an unruffled ease, using words as a framework to disguise the paucity of facts. He rarely paused, and when he did, it was simply to give emphasis to a relevant point. Oh, he was an admirable man really, a politician to the core. Fast on his feet, he knew how to roll with the punches. Already, the conversation was getting beyond her. She'd crammed her head full of facts and figures but it took years of experience to grasp the subtle nuances of the money markets. For all she knew, he might have been spouting gobbledygook. Sooner or later he's going to nail me, she thought.

Perspiration trickled between her shoulder blades as she realised he was gazing at her expectantly. She felt waves of nausea sweeping upwards from her stomach. What in God's name had he been talking about?

The seconds stretched and the Chancellor went on looking at her in the same anticipatory manner. Say something, her brain screamed. Don't let him intimidate you. In desperation, she barked the only word she could think of. "Why?"

He moistened his lips and a tiny pulse began to throb in his temple. He's rattled, she thought with a surge of sudden excitement. I've caught him on the raw. She felt her uncertainty vanish as, icy calm, she moved in for the kill.

The Chancellor tried to back away but she cut him off at every turn, probing his answers with savage persistence. Sweat bathed his face as he weaved and twisted, squirming under her penetrating gaze. By the time the interview was over, he knew he had been well and truly trounced and, flushed with embarrassment, he left the building without a word.

In the Hospitality Room, Editor Noel McCarty was delirious with excitement. "We've had ITN on the line and they want to put out an edited version on their late-night bulletin," he said. "Congratulations, sweetie, you're going national."

Caroline accepted his compliments with a modest smile, then she made her way to the ladies room and vomited noisily into the washbasin.

*   *   *

Caroline dismissed her taxi and set out to walk through the bustling city. She needed time to think, to absorb and reflect. Her first interview had been a sobering experience, and one she wouldn't forget in a hurry. Only a fortuitous twist of circumstance had carried her on to victory. It was a lesson worth remembering.

The city was noisy in the rainy evening. The pavements glistened and wisps of mist gathered above the street lamps. Voices reached her from a nearby pub where the windows blazed with light. It sounded warm inside, warm and comfortable and marvellously alive. My God, she needed a drink. She needed something to soothe her shattered nerves.

She stepped through the door and a rousing cheer arose from the customers, causing her to freeze in embarrassment. She hadn't expected such a raucous reception. Someone slapped her on the shoulder. "Come in, lass. Thoo deserves a dram for what tha's done tonight. That'll larn yon Chancellor t'increase our taxes."

The barman smiled at her sympathetically. "If I was you, love, I'd pop into the Select Room. It's a little less crowded in there and a lot more comfortable."

She thanked him and, waving affably at her admirers, carried her drink through a doorway at the rear. She saw a group of men seated around a table and recognised several members of the NWTV staff. There was sports editor Jake Lenehan, cameraman Lennie Wansworth, two electricians and, to Caroline's surprise, anchor man Edgar Stewart.

Stewart looked healthy and relaxed. He was cradling a whisky glass in his palm and talking earnestly to his companions, his puffy, still-youthful face flushed with animation. There was no sign of the flu bug that had bothered him earlier in the day.

She walked toward him, frowning, and he glanced up with dismay.

"I thought you were sick?"

He shrugged. "False alarm. Turned out to be a flash in the pan."

"Why didn't you come back to the studio? You knew we were short-handed."

"Seemed a bit pointless," he said. "Most of the items had already been assigned."

Bloody liar, she thought. He's been plotting something. The guilt in his eyes was unmistakable.

As if he realised what she was thinking, Jake Lenehan, his eyes slightly out of focus, leaned across the table and said in a loud voice: "Why don'cha tell her the truth, Ed?"

Stewart glanced at him nervously. It was clear that Lenehan was drunk. He had gone beyond the boundaries of civilised behaviour and Caroline felt a tremor pass through her body. Something was happening here, something she couldn't quite decipher. The tension around the table was like a palpable force.

"What are you talking about?" Stewart demanded.

"The reason you pulled out've the programme was so Caroline would get stuck with the Chancellor, right?"

She sucked in her breath. Was it possible? Could Stewart really be so devious? It was clear that Lenehan thought so. He was watching the anchor man with a mischievous grin on his face but there was a look in his eyes that was difficult to decipher.

One of the electricians fidgeted nervously. "Pack it in, Jake," he said.

Stewart glanced at Caroline, visibly shaken by the encounter. Some of the colour had drained from his features and there were beads of sweat on his blue-veined cheeks. "You do talk such bullshit, Jake."

Lenehan laughed. "I thought you had a monopoly on bullshit. You've been dishing it out to the viewers for years."

A faint gasp rippled around the table. As a rule, people did not speak to Edgar Stewart in such a forth-right manner. Despite his bumptiousness, he occupied a special place in the NWTV hierarchy and not even the editor, Noel McCarty, would dream of attacking him to his face.

Lenehan however, seemed oblivious to such niceties. His eyes were filled with a disturbing recklessness and Caroline guessed that, like many of the things he did, his outburst had been made on the spur of the moment.

Stewart moistened his lips with his tongue. His face had turned a deathly grey. He glanced around the silent assembly, trying to think of an appropriate rejoinder. In the end, he whispered: "I hate a man who can't hold his liquor."

"If I'm drunk, it's not on your hospitality, Ed. You've got short arms and deep pockets, which makes for a thirsty evening."

Stewart's niggardliness was legendary but nobody mentioned the fact in his hearing. Lenehan was doing his damndest to turn the encounter into a full-blown punch-up.

Stewart seemed almost beside himself with rage. He rose to his feet, trembling violently. "I'm not staying here to be insulted. Either you apologise, or I'm going home."

"Of course you're going home," Jake told him. "You always go home when it's your shout."

Stewart glared at the others as if calling upon them to witness Lenehan's infamy, then he strode to the door and slammed it loudly behind him. Caroline sensed the embarrassment of the men at the table.

"You shouldn't needle that bastard, Jake," one of the electricians said. "He's a dangerous man."

Too true, she thought. Dangerous and unpredictable. Jake Lenehan had made himself a formidable enemy tonight, but he was probably too plastered to realise it. Eyes glazed with alcohol, he looked ready to lash out in any direction. She decided she'd had enough excitement for one evening and, with a cursory nod at the men at the table, drained her drink and headed toward the door. She heard footsteps behind her and saw to her dismay that Jake Lenehan was following in her wake. "Need a chaperon?" he asked. He looked a good deal less drunk than he had a moment ago.

"I'm walking," she told him dryly. "Think you're capable?"

"I'm soberer than I look."

"Okay. But if you fall in the gutter, I'm leaving you where you lie."

They went out into the street, Lenehan strolling along beside her, his features aesthetic beneath his shock of curly black hair.

"Why did you do that?" she asked after a moment.

"Do what?"

"Attack Stewart?"

He grimaced. "He gets up my nostrils. He's arrogant and insufferable."

"He'll never forgive you for humiliating him tonight."

"To hell with the bastard." He spat on the ground and wiped his mouth with the back of one hand. "He hates you, you know. He'd destroy you if he could."

"I can't imagine why."

"Jealousy, of course."

"I'm not after his job, if that's what he's thinking. I have enough trouble holding onto my own."

"But you have two qualities Stewart will never forgive you for. Youth and talent."

"I do wish he'd behave like a grown-up."

"Well, he shot himself in the foot tonight. You were terrific with the Chancellor."

She glanced at him. "You mean that?"

"I wouldn't say it if I didn't. The bastard pulled every trick in the book but you nailed him neatly. It was a *tour de force*."

She chuckled. "If you want the truth, I hadn't the faintest idea of what he was talking about. I just spotted an opening and moved in for the kill."

"I'd better remember to keep my guard up."

His eyes twinkled in the semidarkness and she studied him curiously. He seemed different somehow, softer, gentler. "Don't you have someone waiting at home?" she asked.

"Not any more." He shrugged. "I *was* married once, a

51

trainee sound engineer I met in London, but it was a total disaster. If I remember correctly, we even quarrelled on our wedding night. Two years, it lasted. Less, if you trim it down to the time we actually spent together. She joined the BBC and fell for one of the cameramen. Hazard of the job, I suppose. It gets a little incestuous when you're on the road. Anyhow, things worked out pretty well considering. I've got my eye on the network and I can't afford unnecessary entanglements."

"I admire a man with a romantic turn of mind," she said with a smile.

He was a strange one in many ways; moody and reflective, sensitive and intelligent, humorous and aggressive. In some respects, he reminded her of her father but there was a wildness in him that was difficult to define. He was clearly hot-tempered and volatile, but he was also funny and compassionate, a man who could be relied upon. She liked him.

They turned at last into Caroline's street and she saw the lights blazing from her apartment block. "Almost home."

"How about inviting me up for a coffee?"

She shook her head. "I don't think that would be a very good idea. You're not the only who doesn't want complications. I intend making it to the top too. I owe it to somebody very dear to me."

"Who's that?"

"My father."

He examined her in silence for a moment as they drew to a halt at her front door, the light from the street lamps giving life to his eyes. "You'll make it," he said after a moment. "Just remain yourself and you'll make it, Caroline. Nothing in the world can interfere with that."

His lips brushed hers and he set off into the darkness, moving on the balls of his feet like a fighter coming out at the opening bell. She watched him vanish along the street, his body solid and compact beneath his bulky donkey jacket, then she opened the door and hurried up to her apartment.

*   *   *

52

For the next few months, Caroline threw herself into her work. The interviews continued and though few of her exchanges were as spectacular as her encounter with the Chancellor, she proved she had a natural instinct for bringing out the best in people. Her style was sympathetic yet tempered with a core of steel when the necessity arose. Guests trusted her. Sometimes they forgot the cameras and divulged – often in emotional terms – jealously guarded secrets. An international movie star wept openly as she described her mental anguish over her inability to bear children. A famous footballer, notorious for his aggressive behaviour on the field, admitted that he was a secret homosexual. The newspaper critics began labelling her "Mother Confessor".

With politicians her approach was markedly different. Then, the TV studio became a coliseum in which the two antagonists circled each other warily. Caroline learned to spot the telltale facial expressions which indicated when an interviewee was under stress, and strike for the jugular. Her groundwork was faultless and soon the newspapers had changed her nickname to "Grand Inquistador".

Inevitably, Caroline's success aroused jealousy in anchor man Edgar Stewart. Stewart had disliked her from the start and now began considering ways in which the threat she posed might be eliminated. He hired a private detective to investigate her background but the detective's report proved disappointing, for Caroline's lifestyle appeared above reproach. She had few boyfriends, and her occasional candlelit dinners and visits to the theatre invariably ended in the same innocuous fashion, with the escort in question dropping her off outside her front door. She was content to spend her evenings at home or visiting her father at his private hospital.

Stewart was filled with frustration as he read through the detective's summary. It seemed beyond credence that anyone's life could be so unblemished. People were people, which meant vices as well as virtues, and wherever Caroline's failing lay Stewart was determined to find it. He examined the section dealing with her father's illness and an idea began to form in his head. He called a reporter on the local newspaper, a man who owed him a personal favour but when he outlined what he had in mind, the reporter was dubious. "Too near the knuckle, old chum. My editor wouldn't touch that with a bargepole."

"I've got the facts right here," Stewart said. "You'll have them on your desk first thing in the morning. Charlie, you owe me this. It's a genuine human interest story, and the public have a right to know. It's your duty as a journalist."

The reporter sighed. "Okay, send me the bumf and I'll see what I can do. But no more favours, understand? I've got my reputation to consider."

Two days later, Caroline was seated at her desk when Noel McCarty came out of his office. He stood for a moment looking down at her, then he dropped the morning newspaper onto her typewriter. "Better take a look at page two."

Caroline saw a photograph of her father seated in his wheelchair somewhere in the hospital grounds. From the picture's quality, it was clear that it had been taken with a telephoto lens. The caption read: "TV Girl's Guilty Secret." And underneath: "Caroline Force Abandons Dying Father To Pursue Glamorous Television Career."

Caroline read the article with astonishment. It was a travesty of the truth and though it stuck to a factual framework, its tone and message – that Caroline had deliberately committed her father to an institution – was outrageously distorted.

Caroline simply couldn't rationalize the article. She went to see a solicitor but whilst the man was sympathetic, he advised caution. "I understand your anger, Miss Force, but I have to confess that in view of the circumstances it would be very difficult to disprove the newspaper's allegations. Strictly speaking, it contains just enough evidence to give it an air of credibility and if we went to court your chances of proving libel could be very shaky indeed."

Caroline was devastated but her anger was minimal compared to that of her father. He telephoned the newspaper and demanded to speak to the editor. The editor, impressed by Force's fury, promised to look into the matter.

Caroline returned from the solicitor's office to find a note ordering her to report at once to Rachel Bartlett's private apartment. It was the first time she had been summoned to a TV executive's home and she was filled with foreboding as she drove through the lunchtime traffic. It wasn't her fault that the newspaper had attacked her. Her father lived in a hospital because he required expert medical attention. The company had no right to pillory her for things which were beyond her control.

Rachel herself opened the apartment door. She smiled when she saw Caroline standing there. "Bang on time. I like that. I have a slow digestive system, and I can't stand tardy guests."

In the centre of the apartment, a table had been laid for two. "I get so tired of eating out," Rachel explained. "Besides, I like to show off once in a while. I'm an excellent cook, you know."

"Your note didn't mention lunch."

Rachel laughed. "Blame my secretary. She's a lovely girl, but a typical northerner. Why use three words when one will do? I hope you like Middle Eastern food, it's rather a speciality of mine." She walked to the cocktail cabinet. "How about a drink?"

"I'd better not. I'm on the air tonight."

"You've got hours yet. Besides, it'll do you good. I should think you'll need a pick-up after reading that bilge this morning."

"You've . . . seen the article?"

"Filthy stuff. If I was the editor, I'd have the reporter's hide."

"I suppose you want me to apologize?"

Rachel looked surprised. "For what?"

"Embarrassing the company."

She gave a laugh. "Don't be an idiot. *Minute-By-Minute*

picks up more viewers in a single evening than the *Gazette* reaches in an entire year. Publicity-wise, we don't give a damn about their spurious allegations. My only regret is that the article's so cleverly worded, it'll be difficult to prove that you've been libelled."

"That's what my solicitor says."

"However . . ." Rachel smiled brightly. "The public's memory is notoriously short and by this time next week they'll have forgotten all about it, so let's relax and enjoy ourselves, shall we?"

Caroline had never seen Rachel so animated. In the television studio she was noted for her sharp tongue and abrasive manner, yet here at home she seemed different somehow, softer and gentler. She talked incessantly over lunch (a delicious mixture of stewed lamb and prunes served on a bed of porridge-like substance which Rachel called couscous) entertaining Caroline with amusing anecdotes from her early days at ITN. She was witty and charming, and despite the unpleasantness of the early morning, Caroline found herself beginning to unwind.

When they had finished dining, Rachel filled two large cognac glasses.

"I really shouldn't," Caroline protested.

"Celebration," Rachel said, cupping her drink in her palm. "You'll have plenty of time to sober up."

"What are we celebrating?"

"You, naturally."

"Me?" Caroline was puzzled.

"I took quite a chance on you in the beginning. If you'd failed, my enemies would have hounded me out of office. But I followed my instincts which I'm happy to say proved gratifyingly sound."

"I'm glad," Caroline told her.

"You have a very great talent, one that's difficult to define. Sometimes, when I watch you conducting an interview, it's like watching a surgeon with a scalpel, only instead of the human anatomy you deal with the human psyche. You're a valuable asset to the company,

56

Caroline, and I'd be a fool to deny that. I'm rewriting your contract."

"In what way?"

"That newspaper story was ugly and grotesque. It was also too well informed to be accidental. Our press department investigated and it appears that the article originated from Edgar Stewart."

Caroline was startled. "I can't believe it."

"I'm afraid it's the truth."

"I knew Edgar didn't like me, but I never dreamed he would stoop so low."

"My dear Caroline, Edgar Stewart is a natural predator. He's prepared, and always has been, to step on anyone who looks like getting in his way. You are much too talented to be treated lightly. He has to destroy you for his own peace of mind, and since he can't attack you in the professional sense he's decided to do it on a personal level. Unfortunately for Edgar, his little plan has backfired. Talking to the press without company clearance is contrary to the terms of his contract. I'm dismissing him forthwith. You will take over the *Minute-By-Minute* anchor chair, commencing tonight."

Caroline almost dropped her brandy glass.

"Well?" Rachel smiled. "Don't you have anything to say?"

"I'm . . . I'm overwhelmed. It's like a dream."

"It's no dream," Rachel said. "From this point on, you'll become the company image – the figurehead, if you like – of everything NWTV stands for. That's an honour in itself, but prestige alone won't pay the rent or help with the grocery bills. I intend to see that your salary is adjusted to reflect your new-found status."

"How can I ever thank you?" Caroline whispered.

"We'll think of something," Rachel purred, gently squeezing her hand.

It was not a blinding revelation. Caroline had suspected the truth for some time now, but it was the moment she was finally brought face to face with it; though she had never questioned Rachel Bartlett's sexuality, there were some things which were difficult to ignore – like the intimate huskiness in her voice, the naked longing in her sultry brown eyes.

A wave of sickness swept up from Caroline's stomach. She rose to her feet, trying to hide her confusion. "I have to get back for the afternoon meeting." She glanced at her wristwatch.

"You've not finished your cognac yet."

"You drink it. Brandy always makes me feel queasy."

Rachel followed her to the door. "We must do this again sometime. I like the informality of meeting away from the office. It seems more relaxed somehow."

"Yes, let's."

Caroline's legs were trembling as she hurried along the passageway and took the elevator to the parking lot downstairs.

Caroline made her anchor debut the very same evening. The following morning, the local newspaper praised her performance and ran a leader by the editor recanting its earlier story. She might have been jubilant if it hadn't been for the thought of Rachel Bartlett. As she contemplated the future ahead, she was filled with a sense of troubled foreboding.

Chapter Four

Rolling crests of sand, some nearly a hundred feet high, rose from the desert floor. In places, the dunes blended as the sun flattened out their creases, turning them into a ghostly heat-haze until it was impossible to tell where the earth ended and the sky began.

High buttes rose to the north, casting vivid shadows across the arid ground as Danny Le Hir guided his truck along the narrow track. In the vehicle rear, his men sat in stony silence. They were clad in battered combat fatigues and their faces were covered with a thin orange dust; at their feet, handcuffed and blindfolded, the three prisoners, two blacks and a white, crouched motionless on the shuddering deck. Even inside the driving cab, Danny could smell the redolence of their fear.

The track skirted a narrow draw flanked by thorn bushes, and Slattery said: "Looks as good a place as any."

Danny stopped the truck and as he jumped to the ground, something scurried through the brush in front – a fox or a jack rabbit, he couldn't tell which. Over west, heat shimmered off the flattened toplands. The three captives, still shackled, were dragged from the vehicle rear and pushed toward the empty gully.

"Fetch the spoons," Slattery ordered, and Spitz drew out three ex-marine shovels complete with telescopic handles, tucking them under his arm.

The prisoners blinked, rubbing their wrists as the handcuffs and blindfolds were removed. "Who are you people?" the white man asked, his voice quivering.

Slattery spat on the ground. There was a slight cast in his eye which gave him a faintly unhinged look. The crumpled forage cap he wore had been tilted rakishly to one side, revealing a massive scar which ran from the crown of his skull to just behind his left ear; Slattery told people he had picked up the scar in Vietnam, but Danny knew he was lying. Slattery had never served in Vietnam.

"We're from the Sanitation Department," Slattery said. "What you might call moral hygienists."

The captives were silent as they digested this information. Sick with fear, they looked inoffensive in the desert sunlight but Danny knew their appearance was deceptive. They represented the dregs of humanity, two drug pushers and a compulsive rapist set free by clever lawyers. Now it was up to Danny and his friends to make society clean again.

One of the negroes, a giant of a man with muscular shoulders, examined Slattery warily. "I got no fight with you folks."

"We got no fight with you neither. This ain't a personal matter." Slattery threw the shovels onto the ground. "Just dig," he ordered. "And make it deep. We don't want the jackals scooping you out for breakfast."

Sweaty and trembling, the three men toiled at the arid earth, the clink of their shovel blades making a discordant symphony on the warm desert air. Danny felt sorry for what they had to do. Some things were too monstrous to contemplate, he reflected, but they had to be faced, coldly and cleanly, if society was to survive.

When the diggers had finished, he pulled out his cheroots and handed them around while Slattery stood to one side, waiting impatiently. He struck a match, shielding the flame with his palm, and lit each of the cigarillos in turn. The captives sucked hard, filling their lungs with smoke.

Slattery drew out his handgun and carefully checked the firing mechanism. The first prisoner crossed himself as Slattery moved behind him. They heard cicedas humming in the scrub nearby and somewhere overhead, a plane droned lazily.

Danny flinched as the handgun barked. He hated this, he'd always hated it. The General had explained a thousand times that pity was a luxury he couldn't afford, but the General didn't have to see the victims, or smell their fear, or soil his hands with the fluxure of their blood.

Slattery's boots scraped as he moved along to the next in line. The second man kept his body very tense as Slattery raised the pistol, his sinews straining against his saturated singlet. An unpleasant odour filled Danny's nostrils as the man's sphincter muscle gave way.

Crack – two down, one to go.

There was a moment in which time seemed to hang suspended, then the remaining survivor, moving with a suddenness that surprised them all, dropped to one side and drove his fist savagely into Slattery's crotch. The move was so unexpected, so shattering in its impact that for a fraction the others could only stand and blink.

Slattery sank to his knees with a ghastly expression, holding onto his genitals, and without waiting for his captors to recover, the muscular negro plunged into the circle of scrub. They heard him crashing through the underbrush, his powerful limbs tearing out plants and tendrils.

Danny took off in the giant's wake, sprinting as hard as he could. He saw the man directly ahead, his powerful shoulders framed against the sky. He was heading for the truck, that was instantly apparent, and Danny remembered with dismay that he had left his driving keys in the dashboard.

The ground tilted and he stepped up his pace, measuring the distance between himself and his quarry. He fixed his gaze on the fugitive's back then sucking in his breath, hurled himself forward in a classic football tackle. His shoulder slammed into the giant's thighs, bringing him down in a breathless tangle but before Danny could move, the giant's fist locked around his windpipe and panic seared his temples as he tore desperately at the corded wrists. The crack of a carbine echoed in his ears and the top of the negro's head lifted off, spraying his cheeks with blood.

Spitz came out of the woods still cradling his carbine, and nudged the body with his boot. "Pretty good shot," he said with satisfaction. "Din' like to risk it with the glare and all, but I figured he was about to rip your head off."

He helped Danny to his feet, wiping the blood from his cheeks and hair. "You okay, chief?"

Danny nodded, not trusting himself to speak. The incident had disturbed him more than he cared to admit.

Spitz spat on the ground and slung the carbine over his shoulder. "Let's get these scumbags under cover 'fore they contaminate the earth they're lying on."

Night was falling when they arrived back at their motel. Danny helped the others unload the truck, then made his way to the reception office. He still felt sick about what had happened. He never seemed to get over that, the feelings of guilt and remorse. It was the one thing the General's counselling failed to alleviate.

The desk clerk looked at them sleepily as he handed out their keys. "How'd the hunting go?"

"Lousy," Slattery told him. "We din' get a single shot."

"Too bad." The clerk rummaged in Danny's pigeon-hole. "I got a message for Mr Le Hir. A Detective Fairfax would like you to contact him in Los Angeles. Said it's urgent. He'll be on duty until after midnight."

Danny was surprised. Fairfax was one of the General's oldest friends; it was rare for him to make contact except in the most dire emergency. He went to his room and called the detective's number. Fairfax's voice sounded strained when he came on the line. "Danny?"

"What's wrong, Matt?"

"We got ourselves a situation here. It's Wayne, the General's son. He's been picked up on a possessions charge."

Danny swore under his breath. "How serious is it this time?"

"Junior league," Fairfax said. "He was caught smoking grass at a kid's party but you know what it'll do to the old man."

Danny did know. General Thirkeld hated the drugs culture more than anything in the world. Hearing that his own son had been using dope would devastate him and Danny couldn't bear that.

He said: "How many officers were involved in this bust, Matt?"

"Only two."

"Arrest sheet been processed yet?"

"It's on the computer now."

"How much will it cost to get the charges squashed?"

There was a pause at the end of the line, then Fairfax said: "Pricey, Danny. There's other guys involved."

"Talk to them. I want this thing erased, understand?"

"Okay, I'll see what I can do."

Danny glanced at his wristwatch. "Can you meet me in the station lobby in a couple of hours? I need to talk to Wayne and straighten things out."

"I'll be there," the detective promised.

Wayne Thirkeld watched sullenly as Danny was ushered into the visitors' room.

Seated behind a wire grill, he wore a faded sweatshirt and a pair of ragged jeans held in place by orange suspenders. His cheeks were sallow, his hair tangled and his chin was covered with silken beard stubble.

"Hello, champ," Danny said.

Wayne ignored the remark. He showed no emotion as Danny sat down. The officer who had escorted him moved to the room rear and leaned against the wall, folding his arms.

"They tell you what happened?" Wayne asked.

"Sure."

"My father know yet?"

"Nope."

Wayne's face was strangely unformed, as if it had been smoothed out of melted clay, leaving only the salient features intact.

"Why'd you do it, coach?" Danny asked.

"I don't know." Wayne thrust his fingers through the

63

wire grill, picking at the strands liked a caged tiger. "For Chrissake, the old man thinks I'm some kind of saint, but I'm a human being with problems of my own."

"Most people work out their problems in a sensible manner."

"Easy for you to talk. All my life – for as long as I can remember – he's been holding you up as his pride and joy. If you want the truth, Danny, there've been times when I've hated your guts. I mean, he doesn't give a damn about what happens to me and Stevie."

"That's a lie. Sometimes you disappoint him, that's all."

Wayne examined Danny darkly through the wire. As a child, he had often resented his adopted brother and even now after all these years, traces of the old enmity still lingered. "You're so controlled," he said. "Don't you have any weaknesses, Danny?"

"I've learned to subdue them. That's something you should try once in a while."

"I bet you'd like that. Seeing me quiet and respectable."

"I won't have you hurting the old man, Wayne."

"Your eyes are blind, Danny," Wayne said exasperatedly. "It isn't the General who's hurting, it's me. He scares the shit out of me. Know why? Because I'm ordinary, that's why."

Danny ignored the outburst. He said: "Where was Julian when the arrest took place?"

Julian was Wayne's homosexual boyfriend. It was a source of bitter contention in the Thirkeld household that the General's youngest son belonged to the Los Angeles gay community.

Thirkeld hated pederasts. He especially hated them as members of his own family. When he'd learned of his son's leanings, he'd ordered him out of the house and forbidden him to return. Even now, though he tolerated Wayne at family gatherings, he made little secret of his disapproval or his contempt.

Wayne said: "At home, where he usually is."

64

"Called him yet?"

"I was afraid the old man might find out."

"He isn't a monster, Wayne," Danny said gently.

Wayne gave a brittle laugh. "Not to you maybe, but he's the devil incarnate to me."

Danny rose to his feet. He liked Wayne, always had. Despite the boy's shortcomings, Danny regarded him as his natural brother. But he knew it was pointless talking to him in his present frame of mind. "I want you to keep this to yourself," he said. "Don't even tell Julian. It'll be a secret between you and me."

"You're not going to bail me out?"

"Not necessary. The charges are being dropped. They're going through the paperwork now."

Danny was halfway to the door when Wayne said: "Hey, coach?"

Danny looked back. Beneath his shock of tangled hair, Wayne's eyes gleamed with a malicious humour. "You can fix anything, can't you, Danny?"

It was after midnight when Danny got back to his motel room. He stripped off his shirt and tossed it onto the bed. He felt drained, mentally and emotionally. It had been a harrowing twelve hours, all things considered.

He sat on the bed and was pulling off his shoes when he heard a sound in the bathroom behind him and turned to see a woman watching him from the doorway. She was red-haired, and clad in a flimsy housecoat belted at the middle. Danny could tell from the way the material fell that her figure would be full and firm.

"Who're you?" he asked.

"My name's Peggy."

"Well, what are you doing here? This is my room." He picked up the key and rattled it meaningfully.

The woman came toward him. Her hair fell on both sides of her face like the folds of a tent, parting in the middle to reveal a pair of startling brown eyes; her breasts jiggled beneath the housecoat and as if she realized the passions such provocativeness could engender she paused,

65

smiling, at the foot of the bed. "Mr Slattery thought you might like some company. I understand you've had a pretty rough day."

Danny moaned. "Please put on your clothes and get out of here. I'm whacked, understand? I need sleep."

"Sure I can't tempt you?"

"Aphrodite couldn't tempt me at this moment."

Still smiling, the woman let the houserobe fall from her shoulders. In the filtered sunlight, her body was strong and beautiful. Danny saw the deep swell of her breasts and the crisp triangle nestling between her legs. A searing urgency gathered in his groin and he felt his stomach tighten. "On second thoughts," he said, rising to his feet, "maybe I'm not as tired as I figured."

The woman chuckled as Danny took her in his arms. She slid her hand down the hard flat wall of his stomach, her fingers groping, clutching, squeezing. "I had a feeling you would perk up somehow."

It was breathlessly hot in the TV control room. The director and PAs sat watching the monitor sets where Caroline was bringing the programme to a close.

"Thirty seconds to end of transmission," the senior PA intoned. "Coming to Caroline in fifteen seconds. Ten seconds for the pay-off then into end credits."

"Stand by studio. Coming out of VT in five . . . four . . . three . . . two . . ."

Jake Lenehan watched Caroline wind up the programme with a reminder that *Minute-By-Minute* would be back on the air at the same time tomorrow. As usual, her timing was impeccable. He felt a surge of approval. Much of Caroline's success, he thought, came from the fact that in a world of pretension she was totally sincere. Had she put on a facade, the merciless eye of the camera would have betrayed it in a twinkling. The viewers realised this and trusted her to the hilt.

He watched the end credits drawing to a close. Caroline was joking with the floor manager, her face smiling and animated. Then the telephone rang on the director's desk and he spoke for a few moments before putting down the receiver, his face deeply troubled. He turned in his chair, addressing the control room at large. "That was the newsroom. They've just had word from Cresthaven Hospital. Caroline's father died forty minutes ago."

A faint gasp arose from the people sitting there and Lenehan felt his stomach contract. Dear God, he thought. He knew that Caroline idolised her father.

"Somebody has to tell her," a girl whispered.

"I know that. Don't you think I know that?" The director was a kindly man but situations like this were beyond his realm of experience.

"It's your responsibility," a PA said firmly. "You're the one in charge."

"Why should it be my responsibility? Noel McCarty's the programme editor."

"I'll do it," Jake offered.

"You?" The director looked at him.

"Unless you'd prefer to handle it yourself?"

"No way." The director paused, looking a little guilty. "Want one of the girls to come along? Give her a shoulder to cry on?"

"No." Jake's voice was adamant. "Go back to the office. She'll need plenty of space until she gets used to the idea. You can pass on your sympathy in the morning."

Caroline was almost at the door when Jake drew her gently to one side.

"What's up?" she asked, smiling. "You look as if they just cancelled your season ticket at Studley Stadium."

"Caroline, I've got some very bad news." He hesitated. "Your father passed away just before the programme started. Some sort of relapse, I gather. I'm terribly sorry."

A strangled sob burst from her lips and he watched a flurry of emotions flooding across her features, horror, disbelief, anguish, dismay. He wanted to gather her into his arms, to comfort and console her, but what could he say – what could anyone say – at such an unbearable moment?

67

He squeezed her wrist, conscious of how warm her body felt through her silken blouse. "I'll take you to the hospital. You'd better not drive, the state you're in."

Caroline spoke little as they sped through the darkened suburbs. She stared at the road ahead, her eyes glassy and impenetrable. Jake felt totally out of his depth. Some things life just didn't prepare you for, he thought, and this was one of them. He was no psychologist, had never professed to be, but some inner part of him longed to take away her pain.

The doctor met them in the hospital lobby, his face filled with sympathy. It was clear that he knew Caroline well.

"It wasn't his illness," he explained, taking her hand. "It was a heart attack. Could have happened to anyone, although of course, we have to assume that your father's condition was a contributory factor. It's a small consolation, I know, but at least he's been spared the final indignities of his disease."

Caroline showed no emotion when she saw her father's body. Michael Force lay on a trolley, his cheeks still tinged with colour. He might have been sleeping, Lenehan thought. Caroline kissed her fingertips and pressed them against the corpse's lips.

She was steady as a rock as they went through the paperwork. Only when they returned to the parking lot did her composure finally crack. She collapsed against the car door, sobbing helplessly, and Jake gathered her into his arms, gently stroking her hair. "I'm taking you to my place," he said. "You shouldn't be left alone tonight."

When they reached his apartment, he sat her in a chair and carefully lit the gas fire. Then he poured a stiff glass of brandy. "Get this down," he ordered, pushing it into her hand.

She shook her head.

"Try it. You need something to pull you together."

Caroline sipped absently, choking a little as the fiery liquid stung her stomach. It was clear that she was dangerously close to breaking point. Suddenly, to Jake's alarm, the glass slipped from her fingers and she began to weep, her shoulders shaking.

He massaged the back of her neck. He had never felt so powerless in his life. He lowered himself until his eyes were level with hers and she stared back at him through a veil of tears. They sat like that for a very long moment, then she cradled his face with her hands and slowly, hesitantly, kissed him on the lips. Jake felt the pressure of her mouth steadily increasing. He felt her fingers touch his neck and move among his clothing. She didn't want to talk nor to hear him talk. She wanted to escape, to lose herself in the timeworn ritual of love and her breath rose with an urgent passion as he gathered her into his arms and carried her tenderly into the bedroom.

For a brief while before and after the funeral, Caroline thought she was losing her contact with reality and probably would have cracked if it hadn't been for Jake who proved a tower of strength during her weeks of grief and bereavement.

Since her earliest childhood, Caroline's father had been the centre of her universe. Now she felt as if some terribly essential part of her being had been summarily amputated. Though she had always realized his death was inevitable, the unexpectedness of it, the sheer incongruity – a heart attack, of all things – seemed the cruellest blow of all.

It was Jake who saved her from emotional disintegration. She moved into his apartment and he cared for her, comforted her, and listened with calm and infinite patience to her impassioned outpourings of anguish and despair. Afterwards, Caroline knew she could never have made it through that terrible period if it hadn't been for Jake's support.

Jake, for his part, realised that Caroline was going through the greatest crisis of her life and resolved to do his damndest to ease her suffering. She was, after all, an extraordinary girl and he counted himself lucky that she had turned to him in her moment of need. However, love featured low on Jake's list of priorities. He had things to do, places to go and despite his feelings, he knew he could travel more swiftly if he made the journey alone.

Rachel Bartlett, meanwhile, was puzzled and concerned. Though she had sent messages of condolence following Michael Force's death, she had received no reply. She knew Caroline was a sensitive girl and wondered if she had overplayed her hand.

One day, she mentioned Caroline's name to the *Minute-By-Minute* editor, Noel McCarty, who laughed.

"Oh, she's coming out of her shell since she took up with our sports editor, Jake Lenehan. Romance is definitely in the air. Wouldn't surprise me a bit if we hear wedding bells in the spring."

Rachel's heart chilled at these words but she forced a smile to her lips and said: "If we do, I'll send them a case of champagne to celebrate."

For the rest of the day her mind was in a turmoil. That evening, she parked her car opposite Jake Lenehan's apartment and sat in the darkness, quietly waiting. She felt ashamed and humiliated, but the situation was beyond her control. Caroline's beauty, her air of cool refinement, had besotted Rachel's senses. She simply couldn't help herself.

Toward midnight, a car pulled into the parking lot and Rachel shivered as she saw Caroline emerge with Jake. She watched them walk up the stairway, holding hands. On the threshold, Jake kissed Caroline passionately on the mouth.

Rachel waited until they had vanished from sight, then drove home in a fury, her body trembling. That night, she lay torn by jealousy and desire. She had to find a way of liberating Caroline from Jake Lenehan's influence.

The following morning, she telephoned a number at the BBC in London. The voice which came on the line was gruff and familiar. Larry Simons had been one of Rachel's lovers during the period she had been trying to deny her sexuality. Their relationship had been doomed to inevitable failure.

"Is that you, Larry?"

There was a moment's pause, then the tone softened. "Rachel? This *is* a surprise. To what do I owe the pleasure?"

"It's business, so don't get any wrong ideas."

"With you, it's always business, Rachel."

She paused. "I hear you're looking for a new reporter on the *Line-Up* programme."

"Who told you that?"

"Word gets around. I've got a possible here you might be interested in. He's been handling our sports desk for the past eighteen months."

"Too specialized. I need someone who knows the drill. *Line-Up*'s the premier current affairs programme in the country and it's my intention to keep it that way."

"I'd be willing to make it worth your while, Larry."

His voice grew curious. "How?"

"He still has four months of his contract to run at NWTV. I'll continue to pay his salary until the expiry date. That way, you can try him out and it won't cost you a penny."

He laughed. "Are you kidding? The BBC would never stand for it."

"Don't tell the BBC. Come on, Larry. You've been in this business long enough to know how to doctor a programme budget. Whoever you engage, you'll be taking a gamble until they prove they can cut the mustard. This way, you'll be doing it for free."

"It's the craziest idea I ever heard. What's in it for you?"

"That's my business. There *is*, however, one proviso."

"What's that?"

"The arrangement is strictly between you and me. No hint of it must leak to the man himself. It has to come out of the blue and he has to start immediately, understand? I'll make sure he gets the necessary clearance."

The voice sounded amused. "What Machiavellian intrigue are you hatching up now, Rachel?"

71

Rachel smiled grimly. "In military terms, I believe it's what's called a fighting retreat."

When the conversation was over, she telephoned the *Minute-By-Minute* editor, Noel McCarty. "Noel, it's the Royal Television Society Ball in London on Thursday. I thought I might take one of our presenters to represent the company."

"Good idea," McCarty agreed. "Bit of flag-waving can't do any harm. Anyone special in mind?"

"Yes. Tell Caroline Force that I'd like her to accompany me."

Chapter Five

When Caroline heard the news, she was filled with alarm. She knew the invitation was nothing more than some curious strategy of Rachel, designed to wittle away her resolve and leave her vulnerable and defenceless.

The next few days passed in a kind of haze. She considered telling Jake but it seemed a despicable measure when she had no real proof. She wondered how she would react if Rachel made unwelcome advances. The programme controller was a powerful and influential woman and she held Caroline's career in the palm of her hand.

Caroline's anxiety mounted as the fateful day approached. To her relief, she saw no sign of Rachel on the southbound train but she found a letter waiting for her at the hotel reception desk. "Caroline," it said, "I'm tied up with business meetings for the afternoon so why don't we meet for cocktails at around six-thirty? That should give us a chance to chat before the festivities get under way."

Mollified, Caroline went up to her bedroom and telephoned Jake. It was Noel McCarty who came on the line. "Jake isn't in today," he told her. "He called about three hours ago to say something important had cropped up."

Caroline was surprised. Jake had been getting ready for work when she'd left his apartment. He was usually so punctilious in matters relating to his job.

She called again after she'd returned from shopping but there was still no reply. Baffled, she showered and dressed for dinner.

At half-past six, she met Rachel in the cocktail bar. Rachel was clad in a simple black evening gown that emphasized her elegant features. When she saw Caroline, she rose from her stool and held out her hand. "This is the first chance I've had to tell you how sorry I was to hear about your father's death," she said. "I sent you a letter at the time, but I'm not sure if it actually arrived."

Caroline felt her cheeks colouring. She had indeed received Rachel's letter but for reasons of her own had decided not to acknowledge it. She said: "I'm afraid everything was so confused . . ."

"I quite understand. Bereavement's a terrible thing. It knocks the whole world out of alignment."

She snapped her fingers at the waiter. "Let's have a drink to fortify ourselves for the circus ahead."

To Caroline's surprise, Rachel was cordial but business-like and by the time they went into dinner she was beginning to relax.

The ball was a sumptuous affair at which the television industry celebrated its achievements. Caroline sat with a group of BBC executives and apart from a brief interlude during which Rachel regaled her with stories of the NWTV Management Board, was able to concentrate on the general conversation.

After the meal, she took advantage of the speechmaking to call Jake's number from the lobby phone booth. Still no answer. It was so unlike Jake to disappear for no reason.

The evening turned out to be both lively and enter-taining, with a steady array of guests touring the dinner tables, greeting old friends and making new ones. Rachel introduced her to a variety of important figures and she did her best to appear witty and charming.

When the band finally played the national anthem, Rachel thanked her by formally shaking her hand. "I appreciate your coming. I know it's a bit of a chore, but I do think it helps the company's image. See you at breakfast in the morning."

A wave of relief swept Caroline as she took the elevator upstairs. All her worries had been for nothing. She let herself into her hotel room and called Jake's number for the final time, but the line buzzed monotonously.

She looked at her wristwatch. It was two o'clock in the morning. Frowning in bafflement, she took off her clothes and slipped into bed.

When Caroline arrived back at NWTV, she found Jake's desk ominously empty. His in-tray, normally an untidy mess, had been scrupulously cleared of papers.

Noel McCarty, reading the *Daily Telegraph*, grinned when he saw her. "How was the ball, Cinderella?"

"Where's Jake?" she asked, ignoring the remark.

"You don't know?" McCarty looked surprised.

"Noel, I've been calling his home for the past twelve hours and I can't get any reply. He's vanished off the face of the earth."

"Jake quit. He got a job as the new roving reporter on the BBC's *Line-Up* programme."

Caroline was stunned. "You're kidding me."

"He didn't tell you?" McCarty dropped his newspaper on the desk. "The offer came out of the blue. Yesterday morning, to be exact."

"And he's started already?"

"That was the deal. Instant availability. He got special dispensation on his contract." A look of concern came into his eyes. "I'm sorry, Caroline. I naturally assumed you'd already discussed it."

Caroline didn't answer. A terrible uneasiness took hold of her as she stared through the window at the river below.

Jake was trying hard not to show his nervousness as he entered the BBC's *Line-Up* office. He had forsaken his customary jeans for a respectable business suit and on a moment of impulse had stopped off at a barber's shop to get his beard trimmed; now he looked, if not elegant exactly, at least a little more presentable than usual.

To his surprise, he found the office empty. He paused on the threshold, his uncertainty deepening. He felt out of his depth, out of his environment. The whole thing had happened so quickly – the telephone call, the mad dash to London – there'd been scarcely time to draw his breath. He hadn't even rung Caroline for Pete's sake, so frantic had been his last few hours. And now, like a classic anticlimax, there wasn't a soul in sight.

As he stared across the deserted desks, a girl walked in from the opposite door and looked at him in puzzlement. He recognized Elizabeth Wheatley, one of *Line-Up*'s leading correspondents.

"Hello," she said. "You must be the new boy."

He nodded, feeling strangely tongue-tied. On-screen, Elizabeth Wheatley exuded a faintly schoolmarmish air but in the flesh she looked ravishing and sensual. "I'm Jake Lenehan," he managed at last.

She smiled, examining him curiously. "We heard you were coming. Bit sudden, wasn't it? I mean, they haven't even advertised the job yet."

"I know. Took me by surprise. They called me yesterday morning."

"Wow, what have we got here? You didn't go through the customary channels?" Her eyes were all over him, absorbing everything at once.

"All I've ever done is sports," he admitted. "I hope I don't fall flat on my face."

"Don't worry." She chuckled. "It's largely a matter of bluff. Give me a call if you need any help."

Was he imagining things or was there a hint of flirtation in her voice? She was an attractive woman to be sure. Not attractive in the way that Caroline was attractive, but alluring certainly, and – the most exciting element of all – clearly available.

At the thought of Caroline, he came out of his reverie. "Listen, is it possible to make an outside call from this place?"

"Sure. Just press 'nine' followed by the number." She reached for her handbag. "I'll pop up to the canteen and let you enjoy your conversation in peace."

He watched admiringly as she walked from the room, moving with a supple grace that almost took his breath away. He hadn't been mistaken; Elizabeth Wheatley was quite a knockout and he whistled softly as he reached for the telephone and punched out NWTV's number. After a pause, a woman's voice came on the line. "Yes?"

"It's Jake Lenehan here," he said. "I'm trying to reach Caroline Force."

"Ah, Jake," the voice said. "This is Rachel Bartlett."

"Miss Bartlett?" Jake was puzzled.

"I asked the girl on the switchboard to reroute all Caroline's calls to my extension. How are things going in London?"

"Well . . . I've only just arrived."

"I'd like to congratulate you. It's what you've always wanted, isn't it? Reporting on the network?"

"Right, Miss Bartlett. And thank you for releasing me. I want you to know how much I appreciate it."

"Oh, I didn't release you, Jake. You still belong to NWTV. For the next four months at least."

He frowned. "I don't understand."

"It's very simple. We pay your salary while *Line-Up* puts you through your paces. If you make the grade, they'll take you on in four months' time. If you don't . . ." She left the sentence unfinished.

Jake said: "But the BBC would never agree to such an arrangement."

"The BBC knows nothing about it. It's a private matter between the editor and myself. It gives him a chance to see you in action and saves him money on his autumn budget."

"Hold on a minute. Why are you doing this?"

"I thought you'd be pleased. After all, you've been pestering me for months about a reporter's job. Now you've got one."

"But what's in it for NWTV?"

"NWTV gets nothing, Jake. I, on the other hand, get a great deal. You took something from me and I want it back."

Jake's bewilderment increased. "Miss Bartlett, I never took anything from you in my life."

"I'm talking about Caroline, Jake. In legal jargon, I believe it's what they call 'enticement'."

An icy coldness gripped Jake's body and he felt the hair on his scalp beginning to prickle. "You're lying," he managed at last.

"She's mine, Jake."

"I don't believe it."

"You've been in television long enough to know how the system works. Do you seriously imagine Caroline could have risen so fast without my loving support?"

He stood perfectly still, trying to dispel the images tumbling into his mind. It had to be a joke, there was no other explanation. If Caroline really had been Rachel's lover, then surely he, of all people, would have realised it? But deep in his heart, he knew that rationality played no part in such things. "What do you want?" he whispered hoarsely.

"Stay away. No letters, no phone calls. Attempt to contact her, exchange so much as a word and you're out on your neck. That's the deal."

Jake's voice sounded strange when he spoke again. "What happens when the four months are up?"

Rachel chuckled. "By that time, Caroline will be mine for good."

The apartment smelled stale when Caroline unlocked the door. It was several weeks since she'd last been home. She dropped her suitcase and moved from room to room, opening up the windows.

She still felt dazed over the events of the past few hours. Though she had called Jake repeatedly, she'd found his line mysteriously engaged. She wasn't a fool, she knew when someone was trying to avoid her and she hated the uncertainty of it all. If he had changed his mind about their relationship, then why couldn't he tell her so? She needed stability in her life and Jake's behaviour was undermining that.

She picked up the telephone and tried again. This time, a girl's voice answered, crisp and businesslike. "BBC's *Line-Up* programme. Elizabeth Wheatley speaking."

"Is Jake Lenehan in the office, please? My name's Caroline Force."

"Ah."

The speaker paused, and Caroline heard her breathing deeply at the end of the line. "I have a message for you, Miss Force."

"Yes?"

"Jake says please don't call again."

Caroline sucked in her breath. It couldn't be true, she thought.

"He's decided to concentrate on his career," the voice went on. "He advises you do the same."

The statement hung in the air, flat, casual, mocking. "That's ridiculous. Jake wouldn't send such a message without discussing it first."

"He sees little point in clinging to the past. Besides . . ." The girl hesitated. "He's already involved with somebody else."

"I don't believe it." Caroline's fingers tightened on the receiver.

The voice softened. "Miss Force, the person he's involved with happens to be me."

Caroline's throat muscles felt oddly paralysed. She stared at the apartment wall where every feature, every dust speck seemed awesomely pronounced. After a moment, the girl went on: "It's painful, I know, but human beings are notoriously mercurial. The sooner you learn to live with that, the happier you'll be."

Caroline heard a click as the speaker replaced the receiver. For a few moments, she stood perfectly still, a terrible emptiness gathering inside her. Then the doorbell rang, and she opened it in a daze.

Rachel stood on the threshold, holding a bottle of champagne. She was dressed in a simple two-piece business suit, and her hair had been swept back to emphasize her angular cheekbones. "Did I ever tell you I was telepathic?" she said with a smile. "I always know when somebody needs a shoulder to cry on."

* * *

79

The guests had already begun to assemble when Danny emerged onto the patio. Dance music drifted across the lawn and coloured lanterns dangled from the trees. Below, the lights of Palm Springs formed a dazzling gridiron in the desert night.

He paused for a moment to light a cheroot then moved down the steps, nodding politely to various acquaintances. The General's birthday party was getting off to a promising start, he thought. He noticed several movie stars among the throng, together with local businessmen and leading members of the Palm Springs artists' community.

Wayne Thirkeld, the general's youngest son, stood with his boyfriend beside the kidney-shaped swimming pool. Wayne had discarded his customary jeans for a smart tuxedo, but he looked incongruous in the elegant setting.

Danny walked toward him. "Glad you could make it."

"An invitation from the General is like a command from the Almighty," Wayne said wryly.

Danny nodded to his companion, Julian, a slender young man with long blond hair and delicate cheekbones. "Welcome to Palm Springs."

Julian fidgeted uncomfortably and grunted a monosyllabic reply.

"Where's Stevie?" Wayne asked, speaking of his older brother.

"He's here someplace. We thought he mightn't make it tonight – he's been pretty busy at the law courts lately – but Gendun said he saw his car arriving."

"I'll bet he did. Even Stephen wouldn't dare ignore the old man's birthday."

Danny looked at him remonstratively. "You insist on talking about your father as if he were some kind of ogre."

"One of these days, Danny, you'll see what the rest of us see. Then you won't feel so complacent any more."

Danny sighed. There was simply no arguing with Wayne once he got an idea into his head; it would take an earthquake to shift it. He slapped his half-brother gently on the shoulder. "Enjoy yourselves, boys," he said, and moved on to mingle with the other guests.

Most of the men knew Danny and it was clear from their wistful looks that most of the women wished they did too, for Danny looked devastating in his immaculately cut tuxedo. He saw Stephen Thirkeld, the General's other son, standing with his wife Sandra at the food table. Stephen was several inches taller than Wayne, but his crinkly black hair was beginning to recede above the temples and he wore a goatee beard to hide his receding chin. He wiped his lips with a napkin as Danny approached.

"Good to see you tonight," Danny said.

"Like the prodigal son." Stephen shook Danny's hand. "Where's the old man?"

"Resting. He'll be down later. First, he has a little business to attend to."

"On his birthday?" exclaimed Sandra, a petite woman in her early thirties.

"The General thought it might be a good idea to hold a committee meeting while all the delegates are gathered in one place."

"Not the Movement again?" Stephen exclaimed. "I thought he'd given up that madness for good."

"The madness, as you call it, lies with society, Stevie. The General's trying to put the madness right."

"Danny, he's got you crazier than he is. He's a crank, for God's sake, and a dangerous crank. He thinks he's omnipotent, a common affliction among military men. In the eyes of the authorities, he isn't a patriot, he's a criminal."

"Your father believes in the future of the United States, and if I may say so, you should try being a little supportive once in a while instead of sneering at everything he does."

"You're brainwashed, Danny. You don't even know what's right any more. You're just a collection of attitudes." Stephen paused, his cheeks flushing with embarrassment. "Listen, forget I said that. The old man represents everything I detest in this world but

81

he's still my father and though this may surprise you, I love him in some strange obsessive way."

Danny saw Gendun, the General's manservant, coming toward them through the crowd. Gendun bowed, his olive face solemn and grave. "General Thirkeld would like you to join him in the conference room," he said. "The meeting is about to begin."

"Tell the General I'll be right there," Danny answered.

"Jump, Fido," Stephen said with a malicious grin.

Danny gave him a cool look, then he nodded at Sandra and made his way into the house interior. For as long as he could remember, Stephen – like Wayne – had fought his father tooth and nail, but Danny loved them both, admired them both, and lamented deeply their fall from grace.

When he reached the conference room, most of the delegates had already assembled. They sat around the polished table, smoking cigars and drinking champagne. They were nondescript men with nondescript faces, their ages ranging from twenty-five to seventy. Thirkeld himself headed the group, and beside Thirkeld was a cadaverous-looking man with a shock of red hair.

"This is Leon Halberstam," the General announced without preamble. "He's a communications adviser and he's going to help us achieve our dreams. However, the price tag promises to be hefty. Several million dollars at first estimate."

One of the committee members whistled. "That's a lot of *dinero*, Walter. Is Huxley worth the price?"

"Arnold Huxley's a weak man, but he's also a malleable one, which makes him invaluable to the Movement."

"What would the money be used for?" another man put in.

Leon Halberstam interjected. "Basically, you'd be buying television space," he explained. "Not for two or three nights, but as part of a carefully regulated campaign. As I understand it, you want to put a man in the White House. Not an easy task with Lawrence Clayman the most popular President in the past fifty years. However,

General Thirkeld assures me that the Vice-Presidency role will suit your purposes for the moment. Our present Vice President, Randolph Guthrie, has already announced that he will not be standing for re-election in three years' time and pressure groups are currently barracking Clayman to accept Huxley as his running mate. What we have to do is persuade the President that Huxley is the only logical choice."

"How?" asked a florid-faced man with a Texas accent.

"By changing his image." Broussard filled his glass from the water jug in the centre of the table. His red hair was so profuse that it made his features look slightly elongated, as if they had begun to sag under the weight. "Senator Huxley's an impressive candidate. He's clean-cut, youthful and athletic. He has a charming wife, two equally charming daughters and a natural penchant for political debate. Unfortunately, he's a little too smooth for the public's liking. There've been rumours of dubious business deals, of extramarital relationships. Now, these may seem unimportant while Huxley's still a senator but caterpult him into the Vice President's chair and it isn't only the FBI who'll be taking a long hard look at his background – the Press will have themselves a field day."

"We'll worry about that when the time comes," General Thirkeld said. "The first, the most important objective is to get Huxley on Clayman's ticket."

"Agreed. That's why television is so important. A political commercial – the right political commercial – can shape people's minds and alter their opinions. There's a knack to it, as Josef Goebbels discovered back in the thirties. Maybe you can't change the voter's viewpoint by bombarding him with television messages but you *can* strengthen beliefs he already holds. First rule . . ." Broussard raised a finger into the air. "Forget politics. Nobody pays attention to the issues anyhow, only to what they see on the screen."

"What d'you think we're running here, a soap opera?" asked the florid-cheeked Texan.

"Exactly. A political campaign is a soap opera using

real people. Even the news commentators can't exist without pictures. Which means that by devising the right visuals, we can virtually choreograph Huxley into the White House."

Glasses clinked on the lawn outside and a woman's laughter, shrill and discordant, echoed in their ears.

A man said: "How we gonna run this campaign without the President realizing?"

Broussard continued: "We concentrate on the basic values – sex, family, income, stability. We tell the American public that Arnold Huxley is basically 'nice people'. We shoot a big production number showing him riding the range like an old-time frontiersman. He's tall and good-looking so he should be pretty snappy in a ten-gallon hat."

"How d'you know he can even sit on a horse?" the Texan demanded.

"We'll teach him. We'll put him through his paces until every time he climbs into a saddle, he looks like John Wayne. It'll go a long way toward dispelling his smoothie image."

"And afterwards?" the General asked.

"Afterwards we humanise him. Show him mingling with children and elderly people. Get the message across that what Huxley stands for is what America stands for. In three years' time, providing we do our job right, Lawrence Clayman will have no choice but to name him as running mate. If he doesn't, he'll be drummed out of office."

Again, a silence descended over the conference table. The delegates looked at each other through the pall of cigar smoke. At last a man said: "I never realized politics could be so dirty."

General Thirkeld chuckled. "Welcome to the club."

By the time the meeting was over, the party was in full swing. Danny heard the sound of laughter as he wandered onto the terrace. He saw a woman in a low-cut gown collapse inelegantly among the flower beds. Her husband

84

dragged her to her feet and steered her unsteadily toward the ladies' room.

A youth was seated alone at the ornamental fountain and Danny recognized Wayne's boyfriend, Julian. Danny liked Julian, he felt sorry for the boy. The General refused pointblank to acknowledge Julian's existence and he always seemed like an outsider at family gatherings.

Danny walked toward him. "Mind if I sit down?"

Julian glanced up and Danny saw that he had been crying.

"Free country."

Danny settled himself on the fountain rim and reached into his pocket for a cheroot. "Any objections to my smoking?"

Julian shook his head and Danny placed the cheroot between his lips and leaned forward to light it. "Where's Wayne?"

"Drinking at the punch bowl. I think he's a little tight."

"Can't you stop him? You know how the General hates drunkenness, especially among members of his own family."

"Wayne can't help himself. That's part of his problem. He can never do anything in moderation. The General raised him to be some kind of Superman but he isn't Superman, he's an ordinary human being."

"The General knows that. He's an exacting man but he's not an unfeeling one. If only Wayne could meet him halfway."

Julian looked at him in the lamplight. "You think Wayne hasn't tried? All his life he's been fighting against his real nature. He's battered his brains out turning himself into the kind of person he thinks his father will admire, but he's wasting his time because nothing he ever does will satisfy that evil old man."

"Don't talk about the General like that," Danny said mildly.

Julian looked down at his feet, sniffing softly. A strand of hair dangled untidily across his forehead. "I can't expect you to see it. You're blind to the General's faults because you're the General's creation, but Wayne's terrified of him."

"That's ridiculous."

"He's terrified, I tell you, terrified of his own father. That should tell you something at least."

"You're exaggerating," Danny said.

Julian laughed shrilly. "What an innocent you are. You see yourself as Lancelot to General Thirkeld's King Arthur, but you don't realize that Camelot is simply Macbeth's castle in disguise." He paused, staring out at the illuminated foliage. "I just wish we could go away for a while, somewhere beyond the General's reach – Europe maybe. It would give Wayne a chance to find himself. He needs to escape from his father's influence."

"Why don't you?" Danny asked. "There's nothing to keep you in Los Angeles. Wayne hasn't a job, and from what I gather, neither of you has any serious commitments."

"Haven't you heard? Flying to Europe costs money."

"Well, you're not exactly on welfare."

Julian snorted. "We might as well be as far as the pittance the General calls an allowance is concerned."

Danny was surprised. He had always found the General generous to a fault. It had never occurred to him that Thirkeld might be somewhat more niggardly with people who didn't please him. "Listen," he said, "if you really mean that, about going to Europe, I can let you have some money."

Julian looked at him. "Seriously?"

"Sure."

"I can't promise we'd ever be able to pay it back."

"I don't want paying back. Wayne is my brother, for Chrissake."

Julian's eyes glistened and he smiled at Danny through the tears. "I knew we could depend on you, Danny. You may be the General's man, but underneath the madness you're still a human being at heart."

Danny heard someone cough behind him and straightened in embarrassment. He saw Gendun watching them in the lamplight. "The General sends his apologies," Gendun said, "and asks if you'll be good enough to join him in his study. He has something important he wishes to discuss."

Danny nodded to Julian and rose to his feet. He made his way to Thirkeld's office and tapped lightly on the door. "It's unlocked," boomed the General's voice from within.

Thirkeld was seated at his desk in front of a mock-Tudor fireplace. The reading lamp had been switched on and its green shade cast mottled patterns across his leathery cheeks. There were dark circles under his armpits and he was filled with a curious testiness that seemed to belie his age. He waved Danny to a chair. "That faggot still on the patio?"

"Julian?"

"Damned ponce. How does Wayne have the effrontery to bring him here?"

"Julian is his partner, General. He feels as loyal to him as he does to you."

"Loyal?" Thirkeld sniffed. "Wayne can't even spell that word. He's perverted and depraved, a disgrace to the human race."

"He's your son, General."

"To my everlasting shame."

Thirkeld fumed silently, his muscular features gleaming. Whenever Wayne's homosexuality entered the conversation, he became apoplectic with rage. Danny knew there was nothing else for it but to let him calm down again.

"What did you think of the meeting?" Thirkeld asked after a moment.

Danny shrugged. "Halberstam's a persuasive man."

"Don't approve of him, huh?"

"I didn't say that."

"You don't have to. I can see it in your eyes."

The General was not a man who believed in mincing words and Danny had always admired that, seeing in

87

his directness a kind of fearless honesty. He waited for Thirkeld to continue.

"You don't think Huxley has a hope in hell, do you?"

"I don't like the man as a politician but if he can be controlled, he might be just the instrument we're looking for. However . . ." Danny hesitated. "Supposing Lawrence Clayman doesn't want him for Vice President?"

"That's the whole point of the television campaign. Somehow, during the next three years, we've got to make Huxley seem so perfect for the role that Clayman won't dare turn him down."

"It'll cost us millions."

"Is any price too high for the redemption of the United States?"

Danny sighed. He hated questioning the General's decisions. He had been raised to accept the man's counsel as beyond reproach and as time had gone by, this conviction had become deeply ingrained in his psyche. "Anything you say is okay with me, General. I'm just pointing out the obstacles, that's all."

"Obstacles are made to be overcome. However, we *do* have a problem, a serious problem."

Danny knew this was the reason the General had summoned him here and he waited patiently for his guardian to proceed.

Thirkeld said: "There's a political stringer in Washington DC named Elliot Behr. He's been digging up dirt on Huxley's business practices."

"Who told you this?"

"Huxley telephoned me less than an hour ago. He's worried sick. The reporter's been snooping around for more than a month now. If he prints what he's got in his dossier, he could blow our campaign sky-high."

"Are you sure we're putting our money on the right jockey, General? Seems to me our Senator has an awful lot of skeletons in his cupboard."

"Huxley's no plaster saint," Thirkeld admitted. "He's gutless and corrupt, but after we get him into power, we'll dictate the rules. First though, we have to ensure that as far as the American public is concerned, the Senator's background is squeaky clean."

He looked down at his hands, folding them on the desktop in front of him. His battered face looked ravaged and embattled. "I hate to ask this, Danny. God knows, you've already done more than enough, but somebody has to handle the problem and you're the only one I can trust."

Danny kept his face expressionless as he said gently: "Don't apologise, General. I'll be happy to iron out the wrinkles for you."

Chapter Six

"Here he comes," Dubinsky said.

Seated in the parked car, Danny watched the Washington journalist, Elliot Behr, emerge from his apartment and stroll up the street toward the Tally Ho Tavern. He was a small man in a shabby raincoat and he walked with a limp like someone recovering from the aftereffects of a stroke.

"He heads for that bar every night, regular as clockwork," Dubinsky said. "Sometimes he stays for an hour, sometimes two. He just sits alone, rummaging through newspapers."

Behr looked a sorry case, Danny thought. His body was stooped, his hair badly in need of a trim. It was hard to believe that such a miserable misfit could pose a serious threat to Senator Arnold Huxley.

"His wife left him nearly five years ago," Dubinksy went on. "He's got a son in Minnesota and a daughter in Idaho, both grown-up. Now he lives alone at the building rear. He's a sad sack really."

Too true, Danny thought. Some people deserved at least one break in their lives but Elliot Behr, regrettably, was entering the final moments of his. Killing diminished a man, blurred the dividing line between self-esteem and self-disgust, but the General wanted the journalist silenced and to Danny that was like a command from God.

"You know what you have to do?" he said.

Dubinsky nodded and stepped from the car, slamming the rear door behind him. Danny watched him scurrying across the street, then he pulled on his raincoat and followed briskly in the journalist's wake.

*   *   *

Elliot Behr had two things on his mind as he headed toward the tavern; the first was his craving for a drink which had been plaguing him for most of the afternoon, and the second was the bulky dossier lying in his apartment which he confidently hoped would boost his career when he offered it to the *Washington Post*. It might even get him a staff job if the signs were right, though he had to admit that with his drinking record, the possibility seemed pretty remote. Still, if the story was syndicated he could look forward to a period of prosperity for a change, which seemed a blessed prospect after the impoverishment of the last few months. Here he was at fifty-six with barely seven thousand dollars to his name; not much to show for a lifetime of dogging the lobbies on Capitol Hill.

Behr was reflecting on this unhappy state of affairs when someone grabbed him from behind and bundled him roughly into a darkened alley. He crashed over a line of garbage pails, blinking in astonishment. A figure moved out of the shadows and fear turned Behr's insides to jelly as he saw a ragged scarecrow towering above him, wielding a wicked-looking clasp knife. "Money, you mother," the apparition said with a menacing hiss.

Behr thought wildly. He had a few dollars in his pocket but if he surrendered them, he would have to spend the rest of the evening alcohol-free and he didn't know if he could survive that. "I'm broke," he choked. "Believe me, I been outta work for nearly a year now."

The scarecrow placed his knife blade against Behr's nostril and gently nicked the skin. Behr's eyes watered and he tasted the salty flavour of blood.

"Money," the scarecrow repeated.

"I already told you," Behr gasped, terrified out of his wits. "If I had any, I'd give it to you but I'm living on welfare, for Chrissake. Look at this raincoat. You think I'd be walking around in a rag like this if I had any choice?"

There was no compassion in the scarecrow's face as he placed the knife against Behr's stomach. "I'm going to open you up, ratface."

Oh Christ, Behr thought. If he wanted to live, now was the time to forfeit his wallet. But he couldn't. He just couldn't.

Suddenly, a figure appeared in the alley opening. A fist lashed out, and to Behr's relief the mugger's knife went spinning into the darkness. The man reeled back against the wall as Behr's rescuer went to work on his stomach. It was clear from the start that the newcomer knew how to handle himself. He picked his targets with consummate ease, striking in a bewildering flurry of punches that left the scarecrow gasping in pain. The fight lasted barely a minute before the mugger, with a strangled moan, lurched out of the alley and staggered off along the deserted street.

Behr's rescuer let him go. He crouched down, wiping blood from the journalist's nose. "You okay?"

"Yeah." Behr eased himself up on his elbow. "That weirdo was trying to kill me."

"So I gathered. Symptom of the times, I'm afraid."

The newcomer helped Behr to his feet and he stood for a moment, holding onto the alley wall. Now that the danger had passed, the ache in his stomach had become an almost unbearable torment. He had to have a drink, he knew, but he couldn't bear the thought of drinking alone.

He examined his rescuer keenly, screwing up his eyes in the subdued lighting. The man was young and athletic-looking with a pleasant, intelligent face.

"Feel like a brew?" Behr said hoarsely.

Surprised, his rescuer hesitated a moment. Then he smiled. "Why the hell not? I got nothing better to do."

"I worked on the *Post* when Ben Bradlee was a rookie," Behr slurred. "People talk about the great years, the 'Golden Age', but I'll tell you – by today's standards, Woodward and Bernstein were a couple of pussies."

Danny looked at his watch. It was almost midnight and the saloon was emptying fast. The bartender kept glancing in their direction as if hoping they would leave. Danny decided Behr had drunk enough. "I think we better go."

92

Behr looked surprised. "Wha'n the hell for?"

"Bartender's waiting to close up."

"Hell, it's barely midnight. We got 'nother coupla hours yet."

Danny motioned at the empty wall-booths and Behr blinked blearily. "Listen," he said. "I got an idea. Why don' we buy a bottle an' go back to my place?"

"I thought you had to work tomorrow."

"Tomorrow I'll be fresh as a daisy. Hangovers are never my problem."

"Okay, anything you say, chief."

Behr's apartment block was falling to bits. The floor was uncarpeted and the entrance hall smelled of stale urine. As Danny helped him up the rackety stairway, lurching dangerously from side to side, Behr began to sing in a cracked, discordant voice: "There was a wild colonial boy, Jack Duggan was his name . . ."

On the second landing, a door opened and a woman stood framed in the lamplight, her hair in rollers. She glared at the two intruders, her face indignant. "Mister Behr, have you any idea what time it is? This is a respectable boarding house and people are trying to get some sleep."

"Go back to bed, you old bat," Behr told her happily.

When they reached the top, he leaned against the wall, fumbling through his pockets for his door key. He was singing again, a different tune this time. "Carry me back to old Virgineeeeeeeey . . ."

The apartment, like the rest of the building, was cramped and seedy. There was a TV set, a thread-bare sofa and an assortment of furniture littered with discarded clothing. A window overlooked an alleyway several floors below.

"Put the whiskey on the table while I get some glasses," Behr said, and shuffled into the kitchen.

Danny took the bottle from his pocket and found a place for it among the unwashed dishes. A draining lassitude had gathered in his limbs. He felt sorry for Behr, but his personal feelings were irrelevant here. He had a job to do. Once instituted, events had to lead to their sad and inevitable conclusion.

He saw a photograph on the apartment wall, a picture of a man smiling ingratiatingly at the camera. Using a pencil, Behr had added a pair of satanic horns. "Hey," Danny said, "isn't this Senator Arnold Huxley?"

"Sure is," Behr called from the kitchen. "I'm doing a special profile for the *Washington Post*."

"Wow, I really admire this guy. I figure he'll end up President some day."

"What, are you kidding me?" Behr came in from the kitchen, staring at Danny with drunken amusement. "You really mean that?"

"Sure, I mean it."

"The guy is a jerk, for Chrissake. You just have to look at him to see he's a jerk. What's more, he's a crooked jerk."

"Hey," Danny said, "this is a face with integrity, with honest-to-goodness virtue."

Behr made a sound like a train whistle. "I can't believe what I'm hearing here. You actually admire this schmuck?"

"Of course I admire him."

"Well, have I got news for you, nephew."

Behr pulled open a drawer and took out a cardboard file. He placed it on the cluttered table and stepped back, motioning Danny toward it. "Take a look," he said. "Go on, take a look."

Danny opened the folder. There were photostat copies of invoices and business letters. "What is this?"

"The sordid truth about Huxley's financial affairs. And believe me, he makes the Mafia look like Sister Theresa."

So there it was, the whole miserable bag of tricks laid out in front of him. Danny couldn't believe it had been so simple.

He said casually: "Kind of dangerous, isn't it, leaving evidence like this lying around? Got any back-up copies?"

Drunk, Behr missed the implication. "Nope. The story's too big to risk some other bastard muscling in."

A wave of sadness swept Danny then, a feeling that came not so much from the prospect of what he had to do as the knowledge that Behr, the perpetual loser, had just played his last tragic hand. He pulled on his gloves as the journalist turned to open the whiskey bottle. A bronze statuette of a naked nymph stood on the cabinet top and he tested it for weight. Twelve or fifteen pounds, he estimated. He saw the journalist's scrawny neck and untidy hair as he walked toward him. At the last moment, Behr, alerted by some infinitesimal movement, glanced over his shoulder and the smile froze abruptly on his face. Danny swung the missile in a vicious arc and a tremor rippled along his arm as Behr's skull splintered in all directions and he collapsed to the floor, his face a glassy mask.

Danny stood for a moment, breathing heavily. The journalist didn't even look human any more, just a bundle of slightly soiled rags. He wiped the ornament clean, then opened the window and leaned out, filling his lungs with air. The images were ingrained in his mind so clearly that he knew he would remember the sight for the rest of his life.

He gathered Behr in his arms and tipped him through the open window, watching the spindly body turning in a slow, unwilling somersault as it hurtled toward the alley floor. It hit the ground with a sickening crunch.

Danny filled a dish with water and placed it, together with a washcloth, on the threadbare carpet as if Behr had fallen whilst cleaning the window. Then he picked up the dossier and quietly left the building.

Howard Anderson, head of the BBC's Current Affairs Department, was a pompous man with a thin, aquiline face whose expression implied that he disliked confronting the banalities of the world. Caroline had the feeling that he disapproved of her in some way though she couldn't say why. She sat in his office, trying to hide her nervousness as he examined her critically over his half-moon spectacles. "I had a call from Noel McCarty," he said. "He appears to regard you as some kind of prodigy."

Caroline was surprised. "I didn't realise you knew Noel."

"We worked together at ITN. Good man. First-rate newshound."

"He's highly thought of at NWTV."

"You too, it seems. Which brings me to my point, Miss Force. Why leave a place where you command so much esteem?"

"Personal reasons," she said.

"Personal?"

"I have to get out. My life is becoming too difficult up north. I need a new start, a fresh direction."

He pursed his lips, humming deep in his throat. His pointed nose seemed to dominate his features, producing a curious Concorde effect. She knew he was intrigued by her, but she knew too that he was entrenched in decades of masculine thinking. "I have to be frank," he said. "Your pedigree is good and Noel's endorsement speaks for itself, but *Eleventh Hour* is a news-orientated programme and looking through your c.v., you've had very little journalistic experience."

"I've been a journalist for nearly two years."

"Electronic journalism, not the printed page. There's a difference. I need correspondents who can scribble a script in the teeth of a howling gale, who can smell a story a mile off and translate that story into television terms."

"I believe I can do that."

"In *Eleventh Hour*, we're not dealing with the glamour end of the business. Our reporters get rained on, spat at and sometimes even physically assaulted but they're expected to get on with their jobs regardless. They belong to the greatest broadcasting organization in the world and that's considered reward enough."

Caroline said: "I didn't come here to get into the glamour end of the business, as you call it, Mr Anderson. I'm not looking for special favours and I don't see myself as

96

a 'TV personality'. If you want the truth, I get embarrassed by that side of things. But I've gone as far as I can at NWTV and I have to move on before I stagnate. In addition, my private life is becoming complicated and that's the major reason why I need this job so badly."

Anderson seemed impressed by her forthright manner. He took out a snuffbox, tapped a small amount of powder onto the back of his hand and sniffed it into his nostrils. She sensed he was using the gesture as a smokescreen while he made the decision that would formulate her future. "Very well," he said at last. "We've looked at your audition tapes and Noel McCarty's perfectly right, you do have a remarkable on-screen presence. I'm prepared to offer you a three-month contract. Prove that you can do the job and I'll extend it to a year. But I must warn you that *Eleventh Hour* has no room for prima donnas."

"I wouldn't expect it to." Caroline met his gaze with perfect equanimity. "I won't let you down, Mr Anderson, I promise."

If *Minute-By-Minute* had seemed chaotic, *Eleventh Hour* was like a volcano waiting to crupt. Throughout the morning, people engaged in raucous arguments with the full-throated exuberance of spectators at a football match. Caroline sat at her desk and tried to look absorbed, but scarcely anyone had spoken to her since her arrival and she was acutely conscious that the unit controller – the man responsible for scheduling the reporters and news teams – was either oblivious to her presence or contemptuous of her existence.

Already, she was beginning to regret her decision to leave NWTV. It had been an impulsive thing, totally spontaneous. Though she hadn't loved Jake, his rejection had wounded her deeply and she'd grown increasingly miserable working on *Minute-By-Minute*. In addition, while Rachel Bartlett had made no direct physical approaches, it had been clear that sooner or later her infatuation would get out of hand, and moving to London had seemed the only sensible answer. To Caroline's dismay, however, her colleagues at the BBC seemed to regard her as some kind of intruder, and filled with misgivings, she watched the atmosphere grow more and more frantic as the morning progressed.

Just before noon, the unit manager slammed down his telephone and addressed the newsroom at large: "I need a reporter. There's a bomb scare at Notting Hill."

Silence fell across the office, then a girl said: "The reporters are all on assignment."

"For Chrissake, the bloody thing's scheduled to go off in forty minutes. This is an emergency."

Caroline rose from her chair. "I'm available."

The man glared at her. "Who the hell are you?"

"The new girl. Caroline Force."

"This is a heavy job. Could be dangerous."

"Well, I can't sit around the office waiting for cosy little fashion stories from Paris. I came to report, so let me report."

He sighed. "Okay, get out to the tube station. The director's name is Andy Purvis. Listen to what he tells you and follow his instructions to the letter, understand?"

Caroline didn't answer. She was already running toward the door.

By the time she reached Notting Hill, the danger area had been cordoned off by teams of uniformed policemen. A few curious onlookers stood behind the barriers, while along the Bayswater Road, the traffic was snarled to a standstill.

Caroline flashed her pass at the constable on duty and he directed her to the camera crew who were busy setting up their equipment. She had rarely felt so nervous in her life. Studio interviewing was one thing, but out here in the field there was little room to manoeuvre, little time to compose oneself for the all-important moment.

The director, a curly-haired young man not much older than Caroline herself, seemed surprised to see her. "Where did you spring from? I thought I knew everyone on *Eleventh Hour*."

"First assignment."

98

"Bloody hell, they're chucking you in at the deep end all right. Nervous?"

"Scared out of my wits," she admitted.

"Don't be. It's a straightforward up-and-down job. First you interview the police officer in charge, basic news stuff. Then we grab some wallpaper shots and afterwards, you write the commentary. Think you can do that?"

Caroline nodded and the director positioned her alongside the camera. The police superintendent was already waiting, a dignified man with grey hair and a trimmed moustache. There was something so casual in the procedure that she found it difficult to believe that just a few feet away, a bomb was scheduled to go off at any moment.

The sound engineer clipped a microphone to her blouse and she cleared her throat, her nervousness deepening.

"Few words for sound," the engineer snapped.

Caroline asked the superintendent what he'd had for breakfast, and he told her.

"Okay, mark it," the director ordered.

The assistant cameraman held up a clapperboard. "Nothing Hill Explosion. Slate Thirteen, Take One."

Purvis cued Caroline and she launched into her question, keeping it simple and direct. She stuck to a basic news approach – clipped queries, factual answers – and it proved easier than she'd expected; in fact, once the dialogue got under way, she forgot her surroundings and the interview continued for several minutes before a police sergeant appeared and called the superintendent away.

Caroline cursed under her breath but the director seemed unperturbed. "Don't worry, we'll fill in the blanks over wildtrack later. Let's try a few 'noddies' while they're sorting things out."

"Noddies?"

"Shots of your reactions. It helps with the editing and makes it look as if we're using two cameras instead of one."

Feeling like an idiot, Caroline stood in front of the camera and forced a rapt expression into her face, gazing intently into space. She went through her questions again, a process which proved trickier than she'd imagined for it was difficult to sound natural while talking to thin air. At last the director yelled "Cut", and she allowed herself to relax. Not too bad for a beginning, she thought. She'd busked the interview, but providing they got the necessary shots, she had enough background material to sustain a comprehensive report.

After a while, a policeman appeared. An explosive device had been found on the platform downstairs and all civilians had been ordered back behind the wire. The director drew Caroline to one side as the crew began dismantling their equipment. "Nobody's guarding the station entrance so I'm sneaking our camera down the back stairway," he said. "Strictly speaking, it's against the rules but we've got nothing to show for this exercise except a few boring wallpaper shots and I'm not going home with an empty can. You head for cover if you'd rather."

Caroline said: "If you go, I'm coming too."

"Good girl. But you'd better hang onto your pantyhose. It could be a bumpy ride."

She had no idea why she'd been so impulsive – mostly, she supposed, it had been a touch of bravado – and her heart was pounding as they crept down the stairway and entered the station foyer. It was quiet, deathly quiet, and the station newsstand looked strangely forlorn and abandoned on the empty concourse. There was no sound of life from the subways below.

"How's the light?" the director asked.

"Bit murky but acceptable," the cameraman told him. "We're picking up sunshine from the fanlight windows."

"Okay, let's roll."

Feet clattered on the escalator in front and Caroline saw a man running toward them, clad in military fatigues. He mounted the stairs two at a time, waving his arms impassionedly. "Get back, get back. Bloody thing's about to pop."

She registered the scene like a frozen tableau; the stairway banister, the advertisement boards with their shiny glass panels, the newcomer's cheeks gleaming with sweat. Then a wave of white-hot air blasted into her face and for no reason she could clearly explain, she was lying on her back staring at the fanlight ceiling. Before her eyes, the glass panes shattered into a million pieces, erupting outwards in a shimmering cascade. She felt the ground vibrate with a tremendous explosion and a pall of thick smoke came belching up from the platforms below. Her eardrums shuddered and for one breathless moment, she thought the top of her skull had come off, then she realized she'd bumped her head against the concrete paving.

"I'll say this for your opening debut." The director was laughing, tears of merriment streaking his smoke-blackened cheeks. "Nobody can claim it didn't go with a bang."

Caroline sat in the BBC canteen, cradling a cup of coffee. She felt drained, her body limp, her mind torpid. The events at the underground station had shaken her badly but they seemed to have had at least one beneficial effect; news of the bomb blast had resulted in a slight thawing among her colleagues and she had the impression that she'd passed some kind of unwritten test. Now she was trying to assimilate her senses while she waited for the video tape to be edited.

She saw a girl coming toward her with a strong, sensual body and a wilful, slightly plumpish face. Something about her features seemed vaguely familiar. She drew to a halt at Caroline's table. "Caroline Force?"

"Yes?"

"I'm Elizabeth Wheatley."

Caroline frowned, noting the anger in the young woman's eyes; it was not a rational anger but a smouldering hysteria that bore little resemblance to logic or reason.

"I understand that you're working here?"

"It's my first day. I've joined *Eleventh Hour*."

"Bit unwise, wouldn't you say?"

"Because of Jake, you mean?"

"Of course because of Jake."

"What's the problem? He isn't even in this building."

"You're bound to run into each other sooner or later."

"I doubt that. We're working on different programmes."

"Oh, you'll find a way, I'm sure."

Caroline said wearily: "If you want the truth, I wouldn't touch Jake Lenehan with a bargepole. It's all over between him and me."

"Expect me to believe that?"

"This may come as a shock to you, but I don't give a damn what you believe."

"Jake's with me now," Wheatley said firmly. "I want there to be no misunderstanding."

"There won't be. I'm happy for you both. Really I am."

"If I hear that you've been anywhere near him, I'll finish you in this business for good. I can be a very vindictive woman and you'll find that I have an extremely low boiling point."

She strode away, her high heels clicking on the uncarpeted floor, and tears of anger filled Caroline's eyes as she watched her join a group of people seated near the canteen doorway. She was sick to death of being pushed around.

She rose to her feet, following in the young woman's wake. A jug of water stood on the serving counter, and on an impulse she snatched it up, heading toward Elizabeth Wheatley's table. Wheatley's companions paused in their conversation and watched quizzically as she approached.

She emptied the jug's contents over the TV reporter's head and Wheatley gasped in astonishment as water slopped over her face, drenching the front of her dress. Her hair hung in tatters across her glistening forehead.

"I too have an extremely low boiling point," Caroline said coolly, and strode out of the canteen.

Chapter Seven

Danny watched the helicopter coming in to land, its plexiglass nose-cone shimmering in the sunlight; the pilot brought it down gently on General Thirkeld's lawn, the draught from his rotors whipping the palm trees and flower beds. Danny glanced at his wristwatch. Eleven forty-five.

He made his way to the conference room and tapped lightly on the door. Members of the executive committee sat waiting expectantly around the elongated table. He said: "The Senator is here."

General Thirkeld motioned him to a chair and thirty seconds later Senator Huxley himself appeared. At fifty-two, he displayed a deceptive youthfulness which belied his age; he had pleasant features and an effusive charm but though his body had once been athletic, it was now on the verge of running to fat. He had romped into the Senate on the back of a state governorship after fighting a vicious battle to unseat the ageing incumbent. Once there, he had taken control of several powerful committees, including banking, intelligence and the armed forces, though he had often been accused of policy vacillation and – to some extent – even dubious morals.

A born politician, Huxley took the initiative from the very first moment, walking forward to shake General Thirkeld's hand. "Walter, you look like a milk-fed quarterback. Why, if it hadn't been for the white hair, I'd swear you weren't a day over forty-five."

General Thirkeld ignored the flattery. "Please take a chair, Arnold."

Huxley seated himself, his tanned cheeks healthy and

relaxed. He glanced around the assembly curiously. "Something wrong?"

"We believe you haven't been entirely honest with us, Senator," Thirkeld told him. "We're all businessmen. We know that it's sometimes necessary to bend the rules a little. But when it comes to the Movement, we have to be absolutely frank with each other."

"I couldn't agree more."

"You may feel that your financial affairs are none of our concern, but since we are spending millions on your political campaign, we believe we have a right to certain sensitive and confidential information."

"I appreciate that."

"Then perhaps you'll also appreciate why it's imperative that you reveal *all* aspects of your business dealings which might prove an embarrassment in the future."

Huxley seemed taken aback. "I don't understand. I already have."

"Not quite."

Thirkeld nodded at Danny who opened a cardboard folder on the table in front of him. "Senator Huxley, have you had any contact with an English businessman named Maurice Ritson?"

Huxley's cheeks blanched. "Ritson?"

"He started in the property business but his interests now range across a wide variety of fields from gasoline to pharmaceuticals. We understand that seven years ago you entered into an enterprise with Mr Ritson which netted you several million dollars. Unfortunately, it happened to be illegal at the time."

"That's preposterous," Huxley breathed weakly.

"We have the evidence right here. You used a complex array of front companies to launder money from illicit gambling interests around the British Isles."

Senator Huxley was no stranger to political scandal, but he realised when he was in dangerous and unfamiliar territory. A sickly gleam came into his eyes. "Where did you get such information?"

"We found it in Elliot Behr's apartment. He was

104

planning to include the details in his profile for the Washington Post."

"God-*damn*."

"Is that all you have to say?" the General asked.

"Walter, I thought it was over and forgotten. It happened seven years ago, for Christ's sake."

"Seven years or seven days, this Englishman is a potential time bomb."

"No, no." Huxley was sweating. "Maurice Ritson would never dream of betraying me. He couldn't, without incriminating himself."

"You and Ritson deliberately broke the law. Can you imagine the impact that news would have if we shoehorned you into the White House? And can you imagine how eager Ritson would be to demand special favours once you were safely in position?"

"When is Behr planning to publish?" the Senator asked.

"Forget Behr. Behr's history. What we have to know – *must* know before we commit another dollar to your future – is the simple, unvarnished truth."

"Walter, I swear to you on the lives of my children . . ."

"Forget your children. Swear on your own life, because that won't be worth a plugged nickel if you lie to us again."

Cheeks ghastly, Huxley said: "I didn't tell you about Ritson because it didn't seem important at the time. We found a loophole in the British law and exploited it, that's all. What we did is no longer viable because the legislation has been changed. However, I've neither seen nor spoken to the man in almost three years."

"Could he have records?"

"Records?"

"Documents, account sheets. Anything which might implicate you?"

"I doubt it. He's hardly likely to leave dangerous evidence lying around."

"We've too much riding on this venture to speculate. For the last and final time, Senator, is there anything else we need to worry about?"

"That's it, Walter, I swear."

"Very well, we'll proceed on schedule." Thirkeld paused, then he added softly: "Danny will take care of Ritson."

Maurice Ritson stared curiously at the young American seated before him. Danny Le Hir was clean-cut and handsome but behind the pleasant exterior he carried a ruthlessness which was difficult to define. A ruthless man himself, Ritson was quick to recognize the symptoms in others. At fifty-one, his carefully studied refinement belied an unscrupulous disposition. He spoke with a clipped English accent which most people put down to a youthful career as an officer in the Guards, but in truth Ritson had never served with the Guards or with any other regiment for that matter. He had grown up in Liverpool, the only son of a modest furniture manufacturer. After borrowing a small loan from his father, he had gone into the property business on his own and by the time he was twenty-three had a portfolio worth four-and-a-half million. Today, Maurice Ritson was conservatively estimated to be worth somewhere in the region of three hundred million British pounds or four hundred and fifty million American dollars.

He examined Danny's business card for a second time, a faint smile playing about his lips. "So how can I help you, Mr Le Hir? Your call from the United States was most intriguing."

Danny said: "I represent a consortium of US business-men who are interested in buying into the pharmaceutical industry."

"The Spencer Group. I've already checked them out."

Danny looked impressed. "I see you believe in doing your homework."

Ritson smiled. "I'm an extremely busy man and I don't give interviews lightly. Despite your proposal – which I have to admit sounded very tempting on the telephone – I had to make sure that you had the means to fulfil it."

"And are you satisfied?"

"Eminently." Ritson folded his hands. "However, I

would like to hear a little more about how this buy-out is supposed to take place."

"It's very simple. The Spencer Group has chosen as its target Manchop Holdings Incorporated. We are planning a carefully orchestrated blitz which could lead to a hundred per-cent takeover of the company."

Ritson looked interested as Danny went on: "We have an outside legal team presided over by Simon Krogel of Friedman and Dupazi. However, what we really need is someone on the inside who can take the initiative. You, Mr Ritson, seem a perfect candidate since you already own a substantial portion of Manchop stock, though not enough to give you any serious headaches should the company switch ownership."

"What is it you're asking me to do, Mr Le Hir?"

"You know all the principal holders, particularly the ones likely to be susceptible to an under-the-counter deal. We would like you to secretly approach a few large individuals. Our initial target is to pick up a minimum of twenty-five per-cent or a maximum of thirty-five per-cent in the first sweep, then follow that up with a second sweep aiming for an extra ten to twenty per-cent."

Ritson said: "That'll hardly pave the way for an all-out takeover."

"Not initially. But it should provide us with just enough stock to give us board representation so that we can check on how well the company's doing. If it stands up to scrutiny, we'll go for a second stage attack involving the entire works."

Ritson looked impressed. He rose to his feet and strolled to the window. "What you're asking me to do could be regarded as reprehensible in certain quarters. I am, after all, a major stockholder and should declare my interests to the board of directors."

Danny said softly: "My executive committee has approved a maximum outlay of four hundred and fifty million dollars. Your commission, together with what you'll make from selling your stock, should rake you somewhere in the region of twenty-six million."

Ritson handled it well, Danny had to give him that, but the muscles along his neck trembled visibly. "I'd like a little time to think about it. A move like this, delicate and sensitive, could prove embarrassing if anything went wrong." He turned from the window. "How long do you intend remaining in Britain?"

"Till the deal is clinched. I'll return to New York when I've secured your cooperation – or your refusal – whichever the case may be."

"Today's Friday. I'm going up to the country for the weekend. I have a house in Dorset which gets me away from the tensions of the city. Why don't I think things over then call your hotel first thing Monday morning?"

"Sounds ideal," Danny said.

Ritson examined him thoughtfully. He liked Danny Le Hir. Despite his youth, the handsome American had handled the encounter with great authority. He was clearly accustomed to dealing with money. He was also intelligent, articulate and charming.

Ritson said: "Look, we're having a few friends up for the weekend. If you've nothing special planned, why don't you join us? It would give you a chance to see something of our English countryside."

Danny looked surprised. "Why, that's very kind of you, Mr Ritson. I'm a country boy myself and cities have a tendency to bore me."

Ritson smiled and punched the button on his intercom machine. "I'll get my secretary to give you the details."

Meldon Towers was a large grey-stoned mansion in the traditional English country style. It stood like a medieval fortress amid spacious lawns and rolling woodland. As Danny slid his rented car to a halt, a grey-haired butler hurried down the steps to greet him.

"Welcome to Meldon, sir. I take it you must be the American gentleman? The other guests, I already know."

The crack of a shotgun reached them from across the lawn and Danny saw a group of people gathered beneath some nearby trees.

"That's Mr Ritson and his wife," the butler explained. "They're shooting clay pigeons. 'Skeet' to you. Mr Ritson is an excellent shot. He's won the Meadowdale Gold Ribbon six seasons in succession."

Danny handed the butler his suitcase. "Will you be kind enough to put this in my room while I pay my respects to Mr Ritson and his family?"

"Of course, sir. We've got you in the Bothwell Suite on the second floor. You really can't miss it."

Danny strolled across the lawn to where the shooting party was preparing for another salvo. Ritson, Danny saw, had forsaken his business suit for a pair of old-fashioned plus fours. With him was an attractive woman in her early forties and a blonde-haired girl in her early twenties. Both women were dressed in tweed skirts and sensible walking shoes.

When Ritson saw Danny, he called out in welcome. "Ah, Mr Le Hir, you managed to find us all right. Please do come and meet my family. This is my wife Mildred and my daughter Wincey."

Danny took Mrs Ritson's hand, noting the firmness in her handshake. Her cheeks were finely chiselled, her eyes slightly aloof. "Welcome to Meldon Towers, Mr Le Hir. I'm delighted you could make it."

Danny turned to the daughter Wincey. There was a hint of devilment in the young girl's gaze as she said: "Thank God you've come. You're the first man under forty I've seen in almost six weeks."

Ritson walked to a table on which lay an assortment of weaponry. He picked up a double-barrelled shotgun, its ornate metalwork intricately carved. "Done any shooting, Mr Le Hir? It's rather a passion of mine. When I was in the army, I was the best shot in the regiment. I used to think that if all else failed, I might make a living at it – giving demonstrations at country fairs, that sort of thing."

He nodded at a retainer standing among the trees and instantly, two clay pigeons shot into the air, curving against the sky. Ritson fired twice and the targets shattered into millions of pieces.

Mrs Ritson laughed. "My husband loves showing off, Mr Le Hir. He's very vain about his marksmanship."

"Perhaps Mr Le Hir would like a try?" suggested Ritson's daughter archly.

"Shotguns aren't my thing, I'm afraid."

"Come over here," Ritson said. "We may have something a little more challenging."

He picked up a silver handgun and held it to the light. "Recognise this?"

Danny took the weapon from Ritson's hand, testing it for balance. He rolled the cylinder with his fingers. "Smith and Wesson Russian .44, the first successful heavy-calibre, hinged-frame revolver ever produced. One of 250,000 made for the Tsar's army between 1870 and 1878, and extremely popular in the United States."

"Bravo, Mr Le Hir. I see you know your handguns. It *is* a Russian .44 and it carries quite a pedigree. It once belonged to the Prince of Wales and according to rumour, he acquired it during a card game with your own President Roosevelt. Care to try it?"

"With such a colourful history, how could I refuse?"

Ritson nodded to his retainer and with a faint whirring sound, two clay pigeons soared into the air. Danny watched them streak across the sky, following a horizontal line above the nearby trees. He made no attempt to raise the pistol. The targets reached the limit of their trajectory and began curving toward a bed of foliage. Danny dropped into a half-crouch, legs spread, shoulders hunched, and squeezed the trigger twice, fanning the hammer Western-style with his palm. The shots were simultaneous and the projectiles vanished in filmy white starbursts.

The spectators applauded spontaneously. "Excellent shooting, Mr Le Hir. There aren't many men I know who could hit two moving targets with an antique handgun they'd never used before. Remind me never to challenge you to a duel."

Mrs Ritson said: "Hadn't we better be getting back to the house, darling? We really ought to be on hand to greet our other guests."

"Quite right." Ritson took the .44 from Danny's hand and placed it on the trestle table. "We'll have another go tomorrow," he promised. "And to make matters interesting, we might add a little something to spice up the pot. Shall we say the best out of ten, stakes to be decided in the morning?"

"I'll look forward to it," Danny said.

The guests began arriving in the early afternoon and the house soon echoed to the sound of animated conversation. Danny did his best to be polite but it quickly became apparent that the newcomers were far more interested in hearing themselves talk than in listening to the views of other people. Several times, he noticed Wincey Ritson watching him from across the room.

Dinner took place in a large baronial hall where, despite the warmth of the summer evening, a log fire bubbled merrily in the grate. Black-skirted waitresses served trout, soup and saddle of lamb. Danny drank sparingly, placing his palm over his wine glass whenever the waiter attempted to refill it.

After the meal was over, he made his way to the outside lawn and lit a small cheroot. It was a beautiful night, the sky clear and filled with stars. The scent of lilac reached him from the neighbouring gardens and a faint breeze rustled the trees nearby.

He heard someone crossing the terrace behind him and saw moonlight gleaming on long blonde hair. It was Ritson's daughter, Wincey. "I wondered where you'd vanished to," she said.

"I needed a smoke."

"You should've waited. Daddy always brings out his Havanas over coffee and brandy."

"Well, to tell the truth, I find it a little claustrophobic in there."

"I know what you mean. Aren't they awful?"

His nostrils caught the fragrance of her perfume as she said: "I really hate this place, you know."

"Meldon Towers?"

"Daddy sees it as a symbol of his success, but it drives

me crazy, it really does. It's nothing more than a rackety old mausoleum."

"Why do you stay?"

"Daddy insists upon it. He brings people here to show the place off and I'm part of the inventory list."

"I can't believe that."

"Oh, I'm sure he loves me in his own idiosyncratic way, but love to Daddy is mainly about possession. He doesn't see me as a human being with feelings of my own. He doesn't realize, for example, just how bored I get sitting around at the end of the world." She moved closer, the wind ruffling her hair. "I'd hoped you might be able to help with that. The boredom."

"I'll be happy to do anything I can."

"Well, you might start by trying to kiss me."

Surprised, he chuckled softly and took her into his arms. He was surprised by the intensity of her reaction. Mewing deep in her throat, she pressed her body against his, her fingers clawing frantically at his hair. He felt the softness of her breasts cushioning his chest, her tongue probing his mouth, her cool palms sliding beneath his shirt to touch his naked skin. His blood quickened and a tightening sensation gathered in his groin.

Then someone emerged on the terrace above, staring at them through the semidarkness. "Wincey?"

It was Mildred, Ritson's wife. Framed against the lamplight, her eyes were expressionless, her mouth a thin hard line.

Wincey drew back, blinking at Danny apologetically. "It's Mother, damnit. She always manages to spoil things."

Embarrassed, Danny took out a handkerchief and wiped the lipstick from his mouth. Mrs Ritson was watching them with the implicit disapproval of a Victorian governess. "I think you had better come inside," she said.

Wincey squeezed Danny's hand. Her face looked sulky in the refracted lamplight. "I'll see you later," she whispered. "Like my father, I never believe in leaving business unfinished."

She kissed her fingertips, pressed them lightly against

112

Danny's lips then trotted across the lawn and vanished into the house. Her mother, after giving Danny a long hard look, followed her through the French windows.

Danny returned self-consciously to the gathering and for the next two hours made conversation with the absent-minded detachment of a man filling in time. Toward midnight, Ritson drew him aside and led him to a private office where he carefully locked the door. He settled behind the desk and waved Danny to an empty chair.

The office was small, and contained little furniture apart from a large computer occupying an entire corner. Ritson's eyes creased with amusement when he saw Danny examining it curiously. "That's my oracle," he explained. "I keep it here so that nobody in the City can hack into it accidentally."

"What's it for?" Danny asked.

"Business records. Being something of an entrepreneur means sailing occasionally close to the wind. For professional reasons, I prefer to keep certain things out of company files. Your own proposition, Mr Le Hir, would fit into that category. Instead, I store them in the oracle. There are no back-up discs. Every deal of a delicate nature which I've made during the past ten years has been secreted away inside that little box of tricks. It allows me to stay on top of the game with a minimum of personal risk."

"Wise precaution," Danny said, seating himself.

A peal of laughter reached them from the drawing room upstairs. "Party seems to be warming up," Danny commented.

Ritson nodded. "I like to see my guests amusing themselves. They're a little overwhelming, I have to admit, but I've always enjoyed the company of extroverts."

Danny said: "Why did you bring me here, Mr Ritson?"

"I've been thinking over your offer and I have a suggestion to make." Ritson paused, pressing his fingertips together. "Why bother with Friedman and Dupazi? I'll be more than happy to handle the role at this end."

Danny stared at him. "Wouldn't that be against the law?"

113

"Not in the real sense. It could be considered a little unsavoury but providing we do it through one of my front companies, there should be no embarrassing comebacks."

"And for this, you would naturally expect a larger cut?"

"No more than your current operators. I am not, by nature, a greedy man."

"Supposing we refuse?"

"Why should you? Get rid of Friedman and Dupazi and you'll have money to burn. If you allow me to handle the legalities, both parties will benefit."

Danny thought for a moment. Ritson was slipperier than he had bargained for. Not content with a substantial portion of the profits, he wanted Friedman and Dupazi's share as well. He marvelled at the Englishman's avarice. It made him an easy man to manipulate. "Agreed," he said at last. "It'll take me a few hours to get the necessary clearance but I'll see that the legal authority is transferred to your name."

"Excellent." Ritson permitted himself a friendly smile. "I like a man who can make quick decisions."

"There's one stipulation however." Danny reached into his pocket and took out a slip of paper. "In case you drop any more surprises in my lap, I'd like your signature on this primary agreement."

"Are you saying you don't trust me, Mr Le Hir?"

"I'm saying I'd feel a whole lot happier if I had your acceptance in print."

Ritson laughed out loud. He read the covering letter quickly, scribbled out his signature and slid the document back to Danny. "Now, shall we rejoin the party?"

Danny switched on the bedside lamp and glanced at his wristwatch. It was two a.m. He slipped into his clothes and eased open the bedroom door. The landing was deserted in both directions. The floorboards creaked as he tiptoed along the passageway, pausing from time to time to listen warily.

114

He reached Ritson's office and as he'd expected, found the door locked. He took out his penknife and jimmied it easily, then he drew the window shades and switched on the desk lamp. A battered old typewriter stood on a metal stand next to a modern word processor and Danny slid a sheet of paper into its platen. The paper was empty except for a name scrawled at the bottom right-hand corner. It was Ritson's signature which Danny had obtained earlier in the evening. He began hammering out a rambling but carefully worded suicide note. It was, he knew, an unconvincing confession, but it should have the effect of confusing the circumstances surrounding the businessman's death.

When he had finished, he slipped the letter into his jacket pocket and switched on the computer. He waited until the screen flashed "entry" then fed a piece of software into the intake slot. The software contained an electronic virus which would corrupt the computer's memory bank in a matter of seconds.

When he was satisfied he had done all he could, he switched off the desk lamp and made his way back along the darkened corridor. He had almost reached his bedroom when he heard someone coming toward him and ducked quickly behind a Victorian cabinet. It was the silver-haired butler who had greeted him on his arrival, carrying a glass of milk on a silver tray.

Danny watched him walk slowly by, then hurried to his door and let himself in. He stood for a moment pressed against the wall, letting his eyes accustom to the gloom. A figure moved out of the darkness and his nostrils caught the faint redolence of perfume. Wincey Ritson, he thought. She was staring at him with the same enigmatic expression she had worn on the terrace earlier that evening. As he struggled to recompose his senses, a sliver of starlight lit up the figure's features and with a sudden shock he realized that it was not Wincey at all, but her mother, Mildred. Mildred's eyes were flat, her finely chiselled cheeks pale and inscrutable. She drew the nightgown she was wearing gently over her head and he saw the aureoles of her nipples forming tiny rosebuds against her creamy breasts. Without uttering a word, she ran her fingers through her hair, stepped into his arms and kissed him passionately on the mouth.

Maurice Ritson opened the *Financial Times* as his chauffeur sped through the misty countryside. He was in an excellent mood. The weekend had proved a splendid success thanks largely to the young American, Danny Le Hir, who looked set to boost Ritson's personal fortune by a staggering thirty million dollars. Not bad for a weekend's work, he reflected. Money was a relative thing to Ritson. He did not regard it, as some men did, in strictly material terms. What he liked – what he loved – was the feeling of power it gave him.

He was contemplating how he would reinvest the proceeds when the car suddenly skidded to a halt and his chauffeur sat peering in puzzlement at the dashboard. Ritson lowered his newspaper, frowning. "What's wrong?"

"I don't know, sir. Sparking plugs don't seem to be firing."

Ritson glanced at his wristwatch. He had an executive conference at eleven o'clock. "Hadn't you better take a look?"

The chauffeur examined the engine for several minutes before returning. "I think the distributor head's been tampered with."

"That's nonsense. Nobody comes near this vehicle without my permission."

"I'm sorry, Mr Ritson, but the engine won't start unless we get a replacement."

Cursing under his breath, Ritson picked up the car phone and punched out a number. "I'd better get Simms to bring out the Bentley."

He sat for a moment with the receiver against his ear but there was no response. He tried again, but the device remained infuriatingly dead. He examined it with exasperation. "Damn thing's crocked," he exclaimed. "Somebody must've been buggering around with it."

He stared at the countryside moodily. Green fields bordered both sides of the road and heather-clad hillslopes vanished into the fog. There was not a vehicle in sight. "How far's the next village?"

"Lindholm's just over the hill," the chauffeur said. "Couple've miles, maybe less. I could telephone from the George and Dragon."

"Do it," Ritson said impatiently. "And hurry, Jason. I can't sit here all day."

The chauffeur vanished and Ritson was about to pick up his newspaper when he saw a yellow Renault approaching in the reflector mirror. His senses quickened as he recognized the rented car in which Danny Le Hir had driven to Meldon Towers. He threw open the door and flagged the vehicle down. He almost cheered when the car drew to a halt and Danny himself came strolling back toward him.

"Thank God," Ritson exclaimed. "I thought you'd be halfway to London by now. I'd be most grateful if you could give me a lift as far as the city. My damned limo's crocked and I have a meeting at eleven."

Danny didn't answer. He leaned through the doorway and pressed something cold against the side of Ritson's head. Ritson blinked in surprise as he recognized the antique handgun which had once belonged to the Prince of Wales. He was about to ask how it came to be in Danny's possession when Danny gently squeezed the trigger. It was the last thing Ritson ever registered for his world exploded in a blinding cataclysm of flame and he flopped back in his seat, his brains splattered across the inside of the car.

Danny wiped the revolver, dropped it with the suicide note into Ritson's bloodsoaked lap and drove off swiftly in the summer morning.

It was almost dark when Danny opened his eyes. He lay for a moment, his temples aching. Through the hotel window he saw the lights of London's West End. The murmur of traffic reached him from the street below, its clamour muted by the double glazing. He moaned as he

117

leaned forward, cradling his chin with both hands. He had slept all day, which was hardly surprising considering how exhausted he'd been.

He rose to his feet, switched on the TV set, then walked into the bathroom and filled the washbasin with cold water. He ducked his face into it, splashing the chilly liquid over his head and neck. The spate of killings seemed unrelenting and his role as executioner was beginning to unnerve him. Sometimes he felt that each time he took a life, an essential part of him died in sympathy. Was duty really such an immutable thing? he wondered.

As he returned to the bedroom, a flicker of movement on the TV screen caught his attention. A young girl with reddish-gold hair was interrogating a politician outside the House of Commons. He watched the encounter curiously as he pulled on his bathrobe. The man was doing his damndest to evade the camera but the girl kept jolting him to a halt and bombarding him with questions.

Danny examined her with interest as he groped for a cheroot. Her face was exquisitely formed, her eyes as penetrating as lasers. She pinned the MP against a metal railing and hung on like a limpet, stripping away the man's facade and leaving his defences in tatters. It was an electrifying performance and Danny was spellbound. She exuded a magnetism that was almost hypnotic. The interview lasted for almost four minutes and when it finally ended, a strange excitement had gathered inside him. He let the air seep from his lungs in a drawn-out sibilant hiss and glanced at his wristwatch. It would be early afternoon in the United States. He picked up the telephone and punched out a California number. After a moment, a voice echoed in his ear and he said: "It's Danny Le Hir here. Do we still have an interest in that New Orleans TV station?"

When the voice confirmed that they had, he took the cheroot from his mouth and stubbed it out in the hotel ashtray. His cheeks were flushed and his eyes blazed with an unusual lustre. "Tell the General that I think I've found our catalyst," he said.

TODAY

Chapter Eight

Caroline fastened her seatbelt and peered through the porthole window as the pilot prepared to land. Down there lay the United States, a new continent, a new beginning.

She tried to control her nervousness. So much had happened during the past few weeks that she almost had to pinch herself to prove it was real. The American offer had come out of the blue.

The two Louisianans – dapper men surprisingly similar in age and appearance (Caroline had mentally labelled them "Tweedledee" and "Tweedledum") – had wasted little time in getting down to business over lunch at the Savoy.

"I am Borden Meadows," the first American had said. "This is my partner Warren Bryant. We run 365-Television, a small cable network in the city of New Orleans. We operate every day of the year, including Christmas, and cater to viewers in the Mississippi Delta."

"We think you have a remarkable talent," the second man put in. "You have 'watchability', a quality that is sadly rare in television today. We consider the BBC exceedingly remiss in failing to exploit your full potential."

And then the offer had come, delivered casually over the hors d'oeuvres.

"We propose to give you a show of your own. We'll transmit it weekly in prime time and we'll call it *'Prime Force'*. We'll run the interviews on a one-to-one basis, the guests drawn from among the top celebrities in the United States. The editorial content will be left to you."

Caroline had been stunned. At the BBC, she knew it

would take her years to achieve such independence. She'd accepted the offer the following morning. It was one thing, however, to make decisions in the cold light of day but quite another to put them into practice. She'd taken a step which was about to change her life and she felt tense, nervous and apprehensive as the plane touched down and she joined the passengers flocking through Passport Control. A young man was waiting for her at the arrivals desk. He was lean and suntanned with merry blue eyes. "Miss Force? I'm Danny Le Hir. Welcome to the United States."

His face was rugged, but filled with a sensitivity that touched Caroline's senses. He wore a floppy old sports jacket and a black silk shirt open at the throat; on another man, the effect might have been sloppy, but he exuded a gracefulness that was impossible to resist. When he moved, his body was fluid – almost like a ballet dancer's.

"This all you've brought?" he asked, taking the suitcase from her hand.

"My baggage is being transferred later."

"Good policy, travelling light."

At least they'd sent somebody to welcome her, she thought as he shepherded her toward the parking lot; it seemed an encouraging sign. "Do you work for 365?" she asked.

"Strictly on an ad hoc basis. Public relations. Meadows and Bryant asked me to roll out the welcome mat and now that I've seen you, I can understand why."

He led her to a waiting sports car and they joined the traffic heading into town. She watched the fields giving way to the first straggling signs of the city outskirts; it seemed little different to her home in Britain, except for the clammy atmosphere.

"Is it always so hot?"

"Humidity. New Orleans is famous for it."

"It'll take me a while to acclimatise. I come from a chilly little island."

He chuckled. "First time in the United States?"

"First time anywhere. I'm not much of a traveller."

"Me neither. I do quite enough of it already. I've got other business interests as well as 365." He glanced at her. "I prefer it that way. There's more diversity."

"Well, diversity's what brought me here."

He was nice, she thought. And extraordinarily good-looking. She watched his hands on the driving wheel, slender hands covered with fine blond hairs which vanished under the silken shirtcuffs. To her relief, he wore no jewellery. Caroline loved jewellery, especially emerald and jade, but on a man she regarded it as affectation.

She noticed that he made no attempt to impress her and found the novelty pleasing. Men, as a rule, tended to posture in her company but she had the feeling that nothing in the world would induce Danny Le Hir to put on a phony "front". He seemed completely himself, easy to relate to, comfortable to be with.

She sat back in her seat, staring out curiously at the American city that was to be her new home. It looked like a city anywhere, sprawling, traffic-ridden, gasoline-infused. "I'll have to find a place to stay," she said.

"Don't worry, your material needs have already been catered for. 365 want you to project the right kind of image so they've rented an apartment in the old French Quarter, just a stone's throw from the studio. I picked it out myself."

"There was no mention of any apartment in my contract."

"Consider it a bonus."

"I'm not sure that I like the idea. It puts me in a difficult position. Supposing I decide to quit?"

"They've already thought of that. The apartment comes with a two-year lease."

"Wow." She whistled softly. "Let's hope I prove to be worth it."

"Speaking as an independent observer," he smiled, "I'd say they've got their money's worth already."

They turned into a network of picturesque streets where Creole restaurants offered crawfish bisque, soft-shell crab, oyster sandwiches and jumbalaya. The sidewalks were packed with sightseers.

"This is the old French Quarter, the Vieux Carré. It used to be a red-light district, but today it's a popular tourist attraction."

He pulled into an elegant cul-de-sac and drew to a halt. "Home sweet home."

Caroline followed him into a leafy courtyard where blue thurnbergia sprouted from every alcove and palm fronds formed a comforting canopy against the sultry sky. In the centre stood an ancient fountain, topped by a crumbling statue of Adonis. Lilies floated on the water's surface.

Danny unlocked a door and stepped back, waving Caroline inside. The apartment was large and lavishly furnished. Everything radiated comfort and refinement. He watched, smiling, as she wandered from room to room, mewing softly under her breath. "It's a palace," she exclaimed.

"I thought you'd like it."

"Must've cost a fortune."

"Pampering ladies is a Louisiana pastime." He placed her suitcase on the floor. "I guess you'll be tired after your journey. I'd better let you settle in."

She was filled with a sudden irrational panic. In the few minutes they had been together, his easy assurance had allayed her doubts and fears. Now they came rushing back with an astonishing force. "When do I start work?" she asked.

"Why don't you call at the studio tomorrow? It's down by the levee, overlooking the river. You really can't miss it."

"Will I see you again?" Her mouth felt dry.

His teeth flashed in a parting smile. "That's something you can count on. I'm what you might call your personal chaperon." The door closed and he was gone.

Danny leaned back in his chair and stated at the two TV executives, Meadows and Bryant. He could tell that the men were angry.

124

"It's the stupidest damn thing I ever heard," Meadows snapped. "You know perfectly well that I'd give my heart and soul for the Movement but this is business Danny, and Walter has no right to interfere with business."

"Every nickel 365 loses on the *Prime Force* programme will be reimbursed by General Thirkeld himself," Danny promised.

"That isn't the point. We have a responsibility toward our viewers."

"Interview shows went out with the Ark," Bryant explained. "Nobody's interested in talking heads any more. People want musicals, extravaganzas. We'll be running a serious risk of alienating our audience."

"I give you my word that won't happen."

"What the hell does that mean, your word? You know nothing about this industry. We were willing to help you coax the girl to the United States, but now that she's here let's call it a day. We're replacing the show with the new Portis series."

"Isn't it a little silly replacing something you haven't even seen yet?"

"We don't have to see it. We know what the viewers want and it certainly isn't *Prime Force*. I'm sorry, Danny, but we are not committing professional suicide."

Danny looked down at his hands, turning them slowly in the light as if examining their texture for wear and tear. When he spoke again, his voice had lost its friendly tone.

"Professional suicide cuts two ways, gentlemen. I wonder how long 365 would last if the TV authorities discovered how your company acquired its initial funding?"

Through the open window, they heard the rattle of a freight train pulling along the waterfront.

"What are you talking about?" Meadows asked after a moment.

"You know damn well what I'm talking about. Almost thirty per-cent of your capital came from illegal stock supplied by Schlieben and Schlieben and never declared to the government."

"That's a lie."

Danny smiled. "General Thirkeld is a meticulous man. He never feels comfortable until he has a lock on people, especially his friends. He runs his own private intelligence network, digging out past indiscretions, forgotten peccadillos. Most of the stuff sits in his computer files, never to be used, but every once in a while when the circumstances seem right, he pulls it out of mothballs."

"You bastard," Bryant said darkly.

Danny seemed unmoved by the insult.

"Stick to our agreement, gentlemen. You have our word that we'll cover any financial deadfalls. However . . ." His blue eyes twinkled. "I have the strangest feeling that far from losing its audience, 365-Television is about to hit the jackpot."

New Orleans proved a revelation to Caroline. In the first place, it was cloudier than she'd expected and it rained often, the skies opening up in dramatic cloudbursts which were followed immediately by dazzling sunshine. A sense of decay permeated the city, especially the old French Quarter where the buildings carried the faded air of a beautiful courtesan who had gone past her prime. She found the free-and-easy atmosphere intoxicating. Sensual by nature, she adored good food and fine wines and New Orleans gave her ample opportunity to enjoy both, though she was careful to follow a sensibly balanced diet for most of the time. She adored hats (cats too, she was fond of saying, though her profession made keeping them a little impractical) and she discovered a milliner's shop on Dauphine Street which specialised in outrageous creations; at home in England her eccentric tastes would have singled her out as a distinct oddity whereas no one in Louisiana seemed to consider her the least bit unusual. She also discovered a French perfumery which specialised in essences direct from Paris; one in particular reminded her of Russian leather, conjuring up images of Cossacks riding the Steppes on crisp wintry nights.

Like many redheads, her skin was near-perfect and the Louisiana sunshine now sprinkled it with a faint smattering

126

of freckles which emphasised the greenness of her eyes. She knew from old photographs that her mother had been beautiful in a delicate kind of way and she herself had inherited some of that beauty with one exception; instead of being delicate, she was bursting with vitality, and her zest for living seemed to find inspiration in New Orleans's old-world ambience. She loved the tourists who thronged the jazz bars on Bourbon Street. She loved the negro children who tap-danced in St Peter's Square. She loved the Mississippi's river traffic which came steaming up from the Delta marshes. She was filled with the sense of leading a bold new life.

365-Television stood on the site of an old repair yard with the river on one side and a railroad junction on the other. It was sparsely staffed to cut down on costs and most of its people did three jobs at once. Caroline was given a private office with two assistants, Milly Garvey and Christine Harding, neither of whom, she was relieved to discover, displayed the kind of aloofness she had encountered at the BBC. One thing puzzled her however; a quick glance at the programme schedules told her that 365 relied for its popularity on a steady diet of light entertainment. With *Prime Force* it was entering new territory. Caroline wondered why Meadows and Bryant had decided to take such a radical step.

Her first interview guest had been carefully selected; he was Zachary Tarpy, a barnstorming evangelist who fronted a popular TV show in America's Bible Belt. Tarpy was a flamboyant figure who had made quite a name for himself by attacking all forms of sexual excess. He had set himself up as the nation's conscience, haranguing the authorities over the proliferation of massage parlours and porno shows, and publicly lamenting the deterioration in moral standards. He had a considerable following among the middle classes and few people underestimated his influence on American public thinking.

Caroline knew Tarpy's appearance would give her show audience appeal, but she also realised that his charismatic manner stood a very good chance of swamping her altogether. One afternoon, she was seated at her desk when the mail girl delivered an unusual package. Caroline examined it for a moment, noting its distinctive wrapping paper. It was yellow in colour and bordered with a pattern of miniscule "T"s. Intrigued, she tore it open. There was no covering letter, only a selection of black-and-white photographs showing Zachary Tarpy talking to a variety of what appeared to be vice-girls. Puzzled, Caroline turned the pictures over. On the back of each one was a location and date. Three of the encounters had taken place outside a notorious New Orleans brothel and it was clear from the subject's expression that he was not merely enquiring the time of day.

She leaned back in her chair, a faint moistness gathering on her temples. What did the photographs mean? Whoever had sent them clearly had a grudge against Zachary Tarpy but how could she be sure that their evidence was genuine?

Caroline disliked subterfuge of any kind; she had a profound compassion for those less fortunate than herself and her compassion extended to all forms of human frailty; she didn't believe in pillorying people for weaknesses they couldn't control. Did she have any moral right to denounce this man?

She strolled to the window and stared down at the muddy river. The question was not an ethical one, she decided. Tarpy had made a fortune by attacking the seamier side of American life. If his own life was equally seamy, then surely it was her duty to expose him publicly. But how could she be sure if the man was innocent or guilty? One way or another, she knew she had to find out.

The cab driver looked worried as he slid to a halt. "Lady, you sure you got the right address? I wun't drop my worst enemy in this neighbourhood."

"This is the place." Caroline peered out at a tumbledown sprawl of pool rooms, pawnshops and beat-up apartment blocks. "Please wait, I'll only be a moment."

The man's eyes rolled against his ebony skin. "This is enemy territory, lady. You wanna ride, yous'll have to flag another cab."

She paid the fare and watched the taxi drive off. She had been crazy, she thought, coming to this part of town unprotected. One glance at her surroundings told her that she was terribly vulnerable. On the opposite side of the street, a group of derelicts stared at her balefully, drinking liquor from bottles concealed in brown paper bags. Keeping her body very erect, she crossed the dirty sidewalk.

Luc's Massage Parlour occupied the ground floor of a converted grocery store; Caroline could still see the faint outline of a poster advertising "Aunt Jemima's Pancake Mix." Underneath, the words "Adults Only" had been painted in scarlet letters.

The smell of cheap perfume assailed her nostrils as she stepped across the threshold. In the squalid entrance lobby, a group of women sat reading magazines and painting their fingernails. They were almost exclusively black.

"Good morning," Caroline said.

The women looked at her, their dark faces luminous in the diffused lighting. Caroline pressed on. "My name's Caroline Force. I'm from 365-TV."

"No shit," answered a heavy-boned negress with an enormous bosom which shivered each time she spoke. "Why, sugar, this ain't no place for a high-tone hooker like you."

Caroline realised the women's amusement was not malicious but that years of humiliation had made them immune to human embarrassment. She was like a visitor from a different planet. "I'm making enquiries about Zachary Tarpy," she said.

The black woman laughed. "You mean the Reverend? Well, you come to the wrong place, honey. What you need is the Salvation Army Hall across the street."

"I understand he visits this establishment on occasion."

"Yeah, who tol' you that?"

"If it's true – if you can confirm it's true – it'll have a

major bearing on how I handle Mr Tarpy when I interview him next week."

There was a slight pause, then a girl said: "Yo' gonna interview Zach Tarpy on TV?"

"That's right. I'd like to discover the truth behind his campaign for moral purity."

The girl laughed. "Why, the purest thing about Zach is dangling right between his legs."

A peal of laughter filled the lobby and Caroline hesitated. What could she say to these women that would allow her to connect? How could she imagine the things they had been forced to experience? How could she appreciate the circumstances which governed what they did?

She was trying to think of a suitable response when suddenly the rear curtains parted and a muscular black man appeared in the opening, staring at her malevolently. A tiny gold ring pierced his left nostril and his air of ferocity was terrifying. Caroline met his gaze coolly. She had the feeling that displaying fear would be like waving a red rag at a bull.

"What you doin' here?" the man growled.

"Just talking."

"I din' give you no permission to come here and talk."

Close, the man was several inches shorter than Caroline but his wiry musculature carried a volatile element that made her stomach squirm. She tried to make her voice relaxed. "I understand that Zachary Tarpy is a regular visitor to your massage parlour, is that true?"

The man pushed his face almost an inch from her own and she smelled the gaminess of his breath. "Go peddle yo ass someplace else," he snapped. "I got all the ho's I can handle here."

Caroline didn't bother to argue. She knew the black man would attack her at the slightest provocation. Cheeks crimson, she backed through the door and hurried to a deli on the street corner where she sat at one of the tables, cradling a cup of coffee. Bad beginning, she thought. She'd gone in with both barrels blazing and

130

run out with her tail between her legs. A fine old mess she'd made of things. She should have taken advice, shown her evidence to higher authority. No wonder the women had laughed at her. She'd have laughed too in their position. But their unwillingness to talk presented her with a difficult dilemma and she was contemplating the situation dispiritedly when the door opened and a young woman came in. Caroline's pulses quickened as she recognized one of the whores from the massage parlour. The girl was scarcely out of her teens and her nose had been badly broken at least twice, giving her a faintly pugilistic air.

She walked up to Caroline's table. "Miss Force?"

"Yes?"

"I'm Mandy Broussard." The girl hesitated. "You's right 'bout Zach Tarpy. He flies in from Memphis two, three times a month, mostly in secret. He likes the specials Luc puts on."

"Specials?" Caroline's voice was barely a whisper.

"I got the marks, if'n you wanna see 'em. He's a cruel man under that Holy Joe pigshit. It's time somebody showed the other side of his face."

A fierce excitement gathered in Caroline. She rose to her feet and pulled up a chair. "Let me get you a coffee, Mandy. I think we should have a little talk."

The studio lights were blinding in their intensity but Caroline scarcely noticed the heat for her mind was totally absorbed with the encounter ahead. With his hooked nose and silvery hair, Zachary Tarpy radiated goodness; he reminded her of an Old Testament prophet and she could see at a glance why he inspired such devotion among his followers. He exuded a powerful theatrical presence which, like an actor, he knew exactly how to project. His voice could be rousing or sepulchral in turns, his eyes challenging or compassionate. Watching him now, seated so comfortably in the interview chair, she found it hard to believe that he had once whipped Mandy Broussard within an inch of her life.

131

"Fifteen seconds to transmission," the director intoned in her earpiece. "Ten, nine, eight, seven . . ."

She heard the introductory music, then the director cued her and reading from the prompter, she went into her opening address. Tarpy smiled confidently as she turned to face him. "Mr Tarpy, you've left us in little doubt about your unhappiness with the state of American society today. Would you care to identify the so-called moral decay which has become the object of your personal crusade?"

He seemed amused by Caroline's earnestness. "Hardly *my* crusade, Miss Force, but the crusade of every God-fearing man and woman in this country. Without morality, society crumbles, and when I look around me and see the depravity lying at the very heart of our daily life, I want to hang my head in shame. We are a nation obsessed with sex. Sex – illicit sex, sex outside marriage, sex that is dirty and unclean – has become our national credo. God has spoken to me about America's plight. He has made me the spearhead of His attack upon the unrighteous. He has endowed me with the task of returning our people to the paths of chastity, decency and virtue."

There was no stopping the man once the floodgates had opened; he talked as if the words intoxicated him in some peculiar way, criticising state legislation which permitted prostitution and deploring the demise of traditional family values. His arguments were cohesive and sprinkled liber-ally with religious sentiment. Caroline waited until he had finished, then she said: "Isn't there a statement in the Bible which runs 'cast not the first stone'?"

Tarpy carried the air of a man confronting a precocious child. "Clemency is an admirable quality, Miss Force, but when Satan himself is in the ring, it's sometimes necessary to fight fire with fire. If I feel the devil's presence around me, I recall the words our blessed Saviour spoke whilst fasting in the wilderness. 'Get thee behind me, Satan.' There is no greater defence against the body's weakness than the edict of our sacred Lord."

"Are you happily married, Mr Tarpy?"

Tarpy seemed surprised. "Why, I believe I am."

"You have a normal relationship with your wife?"

"Within the constrictions of the Lord's word, yes."

"You would never, for example, permit yourself to lust after another woman?"

Tarpy frowned in puzzlement, running his fingers down his silken necktie. "I am a man, like any other. I may be attracted to a sweet face or a gentle disposition, but Martha and I were joined in the eyes of the Lord and that is sacred to me."

"So you've never fallen prey to temptation?"

"I say this with humility rather than pride, for it is the Lord's influence, the Lord's presence within me that keeps me free from sin, that I have never – either in thought or deed – cheated upon the vows I made at the marriage altar."

"Mr Tarpy, are you familiar with a New Orleans establishment called Luc's Massage Parlour?"

He moistened his lips. "Excuse me?"

"Luc's Massage Parlour," Caroline repeated. "I can refresh your memory, if you like. We have photographs of you entering the premises on a number of occasions."

Tarpy handled it well, she had to give him that. He rolled the word around his tongue as if savouring its flavour. "Luc's. Why, now that you mention it, I believe I *have* visited such a place. There was a young lady working there whose tortured soul yearned desperately for deliverance. She turned to me for help."

"Was the lady's name, by any chance, Mandy Broussard?"

"It's so long ago, I really can't recall."

"Mr Tarpy, you were spotted at Luc's only last month."

Tarpy manoeuvred mentally for position. "It's possible," he admitted, his cheeks pale. "Wherever one of God's creatures is crucified on the rack of human degradation, I do my best to bring solace and comfort."

"And how did you bring comfort to Mandy Broussard?"

"Excuse me?"

"How did you bring comfort to Mandy Broussard?"

"I really don't see where this line of questioning is leading us."

"Mr Tarpy, you've commented at some length on America's morality. Isn't it reasonable that your own should also be scrutinised?" She paused, timing her moment. "Is it true that you brought Mandy Broussard solace and comfort by submitting her to a series of sexually deviant acts which involved whipping her so hard that she spent twenty-four hours in the intensive care unit at her local hospital?"

Tarpy looked as if he had been slapped on the face. He slumped in his seat, sucking desperately at the air.

"Isn't it also true that on three separate occasions, your predilection toward sexual violence has led to the hospitalisation of New Orleans's prostitutes?"

"That is a monstrous lie." His voice was a strangled whisper.

"We have sworn statements from the women involved. We also have photographs showing you entering illicit establishments. The gulf between your public image and your private life appears to be several worlds apart, Mr Tarpy."

Tarpy looked ashen. His eyes were glazed and a thin sheen of sweat covered his sickly cheeks. A series of small, almost indiscernible shocks ran through his powerful frame and she thought at first he was having a stroke, but a hint of awareness in his features told her he was merely assessing the situation.

Upstairs in the director's box, the atmosphere was electric. "Close-up on camera three," the director hissed. "Home in on his face, Charlie. Get that blood, for Chrissake. Get it, get it."

Caroline waited for Tarpy to respond. He had scarcely moved, that was the extraordinary thing. His limbs had frozen, as if he had reached a point in time and space where creation itself hung suspended. His expression was strained, not despairing exactly but filled with a desperate intensity as a man might display on a battlefield when the only reasonable course of action is to charge the

134

enemy guns. Confronted with the unthinkable, his brain was weighing odds, measuring options, looking for an escape.

Suddenly to Caroline's surprise, his face began to disintegrate. She watched in wonder as tears streamed down his cheeks and sobs racked his entire body.

He gazed imploringly at the ceiling. "Dear God," he cried in an impassioned voice. "You chose me to be Your instrument and I rejoiced in my heart that of all Your creatures, I should be the one selected to bring the wicked to redemption, but whilst my spirit was strong, oh Lord, my flesh was weak. The devil is a powerful and devious force. He turns a man's mind, corrupts his innocence, leads him into the labyrinths of depravity and madness. Let the people watching this TV show tonight bear witness to the fact that I have sinned before You and before my beloved wife. Let them recognise that I am heartily ashamed for having offended Thee and that in all humility, I beg Your forgiveness for my transgressions, my imperfections and my frailty."

He threw himself from his chair and sprawled full length on the floor, his cries piteous, his repentance overwhelming, and as the cameras focused on his still-quivering frame, Caroline watched the display with an air of reluctant admiration. What an actor, she thought.

Chapter Nine

The story hit the news broadcasts the following morning. Families all over the country switched on their TV sets to witness the extraordinary sight of Zachary Tarby grovelling on the floor in a paroxysm of guilt and shame. 365-Television sold the interview throughout the United States and soon the station's telephone lines were humming. Most people regarded Tarby's behaviour as convincing evidence that he was truly repentant and though a few called for his expulsion as head of the Latter Day Evangelist Church, newspaper columnists predicted that the fire-eating reformer would be back on form before the year was out.

Meadows and Bryant were delighted. *Prime Force* had picked up only modest audience ratings but the proceeds from selling it nationwide had left them with a handsome profit and thanks to the publicity, the series looked set for a spectacular run.

Caroline however, knew her success had been a one-in-a-million shot. The momentum she'd gained from the mysterious photographs had given her a profound advantage but she would need a miracle to encounter such extraordinary fortune again. Still, she was grateful that the luck which had sustained her throughout her British career appeared to have followed her to America.

The following Friday, Danny Le Hir took her out to celebrate. They ate at a little Creole restaurant overlooking the Mississippi. Danny was charming, attentive and devastatingly attractive. She hadn't gone much on looks before – she preferred warmth and kindness in a man –

but Danny's rugged features and the relaxed manner with which he confronted the world were irresistible.

"A star is born," he smiled as the waiter filled her wine glass.

"Some star. That wasn't talent. Just luck."

"Don't knock it. You were sensational."

"I feel such a phony."

She contemplated telling him the truth but some inner core of vanity stopped her; she wanted Danny to admire her, to believe she was truly special.

"Some problem?" he asked.

"I feel inadequate, that's all. Most of the time, I'm just acting out there."

"Well, you have to give a performance to make the thing work. But either you can hack it or you can't, and happily for us, you can."

She smiled at him gratefully. "I don't know what I would have done without you these past couple of weeks."

He raised his wine glass, clinking it against hers.

"To the future."

"I'll drink to that."

The strains of a jazz band came drifting toward them from a paddleboat ploughing its way up-river. Caroline saw people lining the deck rail; several of them waved at the restaurant window and Danny, smiling, waved back, his tanned cheeks picking up reflections from the vessel's lights. She looked at him curiously. "What does the future hold for you?" she asked.

"I never prophesy. It's bad luck."

"Okay, forget the future. Tell me about the past."

"Too boring."

"Too dissolute, you mean? What are you trying to hide, Mr Le Hir?"

He looked amused. "You want to hear the whole David Copperfield thing from start to finish?"

"With no cover-up. If you do, I'll sniff it out. Remember, that's my job."

"You'll be sorry," he told her.

But Caroline wasn't sorry. She was fascinated. Danny

recounted how General Thirkeld had rescued him from the Baton Rouge orphanage, how he had grown up in California as the man's business adviser, confidant and troubleshooter. His voice was flat, almost detached, but she watched, mesmerised, the way his face changed in the candlelight. At times, his eyes were moody and reflective, at others they flashed with a rare rapscallion humour.

When he had finished, she whistled under her breath. "So you're a multimillionaire?"

"My guardian is a multimillionaire," he corrected. "I'm only a hired hand, though I have to admit that he's a generous employer."

She liked the warmth in his voice when he talked about the General. She liked the way he acknowledged the man's influence on his thinking. In fact, she liked everything about him.

"I've had a lovely evening," she said as he escorted her back to her apartment.

"Let's try it again sometime."

"I'd like that." She paused, then added roguishly: "How about tomorrow?"

He laughed. "Can't do, I'm afraid. I'm flying out to California in the morning but I'll call you the minute I get back."

"Okay, I'll look forward to it."

It had been a wonderful evening and her senses were racing as she watched him head back to his car, then let herself into her apartment, but she was puzzled by one thing. If Danny really found her so attractive, why hadn't he attempted to kiss her?

Danny scarcely noticed the beauty of the Californian morning as he got off the plane at Palm Springs and drove into town along Tahquitz Way. He was thinking about Caroline Force. Things were happening inside him he couldn't quite decipher. Okay, so he wouldn't have been human if he hadn't felt the old biology bit – after all, she was a girl in a million – but she'd engaged his senses in a way he would never have believed possible.

Love was not a word that featured much in Danny's vocabulary; he rarely thought of it in rational terms and he did not think of it now except in the loosest, most esoteric sense. He hated the thought that he was falling prey to his emotions. He'd always despised people who did, regarding them as spineless and feckless, but the feelings he was experiencing were so unsettling that he felt he was losing his grip on reality.

Was he even good enough for Caroline? he wondered. He'd never stopped to consider his eligibility before, had always taken it for granted, secure in the knowledge that he was attractive to women. Now for the first time in his life, he was beginning to feel ashamed. It seemed a terrible thing he was doing, a wicked, deplorable, unspeakable thing and the more he thought about it the more disgusted he became.

When he reached the house, he found the General seated in his study. Danny tried to smile as he settled himself in the vacant chair. He didn't want his guardian realising the quandary he was in.

Thirkeld examined him closely as he lit a fresh cigar. "Something wrong? You look a little piquey."

"I got pie-eyed last night."

"Girl starting to get to you, huh?"

Damn the man, Danny thought. General Thirkeld knew him better than he knew himself. "I like her. Is that a crime?"

"No crime. Enjoy yourself all you want, but remember what she's here for. You're a soldier with a battle to win. Everything else is irrelevant."

"Why did you send for me?" Danny was irritated by the General's shrewdness.

The morning sun accentuated Thirkeld's spiky hair and cast vivid shadows across his furrowed cheeks and the twin tendons on his puckered throat. "Bundy's broken away from the Movement," he said.

Danny was surprised. Howard Bundy was one of the organization's founder members. An eccentric man, he had made millions harvesting timber in Washington State.

He was an ardent collector of military memorabilia and bitterly regretted his failure to get into the US Army because of his fallen arches. Since then, he had created his own paramilitary defence force which he trained in the Cascade Mountains. General Thirkeld had always regarded him as a dangerous crank, quirky and unstable, but there was little doubt that the man's financial backing had helped mould the Movement into a potent, cohesive force. Danny knew that if he pulled out now, he could deal a devastating blow to their political ambitions.

"What happened?" he asked, his preoccupation with Caroline suddenly forgotten.

"We argued. You know what the guy's like."

"I thought you'd made up your mind not to antagonise him?"

"He caught me on a bad day. The trouble with Howard is, he just doesn't understand the meaning of compromise."

"Well, compromise is what we need now, General. If Bundy withdraws his support, what happens to the Huxley campaign? Not only is he bankrolling the TV adverts but he could squash the Senator's chances if he had a mind to."

"That's why I want you to talk to him," Thirkeld said. "Bundy likes you, Danny, he'll listen to what you have to say. Fly up to Washington State, tell him I'm sorry that I blew my top and bring him back into the fold."

Danny looked dubious. "When Howard sets his mind on something, it'll take an earthquake to shake it. He's not a man particularly noted for his reasonableness or self-restraint."

"That's why I'm sending you. See if you can walk this kitty back. If you can't . . ." Thirkeld's cheeks were florid as he drew hard on his cigar. 'I guess you'll just have to kill him."

The sign said: "Private Property. No Trespassing. Armed Response."

Howard Bundy certainly didn't believe in rolling out

the welcome mat, Danny thought as he drove slowly up the narrow logging road. The multimillionaire had always been a reclusive man and when it came to his secret passion – the paramilitary defence unit he had nicknamed "Bundy's Babes" – his obsession with security was almost pathological.

The rattle of gunfire reached Danny as he cruised through the avenue of trees. He saw a high-wire buffalo fence and a sentry in camouflaged fatigues whose cheeks had been daubed with paint to blend with the surrounding terrain. He was carrying an Uzi sub-machine-gun and as Danny drew to a halt, he saluted respectfully. "The Colonel is waiting for you, Mr Le Hir. You'll find him in the paddock with some of his men."

"Colonel?" Danny thought wryly as he continued along his way. Bundy had never served with a professional military unit in his life.

The pines fell away and in a small enclosure, he saw a group of men going through vigorous calisthenics. At their head, Howard Bundy was leaping up and down like a man demented, sweat streaming from his face and forming glistening patterns across his naked skull. When he saw Danny, he drew to a halt and nodded to the man alongside him. "Carry on, Sergeant."

Danny climbed from the car as the multimillionaire approached, wiping his face with a ragged hand-towel. Bundy's trim frame belied his fifty-nine years. He looked tanned and fit, and his whipcord muscles rippled impressively beneath his sweat-soaked singlet. His face was elongated as if it had been moulded with plasticine before being deliberately stretched.

He smiled as he shook Danny's hand. "Old man couldn't bear to face me himself, huh?"

"He didn't think you'd listen," Danny said.

"He's right. The sonofabitch gets right up my ass." He jerked his head. "Come on over to the house."

Danny followed him toward the huge log mansion the millionaire had constructed in the style of a Scandinavian palace. Ornate towers sprang from its gable ends, studded

141

with effigies of Norwegian trolls. Bundy liked Scandinavian culture because it reminded him of the Vikings; he admired any race which based its philosophy on the pursuit of war.

As they approached the entrance hall, the rattle of gunfire followed them on the mountain air. "What do you think of my boys?" Bundy asked.

"Impressive."

"Every one of them's ex-Fort Bragg, Special Forces trained. This ain't no chicken-shit brigade. These guys can talk it and walk it."

He ushered Danny into an elegant living room which had been constructed out of polished pine. The smell of resin drifted into Danny's nostrils and he glanced around appreciatively. "Nice."

"Yeah, I got the idea from one of those travel magazines. The King of Norway has a place exactly like it. Whiskey okay?"

"Whiskey's fine."

Bundy poured Danny a drink and waved him to a vacant chair. "Good to see you, Danny. Whatever argument I got with the old man, I still regard you as a favourite nephew."

"I know that."

In the diffused lighting, Bundy's elongated face seemed to accentuate his shaven skull. Everything about the man had been pared away to the barest essentials, as if he couldn't bear fripperies of any kind. He swirled his drink in his glass, his eyes shrewd and calculating. "The General's nuts, I guess you realise that."

"That's hardly fair . . ." Danny began.

Bundy interrupted him. "It's an occupational hazard with military men. I'm nuts too. Look at this."

He drew aside a curtain and in a timbered alcove Danny saw a large table covered with toy soldiers in Civil War uniforms. The table's surface had been moulded into a perfect replica of wooded hillslopes and rolling pastureland. The troops confronted each other menacingly across the miniature landscape.

142

"Battle of Bull Run," Bundy explained. "I been fighting it all week. Military tactics is my forte. I was born to command. That's why it was such a sorry joke when they wouldn't let me into the army." He snorted. "Flat feet? Shit, I could run the butts off half the marine corps and I'm damn near sixty years old. Walter was lucky, he experienced war at first hand."

"He paid the price too, Howard."

"Sure, he lost the use of his limbs. But at least he put his abilities to the test." Bundy looked into his glass as if the amber liquid offered some kind of solace. "Unfortunately, Walter doesn't know where to draw the line. Our Movement's supposed to be democratic and he runs it like God Almighty. Somebody has to stop him, Danny."

Danny knew how volatile Bundy could be and chose his words with care. "The General would never hurt the Movement, Howard. It's the most precious thing in his life."

"You look at Walter through rose-coloured glasses, but I guess I can't blame you for that. He fed you, reared you, and conditioned your mind to ignore all his faults. Oh, I don't dispute Walter's patriotism but he sees the redemption of this country as a one-man crusade and I'll be damned if I'll let him get away with that."

Danny said: "We're entering a critical phase in the Huxley campaign, Howard. Please don't blow it all through some silly sense of rivalry."

"Still don't get it, do you, son? With Huxley in our camp, the stakes are too high to let Walter plough his own private furrow. He's corrupting everything our Movement ever stood for. Put down your glass and come with me. There's something I'd like you to see."

Mystified, Danny followed him along a narrow passage-way. The pine-studded walls were covered with photo-graphs of tanks and other martial equipment. In places, the millionaire had substituted military souvenirs – cavalry sabres, revolutionary muskets and a varied assortment of bric-a-bac.

Bundy led him to a large, theatre-like room at the building's rear, clearly a briefing centre of some kind. On a small stage stood a large TV set, its curved screen occupying the entire rear wall. In front lay several rows of cinema seats.

Danny was puzzled as Bundy waved him to a chair. He took a video tape from a nearby cupboard and fitted it into the playback slot. "I had this made several years ago," he explained. "Until now, I haven't shown it to a living soul."

Baffled, Danny watched the screen flicker into life. The tape had clearly been shot in some kind of motel room. The desultory lighting cast morbid shadows across the drawn window shades and utility-style furniture. Huddled in an armchair, puffing nervously at a cigarette, sat a reedy man in a denim workshirt. His hair stuck out in unruly clumps and his seamed skin was covered with freckles.

There was a faint hissing on the soundtrack, then a voice spoke from slightly off-screen. "State your full name and occupation."

The man fidgeted nervously. "My name is Al Schmelzer," he intoned, breathing out smoke through his lips and nostrils. "I work at a roofing plant in Madison, Wisconsin."

"Where were you on the afternoon of April 6, 1971?"

"I was with the US Army serving in Vietnam."

Danny felt his puzzlement deepening.

The man went on: "My job was training Hmong tribesmen in the Laotian Highlands. On the afternoon of April 6th, we were caught in a firefight about six miles south of the Tasun River. The Charlies pinned us down on a little ridge. We had three men hit, so we radio'd in a Jolly Green."

"Who was in command of your detail?"

"Corporal Randolph Le Hir, sir."

Danny started. He glanced at Bundy who was watching him with a curious intentness.

"Where was Corporal Le Hir at the time this action was taking place?"

"He was lying on the ground with his head in his

arms. He was . . . uh . . . kind of unglued. I guess the attack pushed him over the edge." The man scratched his chin with one bony finger. "We heard a chopper approaching from the south and figured it must be the Jolly Green but then I recognized the markings. It belonged to Major Thirkeld. I'd been with the Major on the Mekong River."

Sweat trickled between Danny's shoulder blades.

"Did you see Major Thirkeld personally?"

"Yeah, I saw him. When the chopper put down, the Major jumped out and waved the casualties on board. That left me'n Corporal Le Hir still on the hilltop." The man fidgeted again and looked embarrassed. "The Corporal was just laying there, shaking and sobbing. I was trying to comfort him when the Major walked up."

"What did the Major do?"

"He asked if the Corporal was wounded. I told him 'no, sir' – not physically anyhow – but he *was* kinda freaked. The Major ordered me back to the chopper and I got on my feet an' took a few paces, then . . ."

The man's voice grew hoarse and a terrible coldness settled in Danny's stomach. "The Major pulled out his handgun and fired three shots into the Corporal's head. I knew he was kilt because of the way his body jumped. You get to recognize that after a while, the impact of a fatal shot."

"What did you do?"

"Nothing. I headed straight for the chopper and they airlifted us out of there."

"So you claim that Major – now General Thirkeld – murdered Corporal Randolph Le Hir in cold blood?"

"Yes, sir. That's how I would describe it. Cold blood."

"Did any of the other men witness this?"

"No, sir. Most of them were already on the aircraft. The sound of the rotors would've muffled the Major's shots."

"Did you report the incident to anyone on your return?"

"No, sir. I figured it was none of my business. Corporal Le Hir was no particular friend of mine and who was gonna believe the word of a p.f.c. anyhow?"

145

"Thank you, Mr Schmelzer. No further questions."

Bundy rose to his feet and switched off the TV set. "You thought Walter rescued you from that orphanage because your father saved his life," he said. "In fact, the opposite was true. The General took it upon himself to execute Corporal Le Hir without recourse to a trial or hearing."

"That's hogwash and you know it. You drummed up this whole thing."

"You're wrong, Danny."

"What kind of schmuck do you take me for? The General's no murderer, Goddamnit."

"Then why did Schmelzer lie?"

"Maybe the guy is some kind of actor. How much did you pay him, Howard? What kind of price tag did you put on your squalid little deception?"

"It was no deception, Danny. What you just heard was the gospel truth."

"Okay, tell me this. If Thirkeld really did kill my father, why did he decide to adopt me after the war was over?"

"Guilt? Remorse? Even Walter must experience such things from time to time."

"Shove it, Howard. I won't have you bad-mouthing the General to my face, I don't care how angry he makes you feel."

"Okay, cling to your fantasies, Danny. Go on telling yourself that General Thirkeld is really Captain America, but deep in your heart you know that video's genuine and I can prove it any time I want by producing the man who made it."

Danny glared moodily at the darkened TV screen. The interview had discomforted him more than he cared to admit. He had never known his father and felt no emotional bond with the man but if what Bundy said was true, it would be the first time in his life the General had knowingly lied to him.

Bundy whistled happily as he came out of the shower and picked up the mug of black coffee which his orderly,

146

Horatio, had left on the breakfast table; like everything else in Bundy's life, the coffee had been served at exactly the right temperature – Horatio knew the precise moment at which his employer would emerge from the bathroom and had timed the coffee accordingly. Bundy approved.

He examined his reflection in the wall mirror as he gulped down the steaming liquid. He didn't look bad for a man approaching sixty, he thought. There was scarcely an ounce of flesh on his bony frame and it was a crying shame that he had been prevented from following his natural vocation through a stupid technicality. Still, he hadn't done badly, all things considered. Thirty-two million he was worth, according to his accountants' last assessment, though all the money in the world couldn't compensate for lost dreams and thwarted ambitions.

The day smelled fresh as he headed into the open air. He saw his men emerging from their quonset huts as he slid into his Ramcharger and started up the engine. Though they numbered less than thirty, every one had been individually trained and he thought of them fondly, possessively, as he might have thought of members of his own family, if he'd ever had one.

He was about to press his foot on the gas pedal when his orderly appeared on the mansion porch. "Mr Bundy? Telephone call for you, sir."

He climbed from the truck and headed back to the house. He had almost reached the porch when a thunderous explosion split the air and he found himself rolling dizzily across the ground. He saw his Ramcharger burst outward in a blinding pumpkin of smoke and flame, hurling fragments of white-hot metal in every direction.

His men came running across the cindered forecourt, levering him into a sitting position. As he stared dazedly at the Ramcharger's smouldering remains, a sense of outrage filled him, starting deep in his chest then spreading outwards till it filled his entire body.

"If that sonofabitch wants war," he said, choking with fury, "then by Christ, we'll give him war."

Chapter Ten

Caroline noticed the package the minute she walked into her office. It lay in the centre of her desk, surrounded by the morning post. Sunlight from the open window shimmered off its yellow wrapping paper. She stood for a moment staring at it, a strange uneasiness gathering inside her. "Madge?" she called.

Her secretary glanced in from the other room.

"Any idea where this came from?"

"It arrived with the mail, same as everything else."

"Anyone sign for it?"

"No need. It was just an ordinary delivery."

"Okay, thanks."

Caroline picked up the package and examined it in the light. Its yellow wrapping paper was bordered with the same distinctive "T"s. Clearly, whoever had sent her the incriminating material on Zachary Tarpy had decided to try again. One exposé she could accept, but two had to be part of a concerted strategy.

Frowning, she tore the package open. Its contents comprised a sheaf of photostated account sheets and she felt her apprehension growing as she studied them closely in the sunlight. Her guest this week was New Orleans Mayor, Lloyd Raymer. Raymer was a popular figure among the poor; his relief programmes had been well documented, largely through the efforts of his aggressive PR team who promoted his image as a latter-day Santa Claus. There had been rumours, however, of shady deals and dubious backhanders, most of which had been swept under the carpet. From what Caroline could gather from the documents in her possession, at least part of the gossip appeared to be true.

She sat back in her chair, staring thoughtfully at the window. If Raymer was a crook, then clearly it was her duty to expose him, but it was equally clear that she was being manipulated by someone from behind the scenes. No longer could she pretend that the first delivery had been a fortuitous twist of circumstances. She had become a pawn in some strange, mysterious game. More worrying still, having been presented with the information, she had little choice but to check it out.

The sound of rock music assailed Caroline's ears as she locked her car. Above the ramshackle building, a neon sign blinked out the club's name: La Cucaracha.

She flashed her press card at the black man on duty. "Mr Dumont in?"

The man frowned. It was clear he wasn't accustomed to receiving visitors from the local media. "Gonna have to check on that."

He returned after a moment, beckoning Caroline to follow. He led her along the back of the club to a seedy office where a crinkly-haired negro examined her business card suspiciously. "What you want?" he demanded without preamble.

"Mr Dumont? I'd like to ask you a few questions."

"I don't know nothing an' I don't hear nothing. I's strictly D and D."

"D and D?" Caroline looked puzzled.

"Deaf 'n' dumb."

The man's bulbous nose, scarred by some ancient adversary, gave him a faintly sinister appearance. Caroline opened her handbag and laid a photostat on the desktop in front of him. "Can you confirm if this is your signature?"

He examined the handwriting, frowning. "So what?"

"You did dispense this money to Borman and Kohlberg at number 18 Hunsiker Buildings, Canal Street?"

"Sure." His yellow eyes fixed on her with the wariness of a cornered rabbit.

"What was the purpose of the payment, Mr Dumont, will you at least tell me that?"

Dumont glanced at his assistant, the scar on his nose becoming more pronounced as the angle of lamplight shifted; viewed sideways, his face looked almost concave in places. "Gratitude," he said after a moment.

"Gratitude? I don't understand."

"They lets me operate, I shows my gratitude."

"You mean you pay out this money in the hope of getting your licence renewed?"

"Yas, tha's right."

Caroline took a deep breath. "Mr Dumont, did you know that Borman and Kohlberg is the name of a front company collecting contributions for the Mayor of New Orleans, Lloyd Raymer?"

"Sure, I knew. Who else would have the juice?"

"Thank you, Mr Dumont. That's all I needed to know."

The house stood in several acres of woodland surrounded by an electrified fence. Caroline stopped her car at the entrance gate where two security guards examined her TV identity card. "Mr Paparelli promised to see me at two o'clock," she told them.

They opened the gate and she cruised up the elegant entrance drive. The house had been built in the style of an ancient Greek temple with marbled pillars and palm-fringed patios. A butler met her as she parked the car.

"Mr Paparelli is expecting you. You'll find him in the garden at the rear of the swimming pool."

Caroline followed a footpath around the side of the house and saw an elderly man in dungarees trimming the rose bushes. He wore a small pair of reading glasses and reminded Caroline of a kindly Swiss clockmaker rather than the hoodlum reputed to control most of Louisiana's underworld rackets.

"Mr Paparelli, I'm Caroline Force."

Paparelli took off his glasses and examined her for a moment, then he motioned toward the house. "Come inside, Miss Force. I recognise you, of course. I watched your debut on TV last week."

His accent was Mediterranean – Greek or Sicilian, Caroline couldn't tell which – and he moved slowly, as if years of past misdemeanours lay heavily on his conscience. He led her to an elegant sitting room and waved to an empty chair. "Shall I order you coffee, Miss Force? I seldom drink alcohol these days. My doctor has forbidden it, and to avoid temptation I keep none around the house."

"Coffee will be fine, Mr Paparelli, thank you."

Paparelli exchanged pleasantries until the coffee arrived then got straight down to business. "How can I help you?"

"Mr Paparelli, what I want to discuss is a little delicate and perhaps even a little impertinent, but certain documents have come into my possession which suggest that you have a long-standing business relationship with our New Orleans Mayor, Lloyd Raymer."

A trace of humour entered his face. Caroline took a deep breath before pressing on. "According to my information, Raymer has been turning a blind eye to some of your activities in return for a percentage of the profits. True or false?"

He began to laugh. "You are very direct, Miss Force. Most of the people I meet tend to pussyfoot around."

He leaned back in his chair, smiling faintly. "Supposing I tell you that it *is* true? Supposing I agree – strictly off the record – that Lloyd Raymer has been taking kickbacks for years?"

Caroline was surprised. She hadn't expected this "rackets" boss to acquiesce so easily. "Then it will be my duty to denounce him."

"Good." He nodded with satisfaction.

"You approve?"

"He's a greedy man, our Mayor. He puts the squeeze on my business enterprises and the more he gets, the more he wants. I would welcome an opportunity to get him off my back."

"But . . ." Caroline was confused. "If Raymer's a problem, why haven't you . . ."

151

Paparelli roared with laughter. "Miss Force, you have been watching too many movies. We do not eliminate people simply because they become an embarrassment. Mayor Raymer is abusing his position and I look to you, as a member of the media, to spotlight his corruption publicly."

"You have my word on that," Caroline said.

The heat in the studio was almost overpowering but Caroline knew it was more than the temperature that was making her perspire. In the opposite armchair sat the Mayor of New Orleans and she could sense his belligerence like a physical force. Lloyd Raymer was a corpulent man with a bloated belly which he assured campaign audiences was the proud result of forty-three years of Cajun cooking, a sentiment the grass roots Louisiana voters heartily approved of. Tonight however, he had lost some of his customary bonhomie and was examining Caroline with the air of a tiger confronting a dangerous reptile.

The studio grew quiet as she heard the PA counting them into transmission. The director cued her and she addressed the camera.

"Four years ago, the charismatic Mayor of New Orleans, Lloyd Raymer, bounded onto the political stage with the flamboyance of a pop star and the oratory of a saint. He promised to lower taxes, create new jobs, revitalise the economy and bring succour to the city's poor. In *Prime Force* tonight, we look at the real result of Raymer's shaky administration – rising street violence, increased poverty and a complex criminal conspiracy rooted firmly in the office of the Mayor himself."

She saw the shock in Raymer's eyes as she swivelled her chair and moved in resolutely for the kill.

At the La Cucaracha, Lennie Dumont watched the encounter, chuckling with jubilation. The Mayor, Lloyd Raymer, purple with rage, was waving a finger at Caroline. "You have no right to accuse me in this fashion. A TV studio is not a court of law. If you have evidence to back up what you're saying, which I passionately refute, then lay your charges through the proper channels."

The camera switched to Caroline, looking icily controlled. "Do you deny that for the past four years you have been collecting rake-off money through the law firm of Borman and Kohlberg in return for issuing nightclub licences to illicit establishments?"

"That's a damn lie," the Mayor choked. "I never in my life accepted a single dime in pay-off money. On the contrary, I helped put the racketeers out of business."

"What would you say if I told you that we have in our possession evidence which shows that Borman and Kohlberg have been making regular payments into your personal bank account from innumerable New Orleans nightclub and strip-joint owners?"

Lennie Dumont roared with laughter, slapping his thigh delightedly. "Thassa stuff, lady," he cried, punching the air in triumph as Lloyd Raymer stared back at Caroline with blank-eyed dismay.

Several miles away on the opposite side of town, Nicky Paparelli, seated on the sofa of his elegant living room, drummed his fingers on the armrest as the programme homed in on the central issue.

"Is it true that last August you accepted a payment of seventy-four thousand dollars from New Orleans businessman Nicholas Paparelli in return for granting him permission to operate a new greyhound stadium?"

"Where did you hear that?"

"From an unimpeachable source."

"Unimpeachable, hell. Tell me where you heard it, and I'll nail the lie right here."

"It came from Mr Paparelli himself."

Raymer's mouth dropped open. He said: "I don't believe it."

"We have the evidence on tape."

"You're bluffing, lady."

"I never bluff, Mr Raymer."

Paparelli watched the interview until the Mayor, driven

beyond endurance, tore the microphone from his lapel and stormed angrily from the studio. Chuckling deep in his throat, Paparelli rubbed his nose for a moment then reached for the telephone. His eyes were laughing and there was a look of deep satisfaction on his face.

"If Lloyd Raymer ever attempts to contact me again," he said to his secretary, "tell him I'm out of town."

The Mayor was impeached the following morning and excerpts from Caroline's interview were screened on most of the major news channels. Reporters who hitherto had been willing to regard the Zachary Tarpy episode as a lucky coincidence now viewed Caroline in a completely different light; one sensational disclosure might have been the hand of providence but two in a row suggested something akin to a miracle. Clearly, here was a girl worth watching.

Suddenly, journalists from all over the country were desperately trying to interview her. The experience did not please Caroline at all, for she was a private person by nature and hadn't prepared herself for the pressures which public scrutiny could bring.

When the press laid siege to her apartment, she stormed to the front door and berated them angrily; she had a fiery temper which could flare up at a moment's notice and though her outbursts were temporary and spasmodic, they could be quite intense. This had little effect upon the media people however, who drowned out her protests with a barrage of questions. Caroline was desperately trying to extricate herself when she saw a car skid to a halt at the crowd's rear.

A voice shouted: "Taxi, lady?" and she recognized Danny grinning through the open window.

"Excuse me."

She pushed her way through the throng, forcing the babbling pressmen aside, and slid breathlessly into the vehicle's passenger seat. Chuckling, Danny stabbed his foot on the gas pedal and roared away from the kerb, leaving the startled journalists behind.

"You looked like you could do with a breather," he said, pulling into the line of traffic.

She whistled softly between her teeth and laid her head against the neck-rest. "The whole world's gone crazy. I do a simple interview and suddenly I'm Joan of Arc."

"That's what this business is all about. The higher your profile, the bigger your success."

"Well, I hate it. They're driving me out of my mind."

"You can't blame them. I saw the show last night, and it was dynamite. You were terrific, Caroline."

She looked at him gratefully. As always, he was a tower of strength. No matter how confused she felt, it was Danny's warmth, Danny's buoyancy, Danny's optimism which constantly sustained her. "Where have you been?" she demanded. "I've been trying to contact you for days."

"I had to go out of town. I told you."

"You said it was just a flying visit."

"Well, it got a little more complicated than I figured."

She hesitated. "I missed you," she said after a moment.

"Likewise." He grinned at her as he headed up Canal Street. "In fact, I thought we might celebrate by taking the rest of the weekend off. After Thursday night, I reckon you deserve it."

General Thirkeld sat on the patio, smoking his fifth cigar. The remains of four others lay scattered around the ground at his feet. Behind him, the house hummed with activity. Men scrambled from room to room or spoke earnestly into telephones. A crisis was taking place. Earlier that morning, Thirkeld's son Wayne had been kidnapped from his Beverly Hills apartment and for the past few hours his men had been trying to contact Danny in New Orleans. Until this moment, General Thirkeld hadn't realised how much he relied upon Danny. Danny was more than his adopted son, he was the only person in the world he could really trust. He was strong, reliable and steady as a rock. His judgement was shrewd, his commitment total and Thirkeld needed him now more than ever before. He calculated swiftly. It was what – late afternoon in Louisiana? It wasn't Danny's nature to stay under cover for long. He was a convivial young man who enjoyed company. He should have surfaced hours ago.

Footsteps clattered on the patio as his bodyguard came out of the study. "General?" The man seemed nervous. "Howard Bundy's on the line. He wants to talk to you."

Thirkeld rolled his wheelchair into the house, and snatched the telephone from Gendun. "Howard?"

"Hello, Walter." Bundy's voice sounded casual and amused.

"What have you done with my boy?" Thirkeld was careful to control his temper. He knew histrionics would get them nowhere.

"He's spending a little time as my guest. A form of insurance, you might say."

"What's on your mind?"

"Talk. We've got to stitch this up, Walter. I took your son as a hostage so that he can guarantee my safety."

Thirkeld breathed deeply, his mind racing. If Bundy wanted to negotiate, maybe he could be outmanoeuvred. "Where is this meeting to take place?"

"You know the old ruined mission house out in the desert, by Mimbreno Wash?"

"I know it."

"Shall we make it five o'clock?"

Thirkeld drew hard on his cigar, his dark eyes glittering fiercely. "I'll be there," he promised.

"Don't be late, Walter. You know how I hate tardiness."

The phone clicked as the line went dead.

Chapter Eleven

The plantation house looked like something out of a picture book. A line of oak trees, solemn and stately, formed an ornate arch to the whitewashed porch. "It reminds me of *Gone With The Wind*," Caroline said.

"At least it's standing. Most of these buildings were destroyed by the Civil War."

They left the car in the parking lot and bought two tickets at the box office before stepping into the elegant entrance hall. Caroline whistled as she gazed at the magnificent stairway.

"The Creole families who settled here brought their ideas direct from Paris," Danny told her. "They created a philosophy based on high living and elaborate manners. These rooms were so large that special furniture had to be constructed to fill them. Ordinary tables and chairs would have been dwarfed by the high walls and ceilings."

She uttered murmurings of delight as they wandered from room to room. "Who lives here now?" she asked.

"I dunno. The estate's privately owned, but the family open it to visitors under the auspices of the Louisiana tourist department."

It was only when they reached the slave quarters that Caroline's enthusiasm wavered. As she looked at the cramped little hovels, a terrible truth dawned upon her. "This is how the plantation owners lived so well. By exploiting the people who worked for them."

"That's right. The world hasn't changed much in the past few hundred years."

"How can you say that? My God, Danny, at least we don't have slavery any more."

"There are still the people who command and the people who obey."

"But they do have freedom of choice."

He laughed. "How much freedom do you think the truck driver has in Toledo, Ohio? Society lays down its rules and the rest of us follow, otherwise we don't survive, it's as simple as that. Since the beginning of time, existence has come down to one thing – eat or be eaten."

It was the first time she had heard him speak in such a manner and she frowned at this new and puzzling development. As a man, he was kind and considerate but there was clearly a feral quality in his make-up, a hint of ruthlessness she'd be foolish to ignore.

"Sometimes you surprise me. Just when I think I know you, you say something that blows my assessment to bits."

His eyes became gentle and familiar again. "I like to be unpredictable," he said.

"You certainly are that."

He took her arm. "C'mon, let's get back to the car. We've seen enough grandeur for one day. I think it's time I introduced you to my past."

Giant cypresses lined both sides of the bayou, their branches dripping with Spanish moss. Lily pads floated on the muddy surface. There was pop ash, custard apple, water lettuce and swamp fern. The smell of vegetation was almost overwhelming.

Caroline sat in the boat prow while Danny expertly handled the tiller. From the sky came the chorus of a million birds. She stared at the luxuriant foliage, trailing her fingers through the cooling backwash. "I'd hate to get lost in here," she said. "How can you tell the difference between one bayou and another?"

"Instinct. I lived here till I was eight."

She looked back at him. "This was your home?"

"Sure. Before my father died."

"You mean you're a Cajun?"

"By birth, yes. I couldn't speak English till I was nearly five."

Caroline was surprised. She'd never thought of him in genealogical terms. Cajuns were dark and Latin and surly. Danny, with his blond hair and open face had to be an anachronism.

"Didn't you get lonely, tucked away in the middle of nowhere?"

"Too lively for that. Look."

He nodded at a flicker of movement across the bow and her stomach chilled as a scaly skin slithered eerily through the shallows.

"An alligator," she exclaimed, jerking her fingers from the water.

"He's a big 'un all right. Too old to pose any threat though. Not much good for the supper pot neither."

She looked at him in disgust. "You mean you'd actually eat that thing?"

"'Gator stew's a delicacy in these parts. You'd be surprised at how good things taste when there's no other food on the table."

Darkness was falling as he steered the boat toward a tiny cabin flanked by giant cypresses. A wooden jetty ran from its verandah and he cut the engine as he drew alongside and made the boat fast to a metal post. "I rented this place for the season," he said. "I like to get away from the city once in a while, and I thought it'd be a good spot to hide from the press. You can use the bedroom. I'll sleep on the sofa in the parlour."

He hauled up a fishing line dangling from the jetty rim, and Caroline saw a wire-mesh container filled with what appeared to be tiny lobsters.

"Crawfish," Danny explained. "Wait till you taste my Crawfish Cardinale. You won't find any finer in the state of Louisiana."

The cabin was small but surprisingly comfortable; a small generator in the rear supplied the building with electricity.

They dined on the verandah as night fell, fireflies dancing in the air and the sounds of the swamp echoing over the darkened bayou. Caroline tried the Cardinale and pronounced it delicious. Danny talked happily, as if returning to the scenes of his boyhood stirred him in some elusive way. He rhapsodised about the beauties of the Gulf and the local wildlife. It was impossible not to fall under his spell.

When dinner was over, they sat on the verandah, staring across the moonlit water. "It's so peaceful here," she said. "New Orleans seems like a million miles away."

"A million years, more likely. This is the way the world was before mankind made his appearance."

"Imagine burying yourself away in this swamp for ever."

"I'd like that. Appeals to my asceticism."

"I'd never have described you as ascetic."

"That's because you don't really know me."

"No." She looked at him with amusement. "I wonder if anyone ever did."

"You make me sound like some kind of ogre."

"Not an ogre. But an enigma, definitely."

"Is that good or bad?"

"Good in one sense. Bad in another. I never know what you're thinking."

"How do you know I'm thinking at all?"

"People always think. It's what you do with it that matters."

She had never felt more relaxed in her life. He had done that, simply by being here. There was little sense in denying it any longer, she thought. She was falling in love with him. It was hardly a blinding revelation. She'd felt it for weeks now, that sense of warmth, of intimacy and dependence. Suddenly, she wanted to tell him everything about her, the good, the bad, the secret, the contemptible.

"Danny?"

"Uh–huh?"

"You know the interviews, Tarpy and Raymer?"

"Yep."

"They were nothing but flukes."

He frowned. "They didn't look like flukes to me."

"I mean, I had help. Specialised help."

Slowly, haltingly, she told him about the mysterious packages, how they'd arrived with the morning mail and how she'd checked out their contents and used their findings in her questioning. "Both those shows were put-up jobs," she finished lamely.

Danny whistled under his breath. "Looks like somebody's trying to use you."

"I feel such a fraud. Without the packages, those interviews wouldn't have worked. I really don't deserve such acclaim."

Danny said: "The packages gave you a break, Caroline, but you grabbed the ball and ran with it. I doubt if there's an interviewer in the country who could have handled those guys the way you did. Don't sell yourself short. You're no phony."

Tears dimmed her eyes as she looked at him gratefully. No matter how bad she felt, he always knew how to reassure her.

A flurry of raindrops came pattering across the porch, then the heavens opened, pounding the cabin in a drenching downpour. Laughing, they leapt to their feet and scrambled furiously indoors.

Caroline lay in bed, thinking about Danny. Never in her life had a man affected her so. He was funny, friendly, sensitive and kind. In the few weeks she had known him, he had become her stabilising force. It had been Danny's strength that had kept her emotionally intact.

She couldn't explain a thing like that, not in any logical sense. She couldn't explain the way she felt either. It wasn't something she had any control over; it was like a virus that had invaded her body and spread throughout her entire system.

She was in love with him, so why not admit it? And if there was one aspect of this situation that didn't make any sense, it was the fact that she was lying here, lonely and reflective, when the man she wanted more than anything in the world lay almost within touching distance.

She came to a swift decision. She was filled with a fierce physical awareness that was unlike anything she had ever experienced before. She threw back the blankets and

161

climbed to her feet. For a moment, she stood naked, trying to quell her nervousness. A flash of lightning split the air as she groped her way to the outer parlour. Her breasts shivered and her nipples rose into rigid points. Desire permeated her body, creating tiny contractions of pleasure which made her head spin and her muscles tremble. The sensation was so unrestrained that its intensity frightened her. Her breathing grew deeper as her knees bumped against the sofa. She felt weak as a kitten.

Danny rolled onto his side and lay for a moment, squinting into the shadows. Then, sensing her presence, he reached up and pulled her gently into his arms.

General Thirkeld's manservant slid the limousine to a halt. Immediately in front lay the ruins of an old Spanish mission house and parked at its side were four Dodge Ramchargers. In every direction, the desert lay shimmering in the heat.

The two men who had flagged them down stood scrutinising their vehicle warily. Both were clad in camouflaged fatigues and carried AKR sniper rifles over their shoulders. General Thirkeld snorted in derision. Bundy's obsession with all things military exasperated him. The man hadn't even qualified for the regular army, for Chrissake, yet he ran his entourage like a crack commando unit.

Thirkeld's nerves were raw and tense. Unknown to Howard Bundy, he had hidden his men in a dried-up river wash barely sixty yards to the east. They had wriggled into position only minutes before Bundy's arrival, but he knew that if anything went wrong, he would have sealed not only his son's fate but his own also. He wished to God Danny had been here. Danny knew how to handle things.

Gendun climbed from the car and opened the rear door. He took out the General's foldable wheelchair and helped his employer into the canvas seat. The two gunmen watched the procedure expressionlessly. One of them ordered Gendun to place his palms on the car roof, then ran his hands over the Vietnamese's clothing.

He turned to Thirkeld with an apologetic shrug. "Sorry, General, but I gotta search you too."

"Go ahead," Thirkeld said, positioning his hands on the armrests.

When the frisking was completed, the man nodded to his companion who spoke briefly into a two-way radio set. He said to Thirkeld, "Colonel Bundy will meet you halfway between here and the mission house. Your manservant stays behind as hostage."

"First I want to see my son."

"Your son is safe, General. He'll be released as soon as the meeting is over."

"I'm meeting no one until I see my son," Thirkeld repeated stubbornly.

The man examined him for a moment, then sighed. He nodded to his companion who spoke briefly into his walkie-talkie. A few seconds later a group of figures emerged from the trucks parked by the ruined mission. One of them was wearing jeans, and Thirkeld recognised his son, Wayne.

He felt his muscles tighten. There was little point in delaying things any longer. He took out a handkerchief and began mopping his glistening cheeks.

The gesture was a signal. Almost instantly, a flurry of shots rang out from the nearby river and two of the men standing at Wayne's rear fell to the ground. The gunmen who were guarding Thirkeld watched the encounter with stricken faces.

Thirkeld groped under the wheelchair to where Gendun had taped his automatic. Ripping it free, he covered them stonily. "Place your carbines on the ground, gentlemen. No sense dying for no reason."

The look in his eyes left little doubt that he would shoot without a moment's hesitation. They dropped their rifles into the dust.

From the dried-up riverbed, Thirkeld's snipers laid down a blistering line of carbine fire. The General's son, Wayne, threw himself on the ground, covering his head with both arms. Bundy's men, caught in the open, fired a few desultory shots then scattered for the waiting trucks, dragging their casualties behind them. A ragged cheer arose from the river as the kidnappers took off, and General Thirkeld watched the trucks vanishing into the distance, grunting with satisfaction. The entire operation had taken less than ninety seconds.

He handed his pistol to Gendun and rolled his wheel-chair along the roadway to where Wayne was still sprawled on the ground, weeping copiously. Thirkeld looked down at his son with an expression of disgust. "Get off your knees, you snivelling wimp. What do you think this is, the last act of *Tosca*?"

"That was the craziest thing I ever saw in my life," Wayne sobbed. "You almost got me killed."

The general scowled, fumbling in his pocket for a fresh cigar. "Probably the best thing that could've happened," he said.

For Caroline, the next few months passed in a kind of haze. Though no further packages arrived, her good fortune continued to accelerate. It was as if a curious precedent had been set and the people who appeared on her shows felt obliged to confide daring and intimate secrets about their lives. Her sympathetic manner induced a frankness that was quite new to American TV. A famous baseball star admitted tearfully that he had once accepted bribes to jeopardise an important game. A celebrated tenor confessed that he was losing his voice. A renowned stage actress, noted for her proprietorial roles, revealed that she had been a prostitute in the backstreets of Naples. Nothing seemed too shocking to withhold from Caroline's delicate probing and though *Prime Force* reached only a small percentage of the viewing audience, it continued to make headlines all over the country.

The station's bosses were delighted. The beauty of it was that the programme was extremely cheap to produce. There were no pricely exteriors, no expensive film sequences and no musicians' union fees; the only costs lay in the guests themselves (most of whom were delighted

164

to appear on such a high-profile show anyhow) and the studio crews who were already on contract.

Caroline, meanwhile, forgot her guilt over the mysterious packages and revelled in her success – though she had to admit that being recognised could be an irritating experience. "Goes with the job," Danny told her cheerfully, and she had to accept that, for during the past few months he had become the most important thing in her life. She loved him passionately, which was a novel sensation for Caroline whose experience of men was severely limited. There had been Jake of course, but her affection for Jake had stemmed from a feeling of gratitude – he had given her support at the moment she'd needed it most – and his subsequent betrayal had destroyed any earlier attachment.

With Danny, it was different. While Jake had been stormy and belligerent, Danny was cool and self-contained. Where Jake had been a bundle of neurosis, Danny was calm and relaxed. He had a crazy sense of humour that somehow matched her own and the solitary things she laughed at became solitary no longer. It was satisfying to find some point of contact in another human being and for a few months they were wildly and gloriously happy. They cycled to the shores of Lake Pontchartrain and swam in the cool, clear waters. They dined at the restaurants in the old Vieux Carré or took powerboat trips along the Mississippi. On sultry evenings, they listened to jazz at Preservation Hall. Never in her life had Caroline felt so sharp and alive. America seemed like a magic place where the craziest dreams really did come true.

At the end of the summer, she was called to the office of the station manager, Borden Meadows, who handed her a glass of expensive champagne.

Caroline looked at him in surprise. "What are we celebrating?"

"The jackpot, my dear." He was filled with an excitement he could barely contain. "CBS have bought *Prime Force*, lock, stock and barrel."

"Can they do that?"

"They can if the price is right."

"What does it mean?"

"It means that beginning next week, your interviews are being transmitted coast to coast."

His eyes twinkled. "We're making history, Caroline. It's unprecedented for a national network to buy in a weekly talk show from a tiny cable company but CBS are paying top dollar. We'll have to drop *Prime Force* from our local schedules, of course – our viewers won't be too happy at paying for programmes which the rest of the country will be watching free – but we'll thrash out the details to everyone's satisfaction. In the meantime, congratulations." He kissed her lightly on the forehead. "You're going national, my dear."

Caroline parked her car outside Danny's apartment and fumbled in her handbag for the front-door key. He had gone into the bayous on a fishing trip but he deserved to hear the news the minute he returned.

Humming under her breath, she made her way to his private study and rummaged through his desk for a notepad. Her eyes fell upon a roll of wrapping paper tucked in his bottom drawer. She froze in her movements, staring at it confusedly. There was something strangely familiar about the paper's eccentric design.

She lifted it out and held it to the light. Its colour was a brilliant yellow, and its border was patterned with dozens of tiny "T"s.

A leaden coldness spread through her body and the world swam mockingly in her vision. She slumped in the chair, staring vacantly into space. She could scarcely believe the evidence of her own eyes. It had been Danny, of all people, who'd been sending her the mysterious packages. Danny who'd been directing her insidiously from behind the scenes. Why? What kind of game was he playing? What could be the purpose behind his sinister little charade?

She'd trusted him to the hilt, loved him and cherished him and now this. Betrayal. She felt strangely soiled, as if the discovery had contaminated her in some peculiar way.

She shook herself dazedly, placed the paper back in the drawer and carefully turned the key. Then she went into the bathroom and splashed cold water over her face. The excitement she'd felt at Borden Meadows' announcement had vanished. Now she was filled with bitterness and confusion. She had to find out the truth. She had to uncover the reason behind Danny's extraordinary subterfuge.

She was trembling visibly when she left the apartment.

The third package arrived the following morning. It was lying on her desk when she walked into her office. Her limbs felt cold as she tore off the yellow wrapping paper. The package contained invoices from a specialist drug company in Huntsville, Alabama. There was no reference to her next interview guest but she knew Danny wouldn't have sent the material if there hadn't been some direct connection. For her coast-to-coast debut, 365-Television had chosen controversial football coach "Pappy" Horvath who, within the space of three short years, had taken his obscure Georgia team from the athletic boondocks into the premier league. He was regarded as one of the most colourful figures in American sport and the only coach in the country whose name was a bigger draw than his own star players.

Caroline toyed with the papers in front of her. Whether she liked the idea or not, she knew she would have to check them out. She stabbed the intercom button with her finger. "Better cancel all my appointments, Sally," she told her secretary. "I'll be out of town for a day or so."

As Caroline expected, the Horvath interview proved a sensation. The celebrated football coach had been elevating his team by supplying them with illegal performance-enhancing drugs and under Caroline's cross-examination, he broke into tears and haltingly confessed the truth. The sporting world was thrown into an uproar and when the ratings report was published the following week, it was revealed that *Prime Force*'s first national broadcast had secured an astonishing fifty-eight per-cent share of the viewing audience, an unheard-of figure for a "talking heads" show. Caroline's impetus gathered momentum. Now that she had gone national, journalists all over the country realised that the promising prodigy with the crisp English accent was turning the TV world on its head and within a matter of days she'd become the subject of twenty-two newspaper profiles. All of which left Caroline cold; her prime concern during this tense, unhappy period was her determination to confront Danny and thrash out the sordid truth.

When he finally did call, he sounded cheery and elated. "How's it going?" he asked.

She paused for a moment, concealing her anger and indignation. "Pretty well. Did you see the show?"

"Not a chance. No TVs on the bayou. I read about it though. I gather you were a sensation."

"Which shouldn't surprise you," she told him coldly.

"Well, I always said you're the best in the business."

"That's not what I'm talking about."

Her cheeks flushed as she prepared to launch into a direct attack but before she could speak, Danny said happily: "Guess what? The General wants to meet you."

She hesitated. "The General?"

"He's invited us both to Palm Springs for the weekend. You'll like him, Caroline. He's a hell of a guy."

She paused, running her fingers through her reddish-gold hair. She realised she was being summoned not by Danny, but by the General himself. Why? she wondered. What role did Thirkeld play in this sordid little conspiracy? Was it possible that Danny's actions belonged to some dubious strategy of the General? Maybe if she handled the situation delicately enough, she might discover the truth.

She came to a quick decision and keeping her voice expressionless, said calmly: "I think that sounds a terrific idea."

Chapter Twelve

A cavalcade of press cars followed their cab all the way to the airport and they had little chance to talk as the driver weaved and twisted through the outflowing traffic. When they reached the concourse, Danny hustled her straight into the departure lounge and it was only after their plane was in the air that they finally managed to relax.

"Woweee," he said, tugging loose his necktie. "Being a celebrity's like living in a goldfish bowl."

"You get used to it," she told him coolly.

He frowned, sensing her hostility. "Feeling okay?"

"Why shouldn't I be?"

"I dunno. You sound kind of . . . unglued. Something's wrong, and it has nothing to do with the gentlemen of the press. Are you going to enlighten me, or what?"

Caroline's face hardened as she said: "Why didn't you tell me it was you sending those packages?"

He examined her shrewdly, rubbing the side of his nose with his thumb. "How did you find out?"

"Never mind how. Just answer the question."

"Thought I'd give you a helping hand, that's all."

"Don't treat me like a fool."

"Okay, I was doing my job. Meadows and Bryant took quite a gamble in hiring you. If the shows hadn't worked, the company would have sunk without a trace. I couldn't afford to let that happen. In case you don't realise it, I get paid to look after 365's interests."

"Are you saying you crucified those people in order to nurture my professional reputation?"

"Hey, let's get things in perspective here. Somebody needed to expose them. Why not you?"

"How did you get your hands on such sensitive material?"

"My guardian. He runs a private intelligence network."

"General Thirkeld deals in espionage?"

"*Industrial* espionage, there's a difference. He's a wealthy man. He'd be a fool if he didn't take steps to protect his interests."

"By spying on people?"

"Open your eyes, Caroline. It's no big deal. All the major companies are doing it. There's nothing sinister in checking out the opposition. It's basic horse sense."

"Does the opposition include football coaches and adulterous evangelists?"

Danny said: "When you run an intelligence operation as complex as the General's, you pick up material from various sources. Much of it's irrelevant, but every once in a while you uncover something that might prove useful in a different context. That's what happened here. I made the connections, set up the interviews and sent you the necessary information. The rest was up to you."

She stared at him in wonder. Nothing stumped Danny. She had a feeling he'd be just as relaxed if he woke up at his own funeral. "You're some operator," she told him.

"Okay, so what I did was a little sneaky, but look at how it's helped your career. Six months ago you were an unknown entity. Today, you're a star."

"I appreciate that," she answered stiffly, "but in future, I'd like it to be my idea."

By the time they reached Palm Springs, Caroline's anger was beginning to subside. True, Danny's methods had been a little underhand but when she came right down to it, what had he done apart from turn her into a national celebrity? She ought to be thanking not criticising him. She was careful, however, to keep her manner reserved as they disembarked at Palm Springs. She didn't want him to think he could wrap her around his little finger.

On the taxi ride from the airport, she stared out curiously at the leafy boulevards. The town seemed like

170

something from a forgotten age, an echo of Hollywood in its prime: brash, sun drenched, luxurious. They drove through elegant shopping malls where smartly dressed women flocked the expensive-looking boutiques. After a while, they turned up a narrow entrance drive where security guards examined the vehicle's occupants before waving the driver on. There were armed patrolmen everywhere and Caroline stared at them in wonder. "It's like arriving at Fort Knox," she exclaimed. "What's General Thirkeld preparing for? World War Three?"

"With the General's money, he'd be a fool not to take a few simple precautions."

"I doubt if the President could whistle up this kind of muscle."

Danny chuckled. "One thing the General learned in Vietnam – never underestimate the enemy."

The house had been constructed in the style of a Spanish hacienda with sloping red roofs, elegant arches and leafy courtyards. The interior was airy and sumptuously furnished. Danny led her to a suite of rooms which reminded her of a film set. The bath, inlaid with marbled tiles, was sunk several feet below floor level, and the windows were covered with exquisite Indian drapes. Heyberdansk sofas surrounded a picturesque stone fireplace.

"Does it meet with your approval?" he asked, watching her reaction.

"It's breathtaking," she exclaimed, shaking her head in wonder.

"And am I forgiven now?"

Her eyes softened as she looked at him. She could never remain angry with Danny for long. She leaned forward and kissed him lightly on the lips. "I'll never mention it again. I promise."

"Good." He slapped her playfully on the bottom. "Now, why don't you dress for dinner while I tell the General that you're here?"

Caroline put the finishing touches to her make-up and examined herself critically in the wall mirror. She didn't

171

look too bad, she decided; better than she'd expected after the trauma of the last few days, but she couldn't stop the qualmish feelings gathering in her stomach. What if General Thirkeld didn't like her? The man exerted such a powerful influence over Danny that he might even have the power to destroy their relationship, a possibility she didn't dare contemplate.

Dusk was falling when Danny came for her. "Wow," he said. "You look terrific."

Caroline smoothed the dress around her hips. "Think the General will like it?"

"He's a man, isn't he?" His eyes crinkled with amusement. "How're you feeling?"

"Petrified. First meeting's are so important. I want to make a good impression."

"Just be yourself. The General adores beautiful women."

Caroline's heart thumped as Danny led her to an elegant library where a man in a wheelchair sat cradling a brandy glass in front of the window. His leathery face was creased in thought and his cropped hair formed a downy membrane over his square, Germanic skull. Even seated, General Thirkeld seemed to dominate the entire room – and yet, he was not particularly tall, Caroline realised, nor was his musculature especially robust. The sense of bulk came from his aura; rarely had she encountered a man with such a strong physical presence.

"General," Danny said, "I'd like to present the young lady who's been gracing our TV screens these past few months, Caroline Force."

Thirkeld kissed her hand with an air of archaic gallantry. "Miss Force, I am delighted to welcome you to my home. It's a privilege to meet you at last."

Caroline laughed in embarrassment. "That's quite a greeting. I hope I manage to live up to it."

"You already have, my dear." Thirkeld snapped his fingers at a manservant waiting in the open doorway. "May I order you a drink?"

"I'll have a daiquiri," Caroline said.

172

"Make it two," Danny put in.

Thirkeld sat back, examining her shrewdly. His skin looked like a football bladder that had recently been deflated but he exuded an easy charm that Caroline sensed could be turned on at will.

"You've made quite an impact since your arrival in the United States."

"Luck, largely."

"Hardly luck, Miss Force. Talent too."

"No. Most of it's bluff under the surface."

"And yet you always look so casual and relaxed."

"That's an act. Usually, my tummy's tied up in knots."

He laughed. "I have a feeling that going on the air's a bit like going into battle. Hell on earth while you're waiting for the opening whistle."

He displayed none of the bitterness she might have expected from someone confined to a wheelchair, yet despite his bonhomie, she sensed a ruthlessness in the man that was difficult to define. She had a feeling that whilst he was trying to be civilised and relaxed, some inner core of savagery was struggling constantly to assert itself.

"Where do you come from, Miss Force?"

"A little town in the north of England called Rolchester."

"I know it. During my youth, I was based for a while at Fylingdales in north Yorkshire."

"I thought Fylingdales was an air-force camp."

"Correct. But for a short time they used army personnel to handle the security and I was one of the people drafted. I like it there, though I have to admit it was a little isolated."

"I know what you mean. I'm a city girl myself now and country places unsettle me."

"Anyhow, you've really put 365-Television on the map. It's been quite an achievement."

Caroline felt her cheeks colouring. "Getting there's easy. Staying's the hard bit."

He laughed. "That's the shrewdest remark I ever heard."

Throughout dinner, Thirkeld entertained her with stories of Vietnam and his early manhood at West Point. Danny, who had clearly heard the tales before, scarcely spoke. After a while, Thirkeld switched tactics, inviting her opinion on practically every topic under the sun. Soothed by the wine, she talked more frankly than she'd intended, a fact which did not seem to surprise him in the slightest. He challenged her constantly, putting forward arguments to see how adeptly she could shoot them down.

"Our country is going to the dogs," he told her. "We have lost direction as a nation. Our ideals are tainted, our society corrupt."

"American society isn't crumbling, General, it's merely evolving – a necessary development. We're all seduced by values which really only existed in our imaginations. Things become stagnant when they don't change."

"I disagree, Miss Force." His voice was mild but his eyes glowed with a peculiar lustre. "If society is to be strong, it must maintain, among other things, a love of God, enough courage to make the right decisions and a belief in its own destiny. Without those standards, civilisation becomes weak. Without strength, it loses purpose."

"Whose purpose, General? Yours or theirs?"

He shrugged. "I have never considered myself a moral arbiter but I do believe there are certain issues which are immutable. The concepts of right and wrong are fundamental to the human psyche and I would like to see this country return to those principles which gave it birth."

"Maybe it never left them, General. Maybe you're chasing a shadow that doesn't exist."

"If enough people care, we'll make it exist. All it takes is the strength and the will."

It was easy to see why General Thirkeld exerted such a powerful influence over Danny. The man was mesmeric in his oratory and it was difficult not to fall under his spell.

Toward eleven, Thirkeld took his leave. "You're a stimulating young woman, Miss Force. However, it's a long time since I talked so exhaustively and I make it a habit to retire early. I'm an old man now, and my powers of concentration are not what they used to be."

"Your concentration seems pretty adroit to me, General," Caroline told him with a smile.

He kissed her hand. "Shall we continue our conversation over breakfast? I'm sure that after a sound night's sleep, I shall acquit myself a good deal more credibly."

Danny waited until the General had gone, then he said: "What did you think of him?"

She whistled. "He's some talker."

"He likes to argue. Keeps people on their toes."

"Think he believes all that stuff?"

"Sure, he believes it."

"Bit extremist, isn't he?"

"An occupational hazard among retired generals. His credo is discipline, hard work and love of country."

"I'd hate to oppose him in a public debate. I have a feeling he could whip up the passions of a crowd faster than an eggbeater."

"That's because, deep inside, most people happen to agree with him."

The phone rang in the other room and Danny went through to answer it. Caroline slid open the French windows and stepped onto the lawn. She felt the evening had gone well, all things considered. Though they hadn't seen eye to eye politically, she was sure that General Thirkeld approved of her.

She walked across the lawn, filling her lungs with air. Beyond the high-wire fence, she could see Palm Springs forming a neon starburst beneath her. The night was warm and scented with blossoms. Over west, the snowcapped San Jacinto summits rose against the stars and she saw the lights of the cablecar station where the aerial tramway ended. Something moved into her line of vision and she narrowed her eyes, squinting hard. Two small dots came gliding eerily across the heavens, taking on shape and substance. She heard the faint murmur of engines. Helicopters.

A strange uneasiness filled her as she stood watching the aircrafts' approach. They grew rapidly larger, sweeping in over the arid flatlands. Without knowing why, she knew they were heading for the Thirkeld mansion. A sudden foreboding took hold of her.

She hurried back to the house and called Danny through the adjoining doorway. He ran toward her, puzzled by the tension in her voice. "What's wrong?"

"Helicopters." She waved at the lawn. "I think they're coming here."

His eyes sharpened. "How many?"

"Two. They're carrying no marker lights."

He ran to the windows, peering into the darkness beyond. The helicopters were almost level now, their rotors creating a vicious downdraught that lashed at the general's flower beds.

Danny cursed, and pressed a small button on the library wall. "Turn off the lights," he snapped.

For one wild moment, she had an eerie conviction that none of this was actually happening, that it was some kind of hallucinatory vision created by the wine, the food and the conviviality of the evening. Then the rattle of gunfire split the air and she saw spurts of flame issuing from the helicopter hatches. My God, they're shooting out there, she thought wildly. It was strange how flat the volley sounded, not deep and sonorous the way gunshots did in the movies, but dry and harsh and curiously discordant.

Searchbeams sliced across the lawn, outlining the helicopters in a dazzling glare and Caroline knew now it was no fantasy – the vessels were real, every line, every detail on their camouflaged hulls awesomely pronounced.

The two machines hovered on the air currents as their pilots struggled to land. Crack–crack. Caroline jumped as Danny fired his heavy revolver. The first helicopter veered sideways and she realized with a stab of panic that the pilot was positioning it for a concentrated broadside. Caught behind the French windows, there was no way she and Danny could escape. Mouth dry, stomach chilled, she spotted armed men framed in the open hatches.

Their bullish faces, daubed to blend more easily with the night, looked even more grotesque behind the tiny lip-mikes protruding from their padded headsets.

A fusilade of gunshots issued from the upstairs windows and one of the machines dipped wildly, swinging back on its axis like a fledgling bird struggling for flight. Caroline caught a glimpse of the pilot battling for altitude, then the man's face disintegrated, spattering pieces of bone, blood and hair across the plexiglass nose-canopy. The helicopter spun sideways in agonizingly slow motion as if, guideless, it was reluctant to move at all, then before Caroline's anguished gaze, it tilted to one side and hit the ground, its rotors splintering. In the same breathless instant, its flanks exploded in a blinding cataclysm of flame, spewing fragments of white-hot metal in every direction.

Caroline began to scream. It was an impulsive protest against the horror of the moment. She was still screaming as the second helicopter, raked by a blistering barrage of gunfire, rose into the air and tore off desperately across the sky.

Caroline shivered as she stood on the patio watching the mopping-up operation. All that remained of the stricken helicopter was a heap of smouldering wreckage. Everywhere, the General's security men were scouring the surrounding grounds. The General himself, wrapped in a silken dressing robe, sat at the edge of the lawn, smoking a cigar.

She swallowed back the bile that kept flooding into her throat. She could still see the helicopters etched against the stars, still hear the awful rattle of machine-gun fire ripping into the warm night air. It had been a nightmare, barbarous and grotesque.

Danny approached from the direction of the gate, his blond hair fluttering in the desert wind. "The police arrived," he told General Thirkeld. "I explained that you'd organised a firework display to entertain your house guest. Chief Brady seemed satisfied."

"I'll go down and see him in the morning," Thirkeld said.

"I think he'd appreciate that, General."

Thirkeld jammed the cigar between his teeth and watched his guards sifting through the still-smoking wreckage, wrinkling their noses as they caught the unmistakable odour of burnt meat. "Any survivors?"

"Nope. We've managed to identify three bodies. Could be more hidden among the ashes, but we'll have to wait for the metal to cool."

"Think it was Bundy?"

"Who else would be crazy enough?"

Thirkeld glanced at Caroline and something in his expression made her shiver impulsively. She had the feeling she'd presented him with a dilemma he didn't know how to handle. "We are grateful for your warning, Miss Force. If you hadn't spotted those aircraft, it could have been quite a different story out here."

Caroline couldn't bring herself to answer. General Thirkeld was no longer the attentive and hospitable host. Now he looked dangerous and unpredictable. His face was hard, almost as if it had been chiselled out of granite and his eyes carried a burning anger. He studied her for a moment, then said to Danny: "Better take your young lady upstairs and let her sleep this off. We'll discuss what to do about it in the morning."

Caroline was silent as Danny escorted her back to the suite. She felt his embarrassment but beneath it all she sensed something else, a hint of brutality she had never recognised before. He had lost his warm and gentle air. Now he was cold and distant, frighteningly aloof.

When she reached their rooms, she confronted him angrily. "What the hell is going on here?"

"Don't get excited."

"I want to know who those people were and where they came from."

"I already told you, the General has powerful business enemies."

"Business enemies who want to kill him?"

"Why not, if the stakes are high enough?"

She closed her eyes, forcing herself to remain calm. "The General's into organised crime, isn't he?"

"Don't be a damned fool."

"It's the only sensible explanation."

Danny looked exasperated. "The General stands for law and order. Surely you realised that?"

"Then why doesn't he go to the police?"

"He will. First thing in the morning."

"Danny, he has to do it *tonight*. Men died on that lawn out there. Even the General isn't above the law."

Danny raised his shoulders in a gesture of helplessness. He tried to take her into his arms but angrily, she pushed him away. "Don't pacify me like some kind of pet poodle. I'm not an idiot and I refuse to be treated like one."

She stormed into the spare bedroom, slamming the door behind her. She knew that whatever was happening here, Danny was in it up to his neck. Her body felt weak, swamped by her emotions.

"Caroline?" He tapped lightly on the door.

"Go away. I'm sleeping alone tonight. I've heard enough of your lies to last me a lifetime."

She slipped off her dress and trembling with anger, slithered into bed.

Sunlight was streaming through the uncurtained window when Caroline rolled onto her side and groped for her wristwatch. It was just after six. She rose to her feet, pressing her forehead against the ornate wall mirror. She had to think. Rationalise. First, she needed to contact the authorities, tell them what had happened here. It wouldn't be easy with the General's security guards all over the place but if she didn't do something, she would be an involuntary accomplice.

She crept to the door and slid back the bolt. Danny was fast asleep in the other bed, his blond hair spread across the pillow. She tiptoed to the wardrobe, selected a pair of jeans and a cotton shirt, then returned to her own room and showered quickly. Her mind was racing as she considered the options ahead. Her first task was to get clear of the immediate area. If she managed that, the rest should be easy.

The house seemed deserted as she made her way downstairs. A group of security guards stood gathered around the burnt-out helicopter, and Caroline tried to look calm and confident as she walked toward them, keeping her features carefully composed. "I have to go into town for a while," she told the man in charge. "I wonder if I might borrow one of the cars?"

He took off his glasses, frowning. "The General awake yet?" he asked.

"Why? Am I a prisoner here?"

"Of course not."

"Well, then?"

He shrugged. "Okay, take the Daimler. You'll find the keys in the dashboard."

Caroline climbed into the driving seat and started up the engine. Relief flooded her as she reached the front gate and the sentries gave her only a cursory glance before waving her through. She was in the clear, thank God, but there was still the problem of convincing the police. When they saw the state she was in, they'd probably think she was out of her mind. She'd taken a basinful over the last few hours. She needed a coffee to soothe her jangled nerves.

She found an early-morning deli and drew into the parking lot but when she got to the takeaway counter, her body began to tremble. It was not an ordinary shivering fit but a paralysing ague that seemed to seep into her very bones. A wave of sickness spread through her stomach and she saw the room beginning to spin.

A man said: "You okay, lady?"

"I'm fine. Really. I slept badly last night. I . . . ."

He took her arm and led her to a nearby table. "Sit down and let me get you something to drink."

Caroline was too ill to argue. Her body seemed limp, her mind torpid. The man returned after a moment, carrying a polyester cup which he placed on the table in front of her. "I hope you like your coffee black. They've run out of cream."

"Black's fine. Thank you."

He was tall and well built, she registered, with slicked-back hair and a thin moustache. His cheeks were olive-coloured and his eyes looked sharp in the morning sunlight.

"What happened last night?" he asked, pulling up a chair. "Somebody try to hit the General?"

The coffee choked in her throat and she stared at him wildly. "Excuse me?"

"I heard the shooting. Sounded like *Gunfight at the OK Corral*. And don't tell me it was just a firework display. I know an Uzi when I hear one."

Panic rose inside her. She brushed back her hair, fighting to maintain control. "Who are you?" she whispered.

"My name's Eric Bullard. I followed you here."

He took out an identity card and placed it on the table in front of her.

"FBI?" She examined him dazedly, her senses reeling. "What do you want with me?"

His eyes were cop's eyes, sympathetic but cool and searching. They were searching her now. "Talk," he said. "There are some people I'd like you to meet."

"What people?"

"Friends, associates, Federal agents. Please finish your coffee, Miss Force, and come with me."

Despite his ridiculous moustache, she had a feeling he could be tough as stamped steel when he had a mind to. In a daze, she drained the cup and followed him out to his waiting car. He took her to a nearby house and ushered her into the kitchen where a group of men sat gathered around the breakfast table. Two were negroes, but apart from their colour, they all seemed similar in age and appearance.

One of the men rose to his feet and offered her a chair. She sat without a word and looked up at them helplessly. Never in her life had she felt so out of her depth.

Bullard lit a cigarette and balanced himself on the table edge, swinging his leg gently to and fro.

"We know who you are, Miss Force," he said at length. "We've seen you on TV. What we don't know is the nature of your relationship with Danny Le Hir."

"We are . . . romantically involved."

"How long's this been going on?"

"Since I arrived in the United States. He's the PR officer at the company for which I work, 365-Television."

"He's no PR officer and no lover-boy either. Frankly, Miss Force, we think you are being cleverly orchestrated."

In the filtered sunlight, his moustache looked strangely out of place, as if he had painted it on as an afterthought. His jacket hung open and Caroline saw a holstered pistol strapped to the leather belt at his waist. His voice sounded disembodied as if she was listening to it from inside a hollow cave.

"What I am going to tell you is strictly confidential," he went on. "If you breathe a word of it, you could jeopardise months of costly police work. We suspect that your host last night, General Walter Thirkeld, is head of a group of screwballs trying to take over the government."

"That's absurd," Caroline said.

"Why's that?"

"I'll admit the General is a little eccentric at times, but he's certainly no subversive . . ."

Or was he? she thought, her voice faltering. Everything she'd witnessed during the past fourteen hours suggested that something sinister was indeed taking place. "Have you any proof?"

Bullard glanced at one of the negroes, a handsome young man in an open-necked skirt. "Our investigations are still at the theorising stage, Miss Force," the negro said, "but we do know that Thirkeld and his friends are trying to establish Senator Arnold Huxley as a candidate for the Vice-Presidency when Laurence Clayman comes up for re-election."

"Huxley is Thirkeld's man?"

"Correct. And since Clayman is almost certain to be returned to office, Huxley will have a free ride into the White House if he can get onto Clayman's ticket."

"Once he's there," Bullard put in, "the President will be assassinated, leaving Thirkeld's puppet to pick up the reins. Pretty ingenious, huh?"

"It's grotesque," she breathed.

"Exactly." Bullard smiled thinly. "Who's going to believe it?"

"The situation is, Miss Force," the young negro continued, "Thirkeld's running a group of neopatriot extremists scattered throughout the country and some of them are pretty important people. Unfortunately, we don't know who they are and we don't have enough evidence to nail them in court."

"Where does Danny fit into all this?" she demanded.

"Right up front," Bullard told her. "Danny Le Hir isn't simply the General's godson. He's also his personal executioner."

"That's a lie." She stared at Bullard wildly.

"What makes you so sure?"

"Because violence isn't in Danny's nature."

Bullard glanced at the young negro who sighed, rubbing his palms against the base of his spine. "I'm sorry, Miss Force, but everything Mr Bullard says is true. A small-time actress named Dulcie Chantresse had an affair with Senator Huxley and then tried to blackmail him by threatening to sell her story to a national newspaper. She was found drowned in the Californian Sierra. Witnesses saw her in the company of a young man resembling Danny Le Hir several hours before her death."

"That's circumstantial," Caroline insisted.

"Maybe. But a few months later, a freelance reporter named Elliot Behr was killed in a fall from his apartment window. Behr had been investigating Senator Huxley's business activities. He too had been seen with a Danny Le Hir lookalike in the period immediately prior to his accident."

"What makes you think those witnesses were telling the truth?"

"What makes you think they weren't?"

"Because I know Danny, that's why."

"There's more, Miss Force," Bullard put in patiently. "Last summer, a British businessman named Maurice Ritson committed suicide by blowing out his brains with an antique revolver. By sheer chance, Danny Le Hir had just spent the weekend at his country mansion. There comes a point when you have to ask yourself – when does a coincidence stop being a coincidence?"

Caroline filled her lungs with air. Danny was too sensitive to be capable of murder, she thought. Or was he? She remembered the way he had fired his revolver at the invading helicopters. "I think I'm going to be sick."

Bullard nodded to one of his companions who held a cup to Caroline's lips. "Drink this."

The scalding coffee warmed her frozen body but her teeth chattered as she stared miserably at the FBI men. "I . . . love . . . him," she told them. "It doesn't matter what he's done. I can't help myself."

Bullard's eyes were sad. "I wish I could let you off the hook, Miss Force, but right now, I'm afraid you're the only card we've got. I don't care how you do it, but I want you to go back to that house and by fair means or foul, find us the evidence we need."

Chapter Thirteen

Caroline drove slowly back to the General's mansion, her mind in a turmoil. The revelations of the past two hours had shaken her to the core; more importantly, they had forced her to reappraise the circumstances in which she had been brought here, for if what Bullard said was true (and she saw little reason to doubt the man) then clearly she was being exploited, though for what purpose remained obscure. The worst thing of all was that Danny himself was at the heart of it. Could he really be responsible for those terrible crimes? She didn't believe it, she'd never believe it. Danny might be many things, but a murderer wasn't one of them.

However, feeling it wasn't enough. She had to *know*. Not because of Bullard, not because of the FBI. She had to know for her own peace of mind.

He came running toward her as she pulled onto the forecourt, his cheeks unshaven, his face strained. She climbed from the car and he examined her anxiously. "Where have you been? We thought you'd gone back to New Orleans."

She tried to keep her manner relaxed – no sense in alerting him unnecessarily – but it was difficult to inject any warmth into her voice as she said: "I wanted to get away for a while. I needed a break. To think."

"The General's been asking about you. He's afraid you might've flipped after what happened last night."

"I'm just a little jaded, that's all. Reaction probably."

"Why don't you come inside and have some breakfast? You'll feel better after you've eaten."

"No, I think I'll go and lie down for a while. I had a restless night. I'll call you later."

She was conscious of Danny watching her as she walked into the house and kept her movements fluid and unhurried. Everything depended on maintaining a placid front. When she reached their suite, she paused outside the door. She heard the sound of a clock ticking on the mantelpiece and a plane droning lazily overhead, but otherwise the place seemed quiet as the grave. She guessed Danny had rejoined General Thirkeld in the breakfast room, but after last night's debacle, the building was probably crawling with security guards. Still, there was little point in delaying things. It was probably the best opportunity she would get.

She was only vaguely aware of the house's layout but she guessed the General's study must lie somewhere on the floor below. She made her way downstairs and froze at the bottom as she heard a security guard coming toward her. A door stood immediately to her right, but she found it locked. A second door opened easily at her touch and she peered into a crowded broom cupboard with a line of overalls hanging along the wall. She slipped behind the crumpled clothing and huddled into the shadows, her pulsebeat quickening.

The footsteps came to a halt, then the door opened and she saw the guard framed against the sunlight. Sweat trickled between her breasts as he selected a pair of overalls and headed off along the passageway. She waited a full ten minutes before moving again.

She crept through the lower house, trying each of the doors in turn until she found the General's study. The shades had been drawn to shut out the heat but through the hazy darkness she discerned a desk and a row of metal filing cabinets.

She switched on the reading lamp and skimmed through the papers in the General's in-tray. They were mostly business letters relating to an oil company takeover in California. She pulled open the drawers and rifled through the documents inside. Nothing.

She turned her attention to the filing cabinets. Again, the contents proved disappointing and she felt her desperation growing. If any evidence existed, this was the obvious place to find it.

When Caroline tried the wall cupboard, she found the door locked. She jimmied it with a letter opener and examined the files on the inside shelves. One contained a list of names and addresses which she pushed down the front of her shirt.

A movement in the passageway outside made her catch her breath. Someone was coming. Switching off the lamp, she wriggled behind the desk, her stomach crawling with tension. The door opened and Gendun came in. He placed something in the in-tray and as he turned to leave, he paused suddenly, sniffing at the air. My perfume, she thought wildly. He can smell my perfume.

Frowning, Gendun tugged open the window drapes. Caroline knew that if she remained where she was, he would spot her the moment his eyes adjusted to the light. She slithered behind one of the General's wheelchairs, gritting her teeth.

Gendun's face was impassive as he checked the contents of the open wall cupboard. She sucked in her breath and pushed the wheelchair savagely forward. It drove into the backs of his thighs, hurling him bodily into the narrow cubicle. Heart thumping, Caroline slammed the door, jammed the wheelchair under its handle, then darted into the corridor and scurried back the way she had come. Too late, she saw a security guard walking toward her from the opposite direction. They collided in a headlong crash, rolling helplessly across the polished floor. The guard clutched his kneecap, cursing loudly, but Caroline didn't give him a chance to recover. She scrambled to her feet and charged off along the empty passageway.

General Thirkeld filled his coffee cup for the second time, dropping in a lump of sugar. His spoon made little clinking sounds against the delicate china as he gently stirred the steaming liquid.

187

"She's not ready," Danny said, seated beside him on the patio.

"She'll do."

"That's crazy, and you know it. We've got eight months before the nominations and we're still in the process of building up her reputation. Launch the interview too soon and you could blow the entire thing."

"After what happened last night, she's become a dangerous liability. Have you considered what will happen if she goes to the police?"

"Leave Caroline to me, General."

"I wish I could, Danny, but that's quite impossible. We have to move quickly before the deal turns sour. I want you to take her back to New Orleans then get onto Huxley's office and set up an interview before the end of the month. Schulman will supply you with the relevant details."

"What details?" Danny asked.

"Business letters, documents, that kind of thing. Forged, of course."

Danny looked puzzled. "You're going to *expose* Huxley?"

"That's what she's noted for, isn't it?"

"But I thought the idea was to bolster his image?"

"What do you imagine the TV campaign was for?"

Danny rubbed his forehead. Somewhere below, a car hooted noisily; the sound, muted by altitude, reached them faintly on the warm desert air. "General, I must be missing something here. Are you saying we're going to nobble our own man?"

"We have a problem with Huxley," Thirkeld explained. "It's a very simple one. He's a crook. You know it and I know it. Okay, so he's already survived an FBI field investigation, but what happens when he's in the full glare of the public spotlight? There are an awful lot of skeletons rattling around in his cupboard. We have to insure ourselves against that."

"How?"

"By getting Miss Force to proclaim his guilt before the world. We'll give the media just enough time to

188

publicly disembowel him then we'll reveal the evidence to be nothing more than a tapestry of lies."

Danny struggled to keep up with the General's reasoning. He felt like a man on a runaway train, helpless, baffled, ineffectual. "I still don't get it."

"We'll expose Miss Force as a shameless charlatan who uses forged documents to destroy people's reputations. We'll muddy the waters so complicatedly that if anyone tries to impute anything dubious to Senator Huxley again, it'll take a miracle to convince the American public."

The sheer deviousness of the plan made Danny's senses reel. He unbuttoned his shirt collar, breathing deeply in the desert air. "We'll destroy Caroline's reputation," he whispered.

"So what? We made her, we'll break her."

A terrible sickness started in Danny's stomach. He hadn't anticipated this, hadn't made allowances. He'd been operating in the dark, imagining one thing, executing another. "I don't think we should do this, General. The girl doesn't deserve to be treated in such a way."

Thirkeld said: "I've often regretted measures I've been called upon to take in the past but I've never shrunk from my duty and neither, if I may say so, should you."

A butterfly fluttered across the lawn and settled on the metal railing; it sat there for a moment, its gossamer wings picking up subtle nuances of sunlight, then it rose into the air and vanished over the scrub below. Danny couldn't believe what a fool he'd been. Innocent and gullible, he'd delivered his lines with the mindless consistency of a computer. Except that he wasn't mindless any longer. And he wasn't dispassionate either. "I'm not going through with it," he declared after a moment.

"After everything I've taught you, you'd let a little piece of ass influence your judgement?"

"I think I'm in love with her."

Thirkeld snorted. "You wouldn't recognise love if you saw it walking up the street. What makes you think this girl is so God-Almighty special?"

"I know she's special."

"She's a dyke, Danny. The only reason she made it in British television was because of a long-standing love affair with a notorious lesbian."

"That's a damned lie." Danny's eyes flashed angrily.

"I have the evidence in my office. I'll be happy to show it to you any time you like."

"What kind of evidence?"

"Signed statements from independent witnesses."

"And you intend making this stuff public?"

"Every last word."

"You'll finish her, Goddamnit."

"Good. With luck, it should have the appropriate effect."

"What effect?"

The General's eyes were uncompromising. "If the girl's emotionally upset, they'll be more likely to record a suicide verdict after you kill her," he said.

Danny found Caroline in their bedroom, busily packing her suitcase. There were spots of colour on her fragile cheeks.

"What are you doing?" he asked.

"Going back to New Orleans."

He hesitated. He couldn't blame her for being upset after all she had gone through. She had a right to feel distressed.

"Listen, if it's because of that little unpleasantness last night . . ."

"It isn't. It's this place. I can't stand it any longer, so don't try to stop me. I've made up my mind."

It was clear she was fighting hard to hold back the tears. He felt a sudden tremor of remorse. All the time, he'd thought he had been helping her, boosting her career while serving the basic interests of the Movement, but the General had used him, coldly and manipulatively, just as he used everyone who came within his power.

Danny had known plenty of women in his life – some of them he'd liked, some he'd even been fond of – but nothing had quite prepared him for Caroline. He had never used the word "love" before, had never considered it in a personal sense (in fact, he hadn't believed he could experience such a mercurial emotion and secretly despised the people who did) but now he saw things in a different light.

She was the best thing that had ever happened to him and he couldn't bear the thought of existing without her.

He opened the wardrobe and took out his suitcase. "I'm coming with you," he said.

Danny scarcely spoke during the brief drive to the airport, for which Caroline felt grateful. She wasn't up to small talk. In fact, if she were absolutely honest about it, she wasn't up to anything, for the events of the past few hours had left her in a kind of limbo.

She felt a change in Danny too; it was barely discernible, but she knew something had happened which had had a profound effect upon his outlook. He had withdrawn into an impenetrable shell with only his thoughts for company. Did he suspect her collaboration with the FBI? It seemed unlikely, but so confused had she become that she was ready to accept almost anything. At least he'd lost his aggressive air, which was something to be thankful for, but she sensed a conflict in his mind and it worried her.

When they reached the airport, he carried their baggage to the check-in counter while she headed for the magazine stall. A figure waved to her from a nearby corner and she recognised Eric Bullard. She glanced back at Danny, then hurried toward him. He took her arm and drew her gently aside. "What's happening?"

"We're going back to New Orleans."

"So soon?"

"I have to get out. Gendun surprised me searching General Thirkeld's study."

"He did?" His eyes flickered. "Find anything?"

She took out the list she had acquired from the stationery cabinet. "I don't know if this is important but it seems to be some kind of register."

Bullard's face glowed. "Good girl. I'll get it analysed right away."

He slipped it into his jacket pocket and scribbled out a telephone number. "If anything crops up, call this extension and ask for Robbo."

"What about you?"

"I'll follow in a couple of days. Just hang loose, and remember – no matter how attractive he may be, Danny Le Hir is still the enemy. Any problems, push the panic button."

She tucked the card into her jacket pocket and with a final squeeze of his hand, headed back toward the check-in counter. It wasn't easy maintaining her equilibrium in such bewildering circumstances, she thought. The game was growing more complicated by the minute.

A sudden commotion on the forecourt made her glance through the tinted windows and her stomach chilled as she saw a fleet of cars skidding to a halt. Men came running across the concourse, pushing the passengers aside to form a cordon around Caroline and Danny. She recognised General Thirkeld's bodyguards.

"What's going on?" Danny asked in surprise.

"Sorry, Danny. The General would like a word with you."

Gendun appeared, bowing politely. "The airport manager has kindly loaned us the use of his office," he said. "Will you please bring your baggage with you?"

"We've just checked it in," Danny told him.

"Then kindly un-check it."

They found the office empty except for General Thirkeld who was seated behind the manager's desk. He waved them inside and motioned at Gendun to lock the door. "What's the rush?" he asked.

"No rush," Danny told him. "We want to get back to New Orleans."

"Without saying goodbye?"

"Come on, General, what the hell is this all about?" There was an angry edge to Danny's voice but Caroline had the impression that he was a good deal less confident than he looked.

Thirkeld said: "Gendun surprised an intruder in my study. An important document is missing."

"What document?"

"That is irrelevant. What matters is that I want it back." He looked at Caroline coldly. "Do you have it, Miss Force?"

Pale-cheeked, Caroline shook her head.

Danny said: "What makes you think it was Caroline?"

"Who else could have penetrated the security system?"

"Anyone, Goddamnit. Maybe one of your guards works for Howard Bundy."

"That's possible," the General agreed, "but at the moment I'm afraid Miss Force is the likeliest game in town." He nodded to his men. "Search her things."

Caroline watched in dismay as her suitcase was opened and her belongings scattered across the desktop. Even the bag's lining was stripped from its leather casing. When it became apparent that the missing document was not among the contents, Thirkeld ordered everyone to leave the room except Danny and Caroline. He told Danny to draw the window shades and switch on the electric light. A tremor ran through Caroline's body as she stared into his vulpine eyes.

"Take off your clothes," he commanded.

A penetrating coldness swept through her. He couldn't be serious, she thought. But it was terrifyingly clear that General Thirkeld *was* serious. He was watching her with the air of a predator assessing its prey.

Danny started to protest but the General silenced him with a wave of his hand. "Make up your mind, Miss Force. I have no intention of allowing you to leave until I am satisfied that you are not the thief. The decision is up to you."

Caroline shivered again, then she sucked in her breath and with trembling fingers, began to unbutton her blouse.

The guards looked at Thirkeld expectantly as Caroline and Danny emerged from the airline office. "The girl's clean," he told them. "Someone else must have the document."

His eyes were not commiseratory exactly but filled with a faint glimmer of regret as if the events of the last few minutes had upset him in some elusive way. He said to Caroline: "I'm sorry that your first visit had to end so distastefully. I hope it will not influence our relationship in the future."

Caroline didn't answer. She wasn't sure if she could trust herself to speak. The humiliation of being examined like a piece of helpless livestock had pushed her dangerously close to the edge. Frightened but trying not to show it, she set off toward the departure gate with Danny hurrying in her wake. When they reached the aircraft, he helped her up the narrow gangplank but she tore her arm angrily away. "Don't touch me," she snapped, glaring down at him. "Don't ever touch me."

"It wasn't my fault, Goddamnit," he protested.

Suddenly, she could restrain herself no longer. Her body began to tremble and tears streamed down her ashen cheeks. It was as if the floodgates had opened, and no matter how hard she tried she couldn't stop the anguished outpouring of emotion. She was still crying as the pilot took off and lifted gracefully into the blazing sky.

Chapter Fourteen

Something changed in Caroline after the Palm Springs episode. It was nothing she could put a name to, but deep down something essential had been knocked out of alignment. She had lost her equilibrium, the mental and emotional stability which enabled her to engage the world on her own terms. Danny noticed the change of course, though she did her best to conceal it. She still loved him in spite of the things he'd done, and she had the feeling that he loved her in return though she could never quite dismiss the terrible suspicion that for all his tenderness, Danny might be a consummate actor.

These instincts seemed confirmed when one morning, she was called to the office of TV executive Borden Meadows, who told her that Senator Huxley had agreed to appear on her show.

"Big deal," she answered dully.

He frowned. "Any interviewer would give his eyeteeth for a crack at Huxley at this specific moment," he said. "He's flavour of the month."

"I'll just bet he is."

She knew the interview was nothing more than a key element in General Thirkeld's baffling strategy. She returned to her own office, called the telephone number Eric Bullard had given her and when a voice answered, explained what was happening. "Don't worry," the voice said. "Eric's flying in from California tomorrow so just hang loose and I'll get him to contact you."

That afternoon, she was sifting through some research notes when Danny himself walked into her office. He placed a package on her desk and she looked at it suspiciously. "What's this?"

"Arnold Huxley's worst nightmare."

"Evidence?"

"The worst kind. Our precious Senator's been playing fast and loose with his business partners for years. When that stuff hits the streets, he'll be on a one-way ticket to obscurity-ville."

"Let me get this straight." She shifted in her chair, trying to make sense of the unexpected development. "You want me to use this material to expose Huxley on television?"

"Well, we can't have a crook in the White House, can we?" Danny answered cheerfully.

Caroline's body felt numb. In one startling moment, the whole scenario had changed. Danny didn't want Huxley nominated, he wanted him pilloried. This entire episode, from start to finish, had been nothing more than an elaborate misunderstanding.

She was filled with a sense of overwhelming relief. She'd been wrong about Danny, everyone had been wrong. The General might well be up to some dubious and highly nefarious enterprise, but there was no evidence – no direct evidence anyhow – that Danny had any part in it.

Overnight, she regained her natural ebullience and when Eric Bullard called her the following morning, she arranged to meet him at a self-service restaurant on Canal Street. She was determined to set the record straight once and for all.

The place was crowded when she arrived but she spotted the FBI agent seated alone in a corner alcove. Humming under her breath, she chose a selection from the salad bar and made her way to his table.

"Somebody's happy," he said as she unloaded her food tray.

"Why not? It's a beautiful day, and I've discovered something quite intoxicating."

"Yeah, what's that?"

"You're investigating an innocent party."

"Meaning?"

"You think Danny wants Senator Huxley nominated for the Vice-Presidency, right?"

"Sure, he does."

"Negative. Danny doesn't want Huxley in politics at all. As a matter of fact, he's given me enough evidence to finish the man's career for good."

Bullard frowned. "What evidence?"

She placed the file on the table in front of him. "Read it and weep. Huxley's been swindling his business partners for years and I intend to expose him on *Prime Force* next Thursday."

Bullard skimmed through the binder, his eyes puzzled. It was clear he did not share Caroline's enthusiasm – which was hardly surprising, she thought, for after all, no man cared to admit that he'd spent months of costly investigative work barking up the wrong alley.

"What makes you so sure that these papers are genuine?" he asked.

"I'll know by the time I get on the air."

"How's that?"

"I'll check them out. That's my job."

"I could verify them a damn sight faster."

"You?" She was surprised.

"I'd get them back to you in plenty of time for Thursday's programme."

"That's a funny idea," she answered uncertainly.

"What's funny about it? It may be a little unorthodox, but I have access to resources you can't even begin to dream about."

"Well . . ."

He smiled at her hesitation. "What's wrong? Scared I'll find out that your boyfriend really is a crook after all?"

Her lips tightened and she nodded in agreement. "Okay, you've got yourself a deal."

Howard Bundy motioned his driver to a halt and climbed stiffly from the Ramcharger rear. Why was New Orleans always so humid? he wondered. Heat, he could stand any day, but this constant mugginess was something else again.

He glared disapprovingly at the tourists thronging the crowded sidewalks. Something in his character abhorred the pursuit of pleasure for its own sake. He believed in discipline, in the harnessing of the will.

His shaved head gleamed as he strolled toward the dimly lit tavern where his men stood huddled beneath the wrought-iron canopy. Willard saluted as he approached. "He's still in there, Colonel. Looking pretty pie-eyed, I'd say."

"Is he alone?"

"Sure. If he warn't, I reckon the bartender would've kicked him out by now."

Bundy glanced at the crowds flocking along Bourbon Street. Bad place for a showdown, he reflected – too many people, too many lights – but he couldn't always choose his arena. He turned back to his men. "Okay, go fetch the drunken bastard."

Danny had lost count of the number of drinks he'd had since the evening began. If the tavern hadn't been empty, he had a hunch the proprietor would probably have refused to serve him, the state he was in.

A terrible depression seized him as he rolled the whiskey glass between his palms. It was a sordid game he was playing, a miserable and demeaning game. What the General wanted was more than flesh and blood could stand. He had devoted his entire existence to the Movement – he was, and always had been, prepared to sacrifice himself at a moment's notice – but he would not destroy the most precious thing in his life simply on the General's say-so.

He downed the whiskey in a single gulp. The pungent liquid stung his stomach and he closed his eyes, breathing in the smoky air. "Another," he slurred.

The bartender looked at him worriedly. He could see that Danny had already gone well past his limit. Danny slapped the counter, glaring at him angrily and with a shrug of resignation, the bartender carefully refilled his glass.

Two customers entered the tavern and drew to a halt at Danny's rear. They wore leather jackets which exuded a faint musky odour that ineptly masked their body sweat.

"Evening, gents," the bartender said. "What can I do for you?"

"We've come to collect our friend," one of the men answered.

The bartender looked relieved. "Beats me how he's managed to stay on that stool so long."

"Come on, Danny," the man said gently. "Time to go home."

Danny squinted in the semidarkness, focusing his gaze on the figures standing behind him. "Who are you guys?" he demanded thickly.

"Why, we're your friends, Danny."

They eased him off the bar stool and steered him roughly toward the door. "I never saw you bums in my life," Danny protested.

When he tried to resist, their fingers tightened on his arms. He braced his legs against the floor and one of the men punched him viciously in the stomach. He heard the murmur of traffic as he was dragged into the street and along the sidewalk to a narrow alley. The smell of garbage was overwhelming.

Through a bleary haze, he saw a group of men surrounding him. His eyes focused on a razor-scraped skull. Howard Bundy.

Bundy was smiling. "Hello, champ."

"Howard?" Danny rubbed his stomach. "What you doin' here, Howard?"

The millionaire's face was obscured by shadow, but Danny could see his mad eyes gleaming. "I need information. Certain things aren't sitting right, and they've got me worried, Danny. I'm beginning to wonder if dear old Walter's losing his marbles."

He held a binder in front of Danny's face. "Recognise this? It's the stuff you gave that TV lady, Caroline Force."

"How'd you get your hands on it?"

"Let me ask the questions, Danny." Bundy tilted his head to one side so that light from the street cast yellow slivers across his elongated features. "I thought the idea was to put Arnold Huxley into the White House? When this shit hits the fan, he'll be lucky to get a job as a lavatory cleaner. Has the General gone nuts or what?"

Danny didn't answer. In the semidarkness, Bundy's face looked infinitely patient. "You better talk to me, kid. You're gonna do it sooner or later and it'll be a lot less unpleasant if you make it now."

After a moment, he spat on the ground. "I guess he wants to try it the hard way. Okay, bring the sonofabitch to the truck."

Danny had no illusions about the seriousness of the situation. Though he and Bundy had always been friends, he knew the man was dangerously unstable and if he could use Danny as a weapon against the General, he wouldn't hesitate for a moment. Danny tried to force himself to think as they tore through the outskirts of New Orleans and into the surrounding countryside.

After a while, they pulled into the car park of a battered motel. An electrified sign, "Orange Grove Apartments", flickered dispiritedly in the clammy darkness. He was hauled from the truck and bundled to a ramshackle cabin surrounded by prickly scrub. The interior smelled of stale coffee and pungent disinfectant. There was a large double bed, a battered dresser and a TV set fixed into the opposite wall.

As Danny entered, a youth came out of the shower, drying his hair with a bath towel. He wore a flimsy robe that reached halfway to his knees.

Danny stared at him in surprise. "Wayne?"

Wayne Thirkeld grinned sheepishly, his damp hair sticking up in every direction. "Hello, Danny."

"What the hell are you doing here?"

"I'm with Howard now. Din' you realise that?"

Bundy came through the door, chuckling at Danny's air of bewilderment. Running his fingers through the boy's matted hair, he kissed him passionately on the mouth.

The move was so grotesque, so unexpected that Danny could only stand and stare. Wayne sagged compliantly while the others stood watching the incident with no sign of embarrassment. The kiss went on for almost a minute and when it finally ended both men were panting breathlessly.

Bundy laughed at Danny's expression. "Shocked, Danny?"

"I always knew you were a little screwballed, Howard," Danny said, "but this . . ."

"This is what made the Spartans invincible, coach. They spurned women, turned to each other for physical comfort and became the greatest fighting force in history."

Danny struggled to recompose himself. He'd let his feelings show and it irritated him. Rule one in interrogational situations; never betray emotion. It gave the questioner an unnecessary advantage. "How long has this been going on?"

"Several months," Wayne said.

"So the kidnapping was a put-up job?"

"More or less."

"You've been working with Bundy against your own father?"

Wayne's eyes flashed. "Can't you understand that I hate the bastard? He's made my whole life a misery."

"That's no excuse for betraying him," Danny said.

"Betrayal?" Bundy laughed shortly. "Walter's the betrayer. He's betraying everything our Movement ever stood for. Wayne knows where his duty lies and if you had any sense, you'd know it too. There's still time to get on the winning side, Danny."

"You always were an asshole, Howard. Now I see that you're a traitorous one as well."

Bundy sighed and motioned to his men. "Hold him."

Danny was flung brutally on the bed as someone tore off his jacket and rolled up his shirtsleeve. Bundy emerged into his line of vision, holding a hypodermic syringe. He raised the needle to the light, testing the plunger briefly, then slid it into Danny's left forearm. Danny felt his senses reeling as the drug entered his bloodstream. He clenched his teeth, trying to blink, but the room blurred, the lights dimmed and his mind sank helplessly into oblivion.

Bullard straightened as he saw Bundy coming toward him. Clad in combat drills, the millionaire looked lean and athletic as he strode across the motel forecourt. Bullard dropped the cigarette he was smoking and quickly straightened his necktie. He knew Bundy hated sloppiness of any kind and would bawl out a man on the slightest provocation for leaving his boots scuffed or his shirt unbuttoned. Bullard always felt uneasy in the millionaire's company. You just never could tell how the guy was going to react. Sometimes he was sweetness itself, but he could blow his top like a raging volcano. "Everything okay, Colonel?" he asked nervously.

"Yeah."

Bundy drew to a halt and Bullard was relieved to see that he was smiling. He was carrying the cardboard binder Bullard had given him the previous afternoon. "We pumped Le Hir full of dextrophylon and he sang like a canary," he said. "And wait till you hear the punch line. This stuff's faked."

"Faked?" Bullard blinked.

"Phonier than a two-dollar bill. A decent lawyer could blow it out of a courtroom in fifteen minutes."

"I don't understand."

"The idea is to set up a smokescreen. Let the Force girl crucify Huxley on TV, then expose the evidence as a pack of lies. Make it complex enough, and it'll take a miracle to ever incriminate Huxley again. Cute, huh?"

Bullard whistled softly under his breath. It was the last thing in the world he had expected.

Bundy spat on the ground. "Just the kind of sneaky double-dealing Walter Thirkeld specialises in. Does the girl still think you're FBI?"

"I imagine so."

"Then give her this." He pushed the binder into Bullard's hand. "Let's play along with Walter for the moment. I want Huxley to win that nomination too. But once the interview's over . . ."

The ring in his voice was unmistakable. Bullard gave him a warning look. "You'll never nail him in Palm Springs," he said.

"Then we'll have to lure him to New Orleans."

"How d'you figure on doing that?"

Bundy laughed. "I'm going to set up his son as bait."

A terrible pain creased Danny's stomach. He groaned softly as he opened his eyes. When he tried to lift his head, he had the unpleasant feeling that the back of his skull had fallen off. Nausea swept his body, disorientating his senses.

He was lying among a pile of garbage, he realised. Thirty feet away, moonlight gleamed on a muddy river. He was on the waterfront, but how long had he lain here?

He remembered the squalid motel room and Bundy pumping him with some kind of drug before the images became hazy and chaotic. He had gone through a mindless reverie with neither substance nor meaning, a voice pounding his consciousness, insistent and demanding.

He tried to move and pain shot through him. He rolled onto his knees, retching as a wave of sickness gripped his stomach. For several minutes he crouched there, racked with misery, then he dragged himself painfully to his feet, his footsteps hollow as he shuffled toward the glow of the nearby city. From time to time, he paused to vomit into the roadside.

Something rose among the shadows ahead: a phone booth. He staggered toward it, dragging a handful of change from his pocket. It seemed to take an eternity before he heard General Thirkeld's familiar voice at the end of the line. "Danny? Is that you?"

"General . . ." Danny sweated copiously as his lips struggled to form the words. "Bundy . . . knows . . . about the Huxley . . . evidence."

The General was silent for a moment. "How can that be?"

"He has the file. Some of his torpedoes grabbed me in a bar on Bourbon Street."

Thirkeld said gently: "How much did you tell him, Danny?"

Danny rubbed his eyes with his fingertips. "I dunno, General. He drugged me up to the eyeballs. I guess I probably told him everything."

Another pause. Danny saw the river blurring in his vision. His heartbeat thudded sickeningly. "There's something else, General. Something you might not want to hear."

"What's that?"

"Wayne's with him."

"Wayne?" Thirkeld sounded incredulous. "That's impossible."

Danny was filled with a bitter reluctance to proceed. He hated what he was doing, but there was simply no other way. "I'm sorry, General. Wayne is Bundy's man. They've been together from the beginning. That kidnap stunt was just a trick." He could scarely bring himself to utter his final disclosure; it seemed the ultimate betrayal of all. "Wayne is Bundy's lover, General."

A police launch chugged by, its pilot light casting patterns across the sleekly flowing river.

When Thirkeld spoke again, his voice was icy and controlled. "Go back to your apartment and wait for me there," he ordered. "I'm flying out to New Orleans tonight."

Caroline was humming softly as she let herself into her apartment. She checked the mailbox, hung up her coat then walked into the sitting room, still humming happily. A gasp issued from her lips as she realised the place was filled with armed men. General Thirkeld sat in his wheelchair, watching her coolly. Behind him stood Danny.

A tiny pulse throbbed in her forehead as a man stepped forward and carefully locked the door. Where had the intruders come from and what were they doing here? She felt naked and vulnerable.

"We've been waiting for you, Miss Force," the General said.

"What's this all about?" she asked, advancing nervously into the living room.

The General's cheeks seemed to sag but there was no sign of weakness in his muscular mouth. "I have to confess that I underestimated you. You deceived us neatly, and you're playing a highly devious game."

He seemed to have aged since she'd seen him last, but his eyes were blazing with a savage fervour as he said: "My godson gave you a number of documents relating to Senator Arnold Huxley, is that true?"

She nodded, staring at Danny in helpless entreaty. She hoped he would give her some kind of signal which might indicate what the encounter was all about but Danny's eyes were inscrutable.

"The purpose of the documents was to enable you to prove that Huxley is unfit to serve in office. Even an imbecile could see that such material was both sensitive and confidential."

A ridge of muscle outlined Thirkeld's lower lip as he leaned forward, gripping the armrests of his wheelchair. "Please tell me why you saw fit to pass those documents to another party?"

She swallowed. "I didn't. I . . ."

"If you value your life, don't lie to me, Miss Force."

Caroline had little doubt he meant what he said. "I gave them to the FBI."

"The FBI?" Thirkeld seemed surprised.

"An agent named Eric Bullard approached me in Palm Springs. He said you'd been under investigation for some time. He . . . he recruited me as an informant."

"And what information did you give him?"

"I found a register in your study. I . . . I gave him that."

General Thirkeld sat back in the wheelchair, thinking hard. She had the feeling he was being motivated by forces beyond his control, forces which bore no relation to temperance or restraint.

"This man Bullard, you must have some means of keeping in touch?"

"I have the telephone number of a go-between. When I want to make contact, I call the number and he sets up a meeting." Her voice sounded little more than a croak.

The General motioned to one of his men who handed him the telephone receiver. He held it toward Caroline. "Bullard is no Federal agent, Miss Force. He passed those documents to a dangerous and highly unstable psychopath. It's essential for all our sakes that he be dealt with as quickly as possible. I want you to call your middleman and arrange a rendezvous for tomorrow morning." To Danny, he added coldly: "You started this mess, so you can finish it."

Chapter Fifteen

The razor made muted squeaking sounds as Howard Bundy drew it delicately across his gleaming skull. It was a ritual he performed every morning and he had come to enjoy the ceremony, as if he was effecting an unburdening of sorts, leaving himself lean and fit for the hours ahead.

Wayne lay watching him from the bed, his eyes still puffy with sleep. Though Bundy frightened him at times, there was something in the man's quirkiness he found fascinating. "Why d'you do that?" he asked.

Bundy grinned at him in the wall mirror. "Makes me look pretty."

"I can't even imagine you with hair."

"Oh, I had hair once." He ran his palm over the top of his head, examining his handiwork. "Made me look like a Goddamn nigger."

"When did you start shaving it off?"

"When they wouldn't let me into the army. Maybe it was kind've a protest, like self-mutilation. Anyhow, after a while I got to like it. Looks kind've military, don't you think?"

Wayne didn't answer. Secretly, he thought it accentuated Bundy's grotesque appearance but he was too discreet to say so.

Someone knocked at the cabin door and Bundy called: "Come on in. It ain't locked."

Eric Bullard entered, his shoulders hunched against the morning rain. His khaki slicker was dripping wet and beads of moisture clung to his thin moustache. "I wasn't sure you'd be up."

"I always rise before dawn," Bundy said. "Any news?"

"We've found out where General Thirkeld's staying. He's rented a houseboat on Lake Pontchartrain."

"A houseboat, huh?"

"I guess he don't trust hotels."

Bundy smiled crookedly. "That's Walter all right. Wary as a rattlesnake. Does this houseboat have a telephone?"

"Sure, I've got the number right here."

Bullard gave him a slip of paper and Bundy examined it for a moment, then sat on the bed and gently stroked Wayne's hair. Something in his eyes made the boy shiver. "I want you to call your father, kid."

"My father?" Wayne was startled.

"I need somebody on the inside, somebody I can trust."

A look of uncertainty entered Wayne's face. "What are you planning, Howard?"

"Talk is all I have in mind. Another meeting. You've got to persuade him to accompany Senator Huxley to that TV station today."

"He's still my father, in spite of the way I feel," Wayne said anxiously. "I don't want him hurt, you understand that?"

"Hey, what d'you take me for? If Walter wasn't such a stubborn cuss, we'd have settled our differences weeks ago."

He patted Wayne's cheek, then reached for the telephone. "Call him," he said with a smile. "Tell him you want to come home, just like the prodigal son."

Danny straightened his necktie and picked up his jacket from the sofa armrest. He had spent the night at Caroline's apartment, sleeping on the floor with two of the General's bodyguards. Now, rested but not refreshed, he was filled with a sense of foreboding as he contemplated the day ahead. It hadn't been easy pressurising Caroline – he still felt guilty about it, even worse than he'd felt last night – but thank God she'd had the sense to cooperate. Had she resisted, who knew how far the General might have gone?

Danny's skin felt clammy when he thought about that, but what worried him now – was driving him to distraction, in fact – was the chilling realisation that General Thirkeld couldn't afford to let Caroline live. Already, she knew too much for comfort and his decision to keep her under armed guard convinced Danny that he regarded her silence as a major priority.

Danny's resentment against the General was rapidly deepening. He owed the man everything, he knew, but there came a point where gratitude ended and anger began.

"I don't want the girl hurt," he warned the bodyguards whose faces looked drawn after their uncomfortable night.

The men glanced at each other. "Nobody's going to touch her, Danny. This is a surveillance job, that's all."

"Keep it that way. Otherwise, you'll answer to me."

He crossed the room and tapped lightly on Caroline's door. When she opened it, he saw to his surprise that she was already dressed. "I have to go now," he said.

"To meet Bullard?"

"Yes."

"You're going to kill him, aren't you?"

He sensed her antagonism like a palpable force.

"He's a dangerous man."

"Bullard may have lied about being FBI, but everything else he said was true. You *are* the General's personal executioner."

Danny knew that this was neither the time nor place to explain things. He said tiredly: "Murray and Evans will accompany you to work, just to make sure that nothing happens."

"You do know I'm going to call the police?"

"Of course. That's why the General's having you watched."

"Well, he can't hold me prisoner for ever. Sooner or later, I'll blow your sordid little conspiracy sky-high, then what will you do?"

His face was sad as he touched her cheek. "Who's going to believe you?" he asked, and quietly left the apartment.

* * *

The morning drizzle cast a shimmering veil over the nearby trees as Bundy pulled to a halt at the side of the road. "This is as far as I go," he said. "The General's houseboat is just around the bend."

Wayne's fingers trembled as he unbuckled his seatbelt. The thought of facing his father worried him deeply but he knew that he daren't defy Bundy. The multimillionaire was wild and unpredictable. If he were strictly honest with himself, he had to admit that it was that very wildness that had attracted him in the beginning but it made for an uncomfortable relationship.

"You know what you have to do?" Bundy asked.

"Yes."

"Don't forget to be contrite. Cry a little if you think it'll help."

Wayne hesitated. "You're not going to hurt him, Howard? You promised."

"I gave you my word, didn't I?"

Bundy leaned forward and kissed him fiercely on the mouth. "Make it good. Walter Thirkeld may be an asshole but I never heard anyone call him a fool."

Wayne saw the houseboat emerging through the trees as he trudged along the rain-soaked highway. Two of the General's bodyguards stood watching him from under hooded ponchos. He recognized Chilton and Bascom.

"Hi." Wayne tried to inject a cheery note into his voice but Bascom spat contemptuously onto the ground. "The General's expecting you," he said.

Wayne felt mildly ridiculous as they pushed him against the handrail and roughly frisked him down.

"Okay," Chilton said at last, motioning him along the wooden catwalk. "You'll find your father in the starboard saloon."

The houseboat smelled musty as Wayne entered, as if it had been unoccupied for a very long time. There were damp patches on the bulkhead and the furnishings were primitive and austere.

Wayne found the cabin cloaked in darkness. For some reason, the drapes had been drawn and he had to narrow his eyes before he discerned the General seated alone in his wheelchair. For one wild, unreasoning moment Wayne thought that his father had died, then the great head moved and his nervousness came flooding back with astonishing force. "Dad?" He tapped on the door. "Dad, are you okay?"

Thirkeld looked at him, his cheeks stitched with lines which crisscrossed bewilderedly like a patchwork quilt. There was no expression on his stolid features. "Where have you been, son?"

"I . . ." Wayne hesitated.

"I missed you."

The voice was guttural, but some of the raw vitality Wayne so abhorred seemed missing from its timbre.

"I'm sorry, Dad."

"When they told me . . . when I heard you were with Howard Bundy . . . I couldn't believe it."

"Dad, I can explain that."

"It was like my whole life had suddenly come apart at the seams."

Even in the darkness, Wayne was shocked by his father's appearance. General Thirkeld looked suddenly old and weary and dispirited.

"Howard's my friend," Wayne said. "He's a good man really, under the surface. I know people find him a little strange at times, but he thinks a lot of you. And what he wants more than anything in the world is to patch up this silly quarrel."

"Bundy's depraved," Thirkeld said flatly.

"You wouldn't say that if you knew him like I do."

"He's corrupt."

"No, Dad."

"He's also a traitor."

Wayne wondered if the General was drunk. He had the air of a man intoxicated, but Wayne had never in his life known his father to be affected by alcohol.

He rubbed his palms down the back of his pants. "I

didn't mean to hurt you, Dad. Howard can be a powerful friend if you'll only give him a chance."

"He's got you so brainwashed you can't even think straight."

"Please try and see this from my side, just for once. I'm sorry I've been such a disappointment to you. I always wanted . . ." He paused. "I wish I could have been the kind of son you hoped for, General."

The deck creaked as water lifted the starboard bow and somewhere across the lake, a motorboat headed lazily westward, the sound of its engine flat and discordant on the damp morning air.

"When you were born," the General said, "I thought you were the most beautiful thing in the world. You looked so much like your mother. You had the same sensitive mouth, the same gentle mannerisms. When I held you in my arms I was the happiest man alive."

Wayne had seen his father in many moods but sentimentality had never been one of them. The General scorned sentiment just as he scorned human frailty. It was one of the unspoken barriers between them, this realisation that, by their very natures, they would always be universes apart.

"You were a good boy," Thirkeld went on reflectively. "You never threw tantrums or clamoured for attention. You lived in your own private world and I have to admit that I worried about that for a time. I felt you had few of the qualities a son of mine ought to display."

"Dad, I . . ." Wayne's voice trailed away. Curses he could have handled. But this . . .?

The General went on as if he had never spoken. "I tried to beat some sense into you, son. Tried to force you to be a man. I thought – the world being what it was – you were too gentle to survive. But I was wrong. Everything I did was wrong. I loved you from that very first moment and I love you now in a way that is tearing me apart inside."

Wayne tried to speak but found that he couldn't. Numbly, he stared around the darkened saloon. Something strange and elongated stood in the centre of the

212

floor supported by a metal frame. Its lid had been removed to reveal a lining of luxurious upholstery and his senses jumped as he realised it was an open coffin. A terrible uneasiness took hold of him. "What's the casket for, Dad?"

Tears formed patterns across General Thirkeld's leathery cheeks and when he spoke, his voice was trembling with emotion. "That's to take you back to California, son."

Danny saw a man waiting on the waterfront. He wore a faded raincoat, belted at the middle, and answered Caroline's description of fake FBI agent Eric Bullard. He was eating peanuts and tossing the shells onto the ground at his feet.

Danny felt a little on edge as he fingered the handgun in his raincoat pocket. There was no question of making the man's death look accidental. It would have to be a straightforward shooting job.

The waterfront was largely deserted, but a handful of tourists stood examining the paddleboats on the nearby quayside. Danny waited until they had withdrawn before commencing his approach. He crossed the wharf, moving quickly, his shoulders hunched against the drizzling rain. His fingers were trembling as he drew out the heavy Walther.

Bullard finished his peanuts, crumpled the bag and tossed it into the nearby river. He wiped his face with a handkerchief and glanced impatiently at his wristwatch. Then he turned. Danny cursed softly as their eyes met. He still had thirty yards to go. He drew to a halt and raised the handgun, watching the puzzlement in Bullard's face change to sudden alarm. Bullard turned, sprinting wildly in the opposite direction, and Danny fired twice, knowing in his heart his shots would miss by a mile. He clenched his teeth and fired again but Bullard reached the open streets, his raincoat billowing in the wind.

Voices echoed behind Danny's head and he saw three men charging toward him from a line of office blocks, wielding lethal-looking .38s. He swore angrily. He should have guessed that Bullard would protect his rear. Now the situation had subtly changed. Now it was he who had become the quarry.

He started to run. A shot rang out and he heard a swishing sound in the air above his head. He darted up a narrow alleyway, the breath rasping painfully in his throat. The alley ended and he saw a railroad siding where the track led to the waterfront unloading bays. Freight cars stood motionless among the scrub. Danny headed toward them, dancing over the rusting rails. The pistol felt slippery in his fingers as he ducked beneath the heavy underbraces. A fine old mess he'd made of things. He should have checked the ground before he made his play. Stupid. Amateurish. No excuse for it.

He found a wagon with its door open and slithered into its musty interior. The walls gave him a sanctuary of sorts, but for how long? A terrible sickness started in his stomach as he sucked desperately at the air.

Footsteps crunched on the adjacent cinders. They were checking the box cars one by one. He eased back further into the shadows, his finger tightening inside the trigger-guard. A spasm of hope rose inside him as a faint rumbling sound echoed in his eyes, growing louder, becoming steady and persistent. A train.

He pulled back the sliding door and saw a diesel approaching, dragging a line of metal gondolas. It was a Class-F twelve-wheeler, its blunt nose covered with grime. Fumes filled his nostrils as the massive contraption thundered by. He waited until the gondolas drew abreast then, positioning himself in the doorway, calculated height and distance and leapt forward, gritting his teeth as he groped for a handhold. His feet clanged against the wagon's underbrace and he hooked his arm over its metal rim, dragging himself painfully onto the cargo of carefully stacked timber.

His three pursuers gave a shout as they spotted him and sprinted madly in the freight train's wake. One loosed off a shot which pinged against the gondola rear, richocheting past Danny's left temple, then the engineer picked up speed and with a sense of blessed relief he watched his attackers vanishing swiftly into the distance.

The cab driver drew to a halt and Danny opened his eyes. The sky was beginning to clear at last, allowing a few desultory sunbeams to filter through. He saw the houseboat moored below, and Chilton and Bascom watching him from the wooden walkway.

Danny paid the taxi fare and strolled toward the narrow companionway, his limbs still shivering with tension. Bascom was staring at him balefully. "The General's gone to the airport to meet Senator Huxley," he said.

Something in his manner alerted Danny's senses. Both Bascom and his companion looked tense and strained. "Everything okay?" he asked.

"Sure. Houseboat's empty, that's all."

Danny frowned. Bascom had spoken a little too quickly, as if he had something to hide. He glanced at the houseboat where water still dripped from its wooden guttering, then without a word he started along the creaking catwalk.

"Don't go in there, Danny," Chilton warned, but Danny ignored him.

The saloon was in semidarkness and he stood for a moment, trying to adjust his eyes. His hair prickled as he discerned the outline of an open coffin. It stood with its mouth facing the cabin door and Danny caught his breath at the sight of a body lying within its padded interior. The corpse's eyes were closed and its long, innocent lashes framed the cheeks like pieces of wispy lace.

A cry of anguish burst from Danny's lips and his features twisted with emotion. Doubling forward, he began to vomit onto the threadbare carpet. For several minutes, he retched helplessly, then he dragged himself to the coffin rim and examined its occupant through a veil of tears.

Chilton and Bascom watched nervously as he re-emerged into the daylight, storming up the narrow companionway. They had opened their jackets to reveal

215

the handles of their .38s. Bascom held up his hand as Danny approached. "We had nothing to do with it, Danny. It was General Thirkeld's decision."

"Why, for Christ's sake? Why?"

"The kid sided with Bundy. He said there could be no other way."

Danny hit him hard between the eyes and Bascom crashed to the ground with a muffled thump. Chilton tore his pistol from its holster, his eyes filled with alarm. He knew Danny was beyond the realm of rational thought. "It was the General's orders, Danny. Nobody wanted to do it."

"Why didn't you stop him, you bastard?"

"He wouldn't listen. He said it was Wayne or the Movement."

Danny held onto his fury with an effort. He was shivering all over, his body cold, his skin sweaty. "Give me your car keys," he snapped.

"What for?"

"To get into town, you asshole."

Chilton tossed him the keys and still reeling with shock, Danny drove in a daze toward the neighbouring city. When he reached his apartment, he filled the washbasin with icy water and plunged his head into it, then dripping with moisture, he examined his face in the bathroom mirror. His pupils were dilated and his cheeks looked like melted wax. He could scarcely believe what had happened. He had watched Wayne grow from spindly child into complex-ridden young man. He had soothed his fears, allayed his feelings of confusion and alienation, and now he was dead – murdered by his own father. What monstrous iniquities was the man capable of?

Danny heard traffic rumbling in the street below but his eyes were turned inward, seeing only himself. All his life he had obeyed his guardian with neither question nor compromise, but the man he had revered was patently insane. If he could sacrifice his own son in such a desultory manner, what in God's name would he do to Caroline?

There was no longer any doubt in Danny's mind that

General Thirkeld intended to have her killed. It would not be an emotional judgement, the General's decisions seldom were. He would do it dispassionately and he would do it tonight, as soon as the television show was over.

No, Danny thought. The things he had done in the Movement's name were beyond atonement, but she was the one thing in his miserable life that was worth a damn and he wouldn't allow the General to destroy that.

He walked into the bedroom, took out a silencer and fitted it to the muzzle of his .38 Special. Then he quickly began to change his clothes.

Chapter Sixteen

Caroline sat in her office, fuming with frustration. The General's custodians were shadowing her like hawks. Both men carried identity cards and though the building was teeming with security guards, they had turned her into a virtual prisoner.

When she reached for the telephone, one of them seized her wrist. "No outside calls," he warned.

"I have to make calls. It's my job."

"Sorry, Miss Force. General's orders."

"I have details to check," she protested. "How do you expect me to operate without talking to people?"

The man prised the receiver out of her fingers and pushed it to the opposite side of the desk. His chipped face was cold and unyielding. "Busk it," he told her flatly.

The guard smiled at Danny as he approached the TV station gate. "Evenin', Mr Le Hir. You're working late tonight."

Danny showed him the film canister he was carrying. "I've got a promo reel for processing." He glanced at the security men checking the station compound. "What's going on here?"

"Ain't you heard? It's the Senator Huxley show tonight. Those guys are from US Secret Service. They been tearing the place apart for days." The guard looked worried. "I hope you got your ID card, Mr Le Hir. I ain't supposed to let anyone in without one whether I know 'em or not."

As Danny fumbled inside his jacket, two SS men came strolling toward the entrance gate, their eyes hidden behind dark glasses.

"This is Mr Le Hir from our PR department," the guard said. "He's called to deliver a reel of promo film."

"Checked his ID?" the first man asked.

"Sure have."

The man turned to Danny. "Will you please place your hands on the gate, Mr Le Hir? We have to search you. It's just a precaution."

Danny laid the film can on the ground and did as he was told. The second SS man ran a small sensor device over the outside of his clothing. "He seems clean enough."

"Would you mind opening your canister?" the first agent said.

"If I do, it'll fog the film," Danny protested.

"Okay, bring it over to the security truck and we'll run it under the X-ray machine."

"X-ray, sunlight, same difference. One shot and the stuff's ruined."

He held his breath as the two SS agents examined the canister, frowning. "You're sure you know this guy?" the first one said to the security guard.

"Mr Le Hir? He's worked here for months."

"Okay, let him through." The man added apologetically: "Sorry about the delay, Mr Le Hir. Just doing our job."

Danny's heart hammered as he headed toward the entrance lobby.

"It's Danny Le Hir," said Larry Heppler, watching the TV station through a pair of night-vision field glasses.

Howard Bundy peered over Heppler's shoulder. The hotel window commanded an excellent view of the TV station's entrance hall. He had chosen it carefully, reserving the room through an intermediary several days earlier and taking care to leave it unoccupied until it had twice been vetted by members of the Security Service. He had fitted infrared telescopic sights to their Lee Enfield sniper rifles and as soon as the TV interview was over, had made up his mind to eliminate General Thirkeld as the Senator's party was leaving the building. It was not a personal thing, he assured himself, for he was not by nature a vindictive man, but he knew the Movement could never function effectively until his rival had been removed.

He saw a slim young man pushing his way through the lobby door, carrying something that looked like a metal soup plate. "That's Danny all right."

"Want me to whack him, Colonel?" Heppler was lining Danny up through the cross-hairs on his sniper scope.

"What for? Danny's no problem. Once Thirkeld's gone, he could prove a useful team-member."

"He could be a messful of trouble too."

"We'll worry about that when the time comes."

The sound of sirens reached them from the street below and Bundy smiled to himself as he saw a fleet of limousines approaching, piloted front and rear by police cars with flashing lights. It was typical of Huxley to make an impressive entrance; the security entourage was more appropriate for a visiting President than a Senator from a down-at-heel state.

He watched the cavalcade draw to a halt and Secret Servicemen tumble into the street. They were followed a moment later by the familiar figure of Senator Huxley himself, his face wreathed in smiles as he waved triumphantly at a handful of observers watching the spectacle from behind the wire barriers.

Bundy spotted General Thirkeld being helped into his wheelchair from a vehicle at the convoy's rear. Thirkeld's features looked coppery against the pristine whiteness of his dinner shirt.

"I could pick him off right now, Colonel." Heppler was eyeing Thirkeld through his telescopic nightsight.

"Wait until the interview's over," Bundy ordered. "We'll nail the bastard as he heads back to his car."

Danny heard the murmur of Secret Servicemen talking on their two-way radios as he moved swiftly along the empty corridor. He let himself into a broom cupboard and locked the door before switching on the electric light. Then he sat on the edge of a packing case and tugged open the metal film canister. Taped inside was the .38 pistol with its elongated silencer. His hands were sweaty as he carefully checked the load before slipping it into his jacket pocket. He heard voices babbling as the Senator's party arrived. It was breathlessly hot inside his cubbyhole and he longed to ease open the door for a breathful of air but he knew that impetuousness could lead to bungling. After a while, the sounds of movement ceased and he glanced at his wristwatch. Time to go.

The passage was empty in both directions as he moved swiftly toward the studio area, keeping the pistol hidden inside his jacket pocket. He had almost reached the turning when he heard the sound of a two-way radio and froze in his tracks. There was an SS agent guarding the entrance hall.

He took a deep breath and rounded the corner confidently. The man was solid and well built with a mass of wavy black hair. He seemed surprised to see Danny.

"Going someplace?"

"Hospitality Room," Danny told him.

"Sorry, friend. Out of bounds until the TV show's over. Only folks with special ID allowed in the studio area tonight."

"I'm a company executive," Danny protested. "I have to present my compliments to the Senator's party."

"Negative. After the show, you can socialise all you want, but right now this part of the building is strictly quarantined. Nobody goes in, nobody comes out."

Danny sighed and turned to go, but before he had taken half a step, he swung sideways in a savage arc and drove his fist hard into the security guard's stomach. The man's cheeks turned ashen as he doubled forward with an agonised gasp. Danny cupped his hands around his victim's head, jerking his knee into the unprotected face. He heard the nose bone splinter and with the same economy of movement, jabbed his elbow viciously into the nape of the agent's neck. The man collapsed to the ground like a stone.

Danny paused for a moment, his heart pounding. There

221

was no sound from the adjoining passageways. He dragged the unconscious agent into a tiny alcove, then took out his pistol and hurried along the deserted corridor.

The atmosphere in the TV studio was tense. Caroline sat opposite Senator Huxley, waiting for the programme countdown. Thirkeld's bloodhounds were watching her from behind the cameras and she had been left in little doubt that if she attempted to deviate from the documents in her possession, she would be shot where she sat.

A terrible anger was gathering inside her. In another few seconds, she would go on the air and play her role with consummate precision. She had little choice. Failure to do so would cost her life. Her muscles quivered as she heard the PA's voice intone: "Roll opening VT."

Inside the Hospitality Room, General Thirkeld watched the programme on the monitor set. Beside him were two of his bodyguards, Foxton and Carpe, and his manservant, Gendun. So engrossed were they in the programme opening that it was only after the door closed that they noticed Danny standing against the nearby wall.

"What the hell . . .?" Thirkeld's mouth dropped open as he spotted the pistol in Danny's hand.

"You'll be going there soon, General."

Without hesitating, Danny raised his weapon and squeezed the trigger. There was a faint plopping sound and Foxton's face crumpled inwards like a battered tin can. His legs somersaulted as he catapulted backwards over his armchair, hitting the floor with a resounding crash.

There was a moment of stunned silence, then Carpe, cursing, leapt to his feet, clawing desperately at his Walther. He tugged it free but the weapon sprang from his fingers and slid along the ground with a metallic rattle. He darted toward the window but Danny fired again, measuring the distance with icy coolness. The bullet took Carpe between the shoulder blades, slamming him into the wall with a sickening thud. He hung there for a moment, both arms outstretched, before sliding to the floor, leaving a crimson streak in his wake.

Gendun lunged across the carpet, moving with a fluid suppleness as he groped for Carpe's discarded pistol. He brought the weapon into alignment but Danny fired again and Gendun's mouth vanished in a welter of blood.

General Thirkeld stared at the scene in horrified amazement, unable to believe his senses. He looked like a man in a state of traumatic shock.

"Surprised?" Danny smiled.

"Have you gone mad?"

"No, General. For the first time in my life, I feel wildly and exhilaratingly sane."

There was no tension inside him now, no strain, only a kind of savage rapture as if all his transgressions were about to be exorcised in one glorious moment. "How long have I lived with you?" he asked.

"How long? I don't know. Since I picked you up from that stinking orphanage, I guess. A long time."

"A very long time. And all those years, I believed everything you ever threw at me. Every damned word."

"Danny, why don't you tell me what this is all about?"

"Truth, is what it's all about."

"You resent the way I've dominated you, is that it?"

"No, I resent the way you've used me. When I think of the things you've made me do, I feel sick to my stomach."

"I made you do nothing, Danny. It was your sense of duty, your commitment."

"You're sick, General. Up here." Danny tapped his temple with his fingertip. "Somebody's got to stop you before the sickness spreads."

"Is that why you murdered three good friends?"

"Was it any worse than murdering your own son?"

Thirkeld's chest seemed to buckle as if some inordinate pressure was bearing down on his ribcage. There was a look in his eyes that was difficult to decipher; it was not hopelessness, Danny reflected, and it certainly wasn't fear, but something inside the man was beginning to disintegrate.

223

"For pity's sake, Danny, he was my own flesh and blood. I loved him more than life itself."

"But he had to be eliminated for the good of the Movement?"

"For the good of the country, damnit."

Danny felt little compassion for the General's anguish. This man was threatening the most precious thing in his life.

Thirkeld ran his palms wearily over his face, massaging the skin as if trying to infuse his features with warmth. He slumped back in the wheelchair, tears glistening in his eyes. "I've lost one son tonight. Don't let me lose two."

"I was never your son, General. That was a fantasy you created. My father didn't save your ass in Vietnam. On the contrary, you blew out his brains in the Laotian Highlands."

"Bundy told you that?"

When Danny nodded, he said: "I want you to know how badly I felt. It was a spur of the moment thing. I lost my head, that's all. The minute I'd squeezed the trigger, I regretted it bitterly."

"Was that the reason you took me out of the orphanage?"

"I guess so. Seemed the least I could do."

Danny felt no anger, that was the curious thing, only a faint sense of regret such as a man might feel on hearing about the death of an old but distant friend. The General had raised him and cared for him, but he had also used him, coldly, shamelessly and manipulatively.

"It's the girl, isn't it?" Thirkeld said. "She's the one who's got your mind in a mess."

"I love her, General. It's that simple."

"You're such a fool, Danny. How many times have I taught you never to let emotions rule your head? You think she'll have you after all this is over?"

"No, I don't. But at least I can make sure that you'll never hurt her again."

Thirkeld smiled, his sweaty cheeks picking up reflections from the TV set nearby. "You can't shoot me, Danny. You know it and I know it."

"You always were a sorry judge of character, General," Danny said, and gently squeezed the trigger.

A red light blazed on the studio door. Beneath it, a notice said: "No Admittance – Live Transmission In Progress".

Sweating hard, Danny burst inside. A handful of technicians stood watching Caroline and the Senator confronting each other across a small coffee table. Danny lunged forward, pushing the men aside. One raised a hand to block his progress, but when he noticed the pistol he stepped back with a sickly grimace.

Danny drew to a halt and raised the .38. Huxley paused in mid-sentence, staring at him curiously. There was no sign of fear in his eyes. He seemed a little bemused but not at all like a man gazing into the face of death. He couldn't believe he was in any danger here.

Danny squeezed the trigger and a small round hole appeared in the centre of Senator Huxley's forehead. His face tilted back, his eyes glassy with shock as blood ran into the hollow beneath his left cheekbone. For a moment, the TV studio was deathly still, then a solitary scream rang out and as if someone had pressed a hidden button, people scattered in every direction, knocking over pieces of furniture and equipment.

Two men came running through the swirling throng and Danny recognized Farber and Stevens, the General's bodyguards. He fired once, quickly, and watched Stevens hit the ground in a tangle of arms and legs. He was on his feet in an instant, hurt but clearly not immobilised. This time Danny took his time, holding his breath as he squeezed the trigger. Stevens leapt into the air, his shirtfront an ugly blotch of blood.

The second man, Farber, brought up his arm in a dizzy blur and Danny saw his .38 Colt Cobra glinting under the arc lamps. He fired swiftly and Farber went down, bloody spittle welling between his lips.

Danny seized Caroline by the wrist and dragged her, struggling, toward the open door. When the studio technicians saw him coming, they scrambled desperately for escape.

"Let me go," Caroline hissed, wriggling and twisting as Danny hauled her into the outside corridor.

"I'm trying to save your life, you little fool."

He saw a man sprinting toward them, wielding a .38, and fired almost by reflex, aiming at their assailant's legs; the man tumbled backwards with a resounding crash.

A stairway opened on their right and Danny charged up it, his lungs bursting. At the top, a single window opened onto the roof parapet. He waved Caroline through and she stared at him in disbelief. "Are you crazy? That's a three hundred foot drop down there."

"It's our only way out," Danny snapped. "Move."

Whimpering under her breath, Caroline wriggled through the constricted opening. She paused, peering down at the parking lot where she could see plain-clothes security men milling about within the high-wire enclosure.

Danny struggled out behind her, motioning with the handgun, and tentatively, fearfully, she began edging along the narrow ledge.

Seated on the roof, Secret Serviceman Leroy Isby listened to the babble of voices issuing from his radio receiver. His face was creased with puzzlement as he struggled to decipher their meaning. It was clear that something extraordinary had happened but so panic-stricken were the transmissions that neither he nor his companion, Special Agent Kevin Kokalis, could make any sense of them.

Isby looked at Kokalis in the neon-lit darkness. "We better check the roof," he said.

"What for?" his partner asked.

"I dunno. We better check, that's all."

As the two men started their circuit of the TV station parapet, they heard the wall of ambulance sirens from the street below. It sounded like the world was coming to an end, Isby thought.

His muscles tightened as he saw two figures moving through the shadows, heading toward the fire escape. One, Isby realised, was carrying a handgun fitted with an elongated silencer.

He threw himself into the classic on-guard position, knees flexed, arms outstretched. "Freeze," he bellowed. "US Secret Service. Drop your weapons and raise your hands."

For a moment, he thought the pair were going to obey. They paused, outlined against the stars, then one of them, moving with a suddenness that surprised Isby, pressed his pistol against his companion's temple. "Back off," he yelled warningly.

A sliver of neon lit the captive's features and Isby recognized the reddish-gold hair of Caroline Force, the TV presenter whose interview guest, Senator Huxley, they had been assigned to protect. A sickly sensation spread through his stomach.

"Do it, or she dies," the man snapped impatiently.

Isby glanced at Kokalis and lowered his pistol, filled with a furious frustration.

"Toss the pieces over the rooftop," the man ordered.

Isby pitched his .38 into the darkness and heard it land with a metallic clatter. Kokalis's followed a moment later.

"Now the radios."

When the radios too had vanished, the man released his hold on the woman and switched his aim to the two security agents. His face was flat and emotionless. "Shoes and pants too."

Isby started to protest. "Now wait a minute . . ."

"Do it."

The voice brooked no argument. Isby hadn't the slightest doubt that the man would fire without hesitation and glancing at his companion, he fumbled angrily with his waistbelt.

Red-faced and trembling, they watched their garments floating into the night. "You asshole," Isby growled, glaring at their captor murderously.

The man ignored the taunt. He shepherded his captive down the darkened stairway, his feet clanging on the metal rungs.

Isby ran to the parapet, leaning over to peer into the floodlit yard below. "They're coming down!" he shouted.

He saw Secret Service agents edging warily backwards as the intruder emerged from the fire escape, holding his pistol to Caroline Force's temple. Suddenly, he realised the fugitive was heading away from the security gate and he followed the route with his eyes, frowning in puzzlement. Where was the bastard going? he wondered. There was nothing at the rear but the Mississippi river.

From his hotel window, Bundy watched the developments through a pair of infrared field glasses. He had seen the shooting on live TV and now he whistled softly as Danny, thrusting his pistol against Caroline Force's cheek, ordered the crew of the SS patrol boat *Monticello* onto the jetty and cast off cheekily, heading up-river. Neat, Bundy thought admiringly. It was the one escape route nobody had bargained for.

Larry Heppler's features were tight with alarm. "Jesus, Howard, how many viewers must've watched that Huxley killing tonight? By this time tomorrow, it'll be world news. When the Feds catch Danny, the shit'll really hit the fan."

"That's why we have to catch him first." Bundy lowered the field glasses. "Get onto Dimitri and tell him we need his helicopter. We've got one big advantage over the Feds. We know where Danny's heading."

"Where the hell's that?"

"Didn't you say he'd rented a cabin in the bayous?"

"Tha's right."

Bundy smiled, rubbing the top of his skull with his palm. "Well, Danny's a Cajun, isn't he? Where the hell else would a Cajun go?"

Chapter Seventeen

Caroline sat in the motorboat prow as Danny steered through the darkened bayou. Spanish moss formed mournful shrouds above their heads and water lilies floated on the steamy surface. She had scarely spoken since their desperate retreat from the television building. Once, she had tried to protest when Danny used a monkey wrench to lop the high heels from her Italian-made shoes but the look in his eyes convinced her that he was in no mood to argue.

The scene in the studio was etched into her mind like an indelible tableau. She could still see the Senator's face as Danny's bullet had shattered his brain. He had slaughtered Senator Huxley in front of millions of people with as much emotion as he might have displayed in swatting a bothersome mosquito.

She stared into the darkness ahead where tufted islands formed spiky backdrops against the starlit sky. Danny appeared to steer by instinct, as if the baffling complexity of waterways had been sealed for ever into his consciousness. He knew the swamplands like his own backyard, she thought.

He was sprawled in the stern with one leg hooked over the gunwale, watching the water ahead. There was no expression on his face.

"Why did you do it?" she asked after a moment.

He looked surprised. It was the first time she had spoken in more than three hours. "Do what?"

"Kill Huxley?"

"He was a dangerous man."

"Couldn't you have simply notified the authorities?"

"With General Thirkeld's kind of money, you can buy anything, even silence."

Caroline said: "You realise the whole country will be looking for you? You committed that crime in front of millions of witnesses."

"It was the only way. He was too well guarded."

Caroline heard the trees stirring on the opposite bank. She paused, not wanting to ask the next question, knowing that she'd already guessed the answer but desperately needing to verify it for her own peace of mind.

"Did you kill the General too?"

"Yes," he said after a moment.

"I thought you loved him. He saved you from that orphanage. He taught you everything you know."

"He murdered my father and my brother. He twisted my mind and made me do unspeakable things. Besides, if I hadn't, you'd never have lasted the night. As soon as the interview was over, he was planning to kill you."

"I don't know whether to believe you or not."

But she knew he was telling the truth. He was too unemotional not to be. His eyes, normally so warm, had retreated to some indeterminate corner of his brain. If he felt any regret, any sadness at the killing of the man who had been his friend and guardian, he certainly wasn't showing it.

"If the General's dead, why are we running?"

"Because the General had a rival, a man named Howard Bundy. As long as we remain alive, Bundy's future is dangerously shaky. Put bluntly, we know too much."

"Then let's go to the police."

"Won't help. Bundy can bribe his way into or out of anything."

Despite the warmth of the night, Caroline felt a chill seeping through her. Danny seemed so resigned, as if everything was cut and dried. She folded her arms, shivering. "What are we going to do?"

He motioned into the darkness and she saw a jetty protruding from a nearby island. Framed against the sky was a tiny cabin. She recognized it as the building in which she and Danny had spent their first weekend together.

"We'll hole up here for a day or two while I figure out our next move."

Caroline sat at the table, staring dispiritedly at their empty dinner plates. They had found some canned chilli stashed inside the food locker and Danny had cooked supper on the tiny spirit stove. It had been an unappetising meal but they'd needed something to quell their hunger. Now he had gone onto the jetty to smoke a cheroot.

Never in her life had Caroline felt so confused. She loved him more than she'd ever believed possible but the real Danny was someone she didn't even recognise, vicious, cruel and unpredictable. He could smile with the charm of an angel and murder like a well-oiled machine. God knew, she had little reason to lament the death of General Walter Thirkeld but the very fact that Danny was capable of such an act showed how savage he could be. And yet, if she were honest with herself, totally and clinically honest, was she in any position to judge the man when without his cold-blooded implacability she would probably be dead at this very moment?

She shuddered at the thought of that. Viewed in such a light, his actions had hardly been those of a ruthless psychopath but of a man prepared to sacrifice everything to protect the person he loved.

Through the open window, she heard the breeze lifting the nearby trees. Spanish moss dripped from the cypress branches and the night air was scented with blossoms. A faint mist hung over the water's surface as she walked onto the porch.

Danny was sitting with his legs dangling over the jetty, staring moodily at the stars. The boards creaked as she took off her shoes and slithered down beside him, trailing her toes in the inky shallows. Somewhere far off, an owl hooted mournfully, its cry sad and discordant like the wailing of children heard through the night.

For a long moment, neither of them spoke, then Caroline reached out and gently, tenderly, took his hand.

Dawn came with a curious drabness that bathed the swamplands in mist; the sky hung like a soggy blanket just above the cypress tips and the smell of moisture was overwhelming. Bundy peered through his helicopter nose-cone at the bristling foliage below. Behind him in the rear, his three followers sat perched in bucket seats along the hull. For the past two hours, he had zigzagged over the surrounding area, following a process chopper veterans called "mowing the lawn", but so far their search had proved disappointingly negative.

Eric Bullard motioned downwards through the plexiglass canopy and his senses quickened as he spotted a tiny cabin with a sleek, single-masted motor cruiser moored at its jetty; it was the SS patrol boat Danny had stolen the evening before. Bull's-eye, he thought triumphantly.

He circled over the adjacent terrain, examining the forest for a possible landing spot. A small clearing formed a pear-shaped tear among the foliage and nudging the cyclic-stick, Bundy started to descend.

Caroline opened her eyes and held her breath, listening intently. The sound came again, faint and rhythmic, leaving a resonance on the still, moist air. Helicopter rotors.

She shook Danny and he sat up in bed. "What is it?"

"Listen."

He cocked his head to one side, his eyes tense with alarm, then he scrambled across the room and tore open the window drapes. Caroline saw the aircraft like a monstrous firefly, descending into the nearby brush. It looked close, terrifyingly close.

"Come on," Danny snapped.

They struggled into their clothes and raced along the jetty, untying the motor launch. Caroline heard the helicopter coming to a rest in the neighbouring timber as Danny fought to get the engine going. It roared into life, hiccupped and died. He tried again. A series of asthmatic splutters rose from the metal casing.

"What's wrong?" she cried.

"Maybe we've got water in the fuel valve."

"Can't you fix it?"

"Sure. If I had time, I could take the whole thing to bits and dry it out piece by piece, but right now the meter's running."

He hit the starter button again and Caroline's stomach tensed as the motor flared briefly before hissing into silence. Skin crawling, she watched in an agony of frustration as Danny battled to breathe life into their stricken engine.

Bundy tore through the jungle like a man possessed. He had trained for this a million times and now at last he was getting a chance to put his expertise into practice. He relished the roughness of the terrain as if the sharp scrub and spiky branches invigorated him in some curious way. Behind him, his three associates struggled to keep up.

His heartbeat quickened as he saw a power boat bobbing impotently on a stretch of scum-covered water. He heard the rattle of the motor struggling to ignite and slid to halt. "Gimme the Redeye," he snapped.

Starkey passed him the missile tube and Bundy balanced the weapon across his left shoulder, eyeing the vessel through the cross-hairs on the firing sight. He flicked the battery-coolant switch with his thumb, hearing a faint buzzing sound as the homer engaged. Keeping the tube level, he slipped his fist around the firing grip and sucking in his breath, gently squeezed the trigger. The tube tilted upwards with a violent swishing sound and the missile streaked from its mouth, igniting in a shower of sparks. Bundy's mouth turned dry as he watched its awesome trajectory. It hit the power boat just beneath the water line and the vessel erupted in a shattering explosion. Bundy watched the flames billowing skyward, multiplying with terrifying ferocity. "Sweet suffering Jesus," he whispered, gazing numbly at the frenzied inferno.

*   *   *

When Caroline broke the surface, the daylight took her by surprise. She'd been unconscious, she realised, and might actually have drowned just now if the chilly water hadn't revived her. She remembered hearing the sound of movement, then the world had erupted in a blinding pumpkin of flame. There had been no pain, only a peculiar numbness, like the aftereffects of a dental injection.

She trod water, staring at the blazing wreckage. She wasn't hurt, thank God, at least not as far as she could tell (her limbs appeared to be working normally and her brain was beginning to function at last) but where in God's name was Danny?

A head broke through the water lilies and she swam toward it, whimpering. Danny's eyes were closed and an ugly gash creased his skull, oozing blood into the muddy current. He was out for the count, but still alive and breathing.

Her skirt billowed around her waist as she slipped her hands under his armpits and swam toward the nearest shoreline. On the opposite side of the bayou she saw four men emerge from the thicket and come splashing noisily through the shallows. They were clad military-style and carrying sub-machine-guns which they held crosswise against their chests.

She cast an anxious glance over her shoulder and spotted a narrow water channel, cluttered with sawgrass. Tentatively, she lowered her legs, breathing a sigh of relief as her feet sank into the muddy silt. Panting hard, she hooked Danny's arm over her shoulder and steered him awkwardly into the channel entrance. Sawgrass gathered around them, the spiky stems crackling and rustling as she manoeuvred Danny deeper and deeper into the watery inlet.

Behind them, their four pursuers called to each other as they spread out across the bayou, forming a human cordon to shut off the fugitives' escape.

"What's happening?" Danny panted, coming awake at last.

She looked at him with relief. His eyes were still dazed but there was a hint of awareness in his bloodstained face and she sensed, rather than saw, his body struggling to restabilize itself.

"They hit the power boat. Some kind of missile launcher, I think. You've been hurt. Shrapnel, probably."

"Where are they now?" His cheeks looked sickly under their tan.

"Swimming across the bayou. I don't think they've spotted us yet."

"How many?"

"Four."

The channel came to a halt and she saw a steep bank leading into the thicket. "We've got to get out of the water. Think you can climb up that rise?"

Danny eyed the incline through the blood streaming from his brow.

"Sure. Just gimme a hand."

Somehow, gasping and choking, she wrestled him up the scum-covered slope and followed inelegantly in her bedraggled clothing. Danny was examining his chest where blood oozed from at least a dozen puncture holes, producing a curious colander-like effect.

"How bad is it?" she whispered.

"Christ knows. My ribs hurt, but I don't think they're busted." His hair, plastered with mud, was caked over his head like a woolly skullcap; only his eyes gave any indication that he was still functioning as a human being.

"What are we going to do?" she asked.

They heard their pursuers whistling to each other as they entered the jungle at thirty-foot intervals, using their weapons to probe the underbrush. "We've got to get ourselves a shooter," he said.

Mel Starkey moved cautiously through the underbrush, jabbing the leaves with his Uzi muzzle. He disliked operating in such cluttered terrain; preferred the freedom of the wide open spaces. Jungle smothered a man, distorted his sense of perspective and hid a million dangers, snakes, alligators and God knew what.

He did not share Bundy's enthusiasm for this ill-conceived adventure. Better by far to have staked out Danny's home in Palm Springs. But Bundy had been adamant. He liked this kind of thing. Small group penetration. Hunting. Tracking. Bundy was having a good time.

Starkey's senses sharpened as he spotted something in the greenery ahead. Several blades of sawgrass had been brushed aside and he saw footprints leading through the reddish-brown mud.

He circled to the right, stepping warily, then the leaves fell back and he saw Caroline propped against a treetrunk, her sodden dress moulded like cellophane around her body.

He gave a snort of triumph and bellowed loudly: "Over here. I've got the girl."

Something moved in the underbrush behind him and, startled, he glanced over his shoulder. Danny towered at his rear, covered with blood and wielding a massive log. It was the last thing Starkey ever saw before Danny, moving with a neat, economical, swinging motion, lunged forward and dashed out his brains.

Caroline stared in horror at the ugly crater in Starkey's skull. "You've killed him."

Danny shrugged. He had confiscated the man's Uzi and was fumbling through his tunic for ammunition clips. "It was him or us."

"You didn't need to hit him so hard."

"What did you think he was going to do, slap our wrists? Either we fight back or we're dead, it's as simple as that."

Caroline's skin turned clammy as she heard someone crashing toward them through the underbrush. "They're coming."

Danny clutched the Uzi against his hip, his eyes scanning the foliage. A figure appeared, and Caroline jumped impulsively as Danny's machine gun purred, spitting out smoke and flame. She saw the intruder flip backwards, the front of his tunic stitched with blood.

"Come on."

Danny seized her wrist and tore into the jungle with Caroline trying desperately to keep up. Spiky thorn bushes lacerated her legs and ripped the hem of her bedraggled skirt. She swallowed back bile spurting into her mouth and gasped painfully as her chest struggled for oxygen. She heard their pursuers crashing through the scrub behind. "They're gaining," she panted.

Danny didn't answer. Despite the exhaustion she knew he must be feeling, he seemed obsessed with the need to keep moving. His face was a haggard, tortured mask as he twisted and turned through the labyrinth of greenery.

A shot rang out and Caroline heard the bullet thud into a nearby tree. She spotted the rifleman at their rear. "Danny!" she screamed.

Danny spun sideways in a dizzy arc, firing rapidly. Bullets ripped through the trees, tearing off bark-chips and tattered clumps of foliage. Caroline pressed her hands against her mouth as she watched the bullets slice the rifleman's body in two.

A machine gun clattered among the cypresses and she saw Danny slam backwards into the mud, blood spurting from a ragged wound in his left side. She fell to her knees, gathering up her dress and bunching it over the blue-rimmed wound in a desperate effort to stem the bleeding.

"Get me under cover, quick," he snapped.

Sobbing, she dragged him against a cypress tree and, grimacing with pain, he slammed a fresh magazine expertly into the Uzi. He seemed paralysed from the waist down. His flesh, where the bullet had entered, carried the texture of raw liver, but when Caroline tried to open his shirt he thrust her roughly aside. "Forget it. I'm done for anyhow."

"No." Tears streamed down her cheeks. "No, no, no."

Amid the bloody devastation of his face, his eyes were icy calm. "Listen to me. There's no sense in both of us dying. You've got to get out of here. I'll hold the bastards back."

"I can't leave you like this. I'd never . . ."

"Don't be a fool. You're the only one who can tell the world the truth. Stay, and Bundy wins."

"We go together or we die together."

"No." His fingers tightened on her arm. "If I have to die, I'd at least like to think there'll be some purpose behind it. You can give me that purpose, Caroline, by leaving now."

She shook her head, sobbing breathlessly. "I can't," she wailed. "I love you."

"I'm dying, Caroline. I'm dying, whatever happens. But you've still got a chance. If Bundy kills us both, there'll be nothing left, but if you survive, then a little part of me will survive too."

"You're crazy."

"You owe me this, Caroline. Let me live in you."

He seized her by the neck and she felt blood from his cheeks running into her mouth as they kissed. She was still weeping when he let her go.

"Go now," he said gently. "While there's still time. Don't look back and don't slow down."

Bullets ripped through the trees above their heads and Danny returned the fire, spraying the foliage with short, staccato bursts.

"Move!" he bellowed. "Don't sit there like a whimpering idiot. I don't know how long I can keep this up."

With tears blinding her eyes, she rolled onto her stomach and slithered despairingly through the underbrush.

Chapter Eighteen

Fuzzy clouds drifted above the treetops as Danny opened his eyes, sniffing at the air. Rain soon, he thought. He wondered how long he had been asleep. His mind kept drifting, wandering childlike through fields of memory. It was difficult to distinguish fantasy from reality.

The blood from the shrapnel wounds had begun to congeal into a brittle crust which was something of a blessing since it had stopped the damned stuff trickling into his eyes, but a terrible aching sensation filled his head.

He was still lying where Caroline had left him, his spine propped stiffly against the tree trunk. Bad policy, he realised, for when his attackers came through the trees, they would pick him off like a sitting pigeon. Better on his belly, hidden in the bushes with the machine gun braced on the ground in front of him. There were only two pursuers left. If he stayed loose and kept his head, maybe with luck he could dispatch them both. Not that it would help him any. Too late now to save his ass. That bullet had hamburgered his insides, but he was lucky in one respect – there was no pain, only a debilitating numbness permeating his entire body.

He was finished, whatever happened, he told himself wearily. If his stomach didn't kill him, his head sure as hell would. Only Caroline mattered now. He wished things could have worked out differently between them, but if he'd been honest with himself, there had never been a future with Caroline Force. No, by God, his future had already been preordained by General Walter bloody Thirkeld. He wasn't good enough for Caroline, and that was the simple truth. The things he'd done, the terrible, unmentionable, unthinkable things would always have presented a barrier between them. Better like this, simple and unadorned. He didn't mind dying, he had no fear of it. Everyone had to face this moment sooner or later. The saddest bit was thinking of the things which might have been.

A faint rustling drifted from the woods nearby and Danny blinked, focusing his eyes. He watched the branches swivel into alignment. Someone was coming. He had to get into a more secure position.

He rolled onto his side, grimacing as spasms of pain ripped through his upper body. He hoped to God he didn't pass out.

The rustling came again. Faint, menacing, barely discernable. He contemplated firing a burst into the thicket – a lucky bullet might find its mark – but he had no idea of where his pursuers were hiding and if he betrayed his presence he would make an easy target.

Danny contemplated the landscape around him. On one side, a ragged channel sliced through the underbrush to join the main bayou somewhere at his rear. A sudden thought struck him. Here on land he was useless and disabled, but in the water he would still have the advantage of buoyancy.

Grunting with pain, he used his elbows to drag himself to the water's edge, then wriggled, panting, into the slimy scum. He felt his brain beginning to swoon as the cool liquid stung his lacerated body, and he clenched his teeth, holding onto his senses with an effort. Mustn't pass out. Not yet. He had things to do. Important things.

He saw the channel curving to the right and worked his way laboriously around it. Birdsong, chattered in his ears, then something moved on the bank above and he saw Howard Bundy smiling down at him, his machine gun trained on Danny's chest. Bundy's battered forage cap looked mildly incongruous on his razor-scraped skull. "Drop the piece, Danny."

Danny brought his Uzi forward in a rapid arc, his finger sliding inside the trigger guard. He fired once, not bothering to aim, but dismay filled him as the weapon jammed.

Bundy's smile grew broader. "Nice try, Danny. I guess this just isn't your day. Now drop the piece before I open up your insides."

Danny let the Uzi slide into the water.

"Where's the girl?" Bundy towered above him like a giant Colossus.

"Gone," Danny said.

"I can see that. Gone where?"

"Out of . . . reach . . . you skin-headed bastard."

Bundy chuckled softly. He seemed genuinely amused by the situation. "I always liked you, Danny. I wish we could've been friends, but after what you did to the General – a man who'd raised you like his own son – I guess I'd never be able to trust you again."

Danny didn't answer. Why didn't Bundy get on with it? he thought. Why didn't he blow the final whistle and head for home?

Bundy cradled the sub-machine-gun against his chest, a look of sadness entering his fiery mad eyes. "Goodbye, Danny," he said, gently squeezing the trigger.

Danny's muscles relaxed as he sank peacefully into the water.

Mile after mile, the country repeated itself, trees and scrub, trees and scrub. Caroline lost count of the hours she had been walking. She moved by instinct, every part of her body scratched, bleeding and racked with pain.

She had no idea if she was heading in the right direction or if her aimless headlong flight was leading her deeper and deeper into the wilderness. All she could think of, all she could focus on was the relentless need to keep moving. She tried not to think about Danny. She would think about him later, when the time was right. For the moment, she had to concentrate on survival.

Flies formed a constant cloud around her head and the shrubbery gathered about her, dense and suffocating. The trees seemed interminable and she had the destabilising feeling that they might continue for ever, reaching all the way to the end of the world itself. What a nonsense her life had been. All the things she'd once thought important seemed suddenly meaningless and futile. If only her father had been here to tell it to. She could have explained how, in the end, everything came down to living or dying. Nothing else mattered.

She looked at her dress which was hanging from her body in mud-stained tatters. Her Italian shoes (from which Danny had thankfully chopped the heels) would soon disintegrate; then what would she do? She could hardly move through the underbrush barefooted.

She saw the pale gleam of the bayou shimmering among the trees and a sudden idea struck her. In the water, she might stand a better chance. Here, the vegetation was so thick and tangled that she was constantly having to retrace her steps.

Whimpering, she splashed into the shallows, her feet sinking into the silt-covered bottom. The surface rose to her knees, causing the frayed remnants of her skirt to billow upwards. She moved tentatively at first, but as her confidence grew her progress quickened. The flies still followed her, but here at least she could see where she was going.

An hour passed. Another. A terrible lassitude gathered in her limbs. How long could she keep this up, floundering wearily among the water lilies? Sooner or later, her strength would give out and then she would probably drown.

Something moved in the shallows ahead and alarm stabbed her as she saw V-shaped ripples slicing the placid water. Alligators.

A promontory rose to her left, its ragged hump cluttered with vegetation. Panting, she seized an overhanging branch and dragged herself up the slippery incline. She burrowed into the foliage until she found a small clearing surrounded by trees, then she flopped to the ground with a thankful gasp and rolled onto her back, staring at the sky. A few drops of rain pattered against her cheeks but she scarcely felt them. Her eyes closed and her breathing steadied as, shattered and exhausted, she drifted into a tortured sleep.

Caroline awoke to the sound of rustling. Around her, the familiar swamp sounds had disappeared. The trees were dark and still, and some inner sense brought her instantly alert.

The rustling started again, faint and furtive. It was coming from the direction of the bayou. She rolled onto her side, staring fearfully at the scrub. Drained by exhaustion, she no longer had the capacity to rise.

Her mouth felt dry as she counted the passing of the seconds. Time seemed elongated as if the entire universe had shuddered to a standstill and everything was happening in slow motion.

A man stepped into her line of vision, carrying a sub-machine-gun. Her stomach quivered as she recognized Eric Bullard. Bullard looked different from the way he'd looked in Palm Springs. His moustache was coated with mud and his eyes were cold and pitiless.

A second man emerged into the clearing. This man was taller than Bullard and his face was long and lantern-jawed. He wore a battered forage cap on top of a scrupulously shaved skull. From Danny's description, she guessed it must be Howard Bundy.

Bundy glanced from Bullard to her, then back again. "What are you waiting for? Shoot her, you fool."

Caroline swallowed. She didn't even feel scared any more, that was the curious thing. Her mind and her body were too bruised to care what was happening to her. She tried to imagine how it would feel when the bullets entered her insides. Would death be quick? she wondered. Instantaneous? She hoped so. She hated the thought of pain.

Bullard made no attempt to squeeze his trigger and Bundy, exasperated, snapped: "Shoot, Goddamnit. Have you gone deaf?"

Cursing, he tore his own machine gun from his shoulder

243

and Caroline watched him checking the firing mechanism. There was an air of fiery determination in his movements that paralysed her senses. She saw the Uzi swivel into alignment, its snub-nosed barrel blunt and menacing. Moistening her lips, she met his gaze with a defiant expression. Let him look into her face while he was killing her, she thought. She would give him something to remember her by.

Suddenly, inexplicably, she saw his left eye vanish in a spurt of blood. The sight was so incongruous that for a moment she thought she was imagining things. Then she heard the shot and jumped impulsively as Bundy's forage cap lifted into the air and the bullet emerged through the rear of his skull. He hit the ground in an undignified tangle, bouncing once before coming to a rest, gazing sightlessly at the sky.

A faint flume of smoke drifted from Bullard's machine-gun barrel. He leaned forward, pulling Caroline to her feet and she looked at him dazedly, as if Bundy's death had blunted her sense of perception. "You killed him."

"I had to. He was going to shoot you."

"I don't understand."

"It was you or him, it's as simple as that."

"But . . . but you're on Bundy's side."

"Where did you get that idea?"

She rubbed one hand against her forehead as her brain slowly swivelled into focus. "You mean . . . you really *are* FBI?"

"Sure. The Bureau's finest."

Caroline began to cry. She just couldn't help herself. The events of the past few hours had pushed her beyond the bounds of personal endurance. Tears coursed down her face, forming little rivulets among the dirt which had caked there during the day.

Embarrassed, Bullard took out a handkerchief and began to dry her eyes. "Better save your energy," he said. "It's a long hike back to the helicopter."

* * *

It was raining in the little cemetery when Caroline and

Bullard got out of the car. Moisture dripped mournfully from the tree branches and the skies formed a dispiriting backcloth which blended into the neighbouring streets with no apparent dividing line.

The double funeral was already in progress. They saw mourners gathered around the adjacent graves, their shoulders hunched against the leaden drizzle. They looked uniform in grief, their features curiously detached as if each individual had withdrawn into some secret corner of his mind.

Bullard opened an umbrella to protect Caroline from the rain. "Sure you want to go through with this?"

She nodded wordlessly. She scarcely knew what she was doing here – General Thirkeld had never been a friend of hers and she hadn't even met his late son, Wayne – but Danny would have wanted it. Death brought all things into perspective, she thought, and despite what the man had done, the kindness he had displayed toward Danny was as immutable now as it had been in life, perhaps even more so. Besides, Danny was lost for ever in that interminable swamp. This was the only way she had of saying goodbye.

Several of the mourners made way for her on the wooden boardwalk and she stood under Bullard's umbrella, listening to the clergyman's sermon. It had been the decision of General Thirkeld's last remaining son to have his father and brother buried in New Orleans instead of flying the corpses back to their Californian home and only a few close family members had made the journey from Palm Springs.

The clergyman led the congregation in prayer. "Almighty Father, everlasting God, in whose hands we are, in life as in death . . ."

Caroline felt hollowed-out inside as if what had happened in the bayous had gutted her in some peculiar way. Physically, at least, her body was as good as new – even her scratches were beginning to heal – but her emotions were another matter. It was impossible to undo the way she felt. She would never forget the memory of Danny. God, she'd loved him so, loved him then and loved him still despite the terrible things he'd done. He would never

245

leave her, not in the real sense. He would always be there, lurking just beneath her consciousness, his lazy, enigmatic smile teasing her playfully through every day of her life. Love wasn't something you took or left according to circumstance; it was all-consuming, all-embracing, and no matter how hard you tried, love itself dictated the rules.

The clergyman finished and she joined the mourners as they flocked toward the cemetery gates. She felt no sense of belonging here. Her life in New Orleans was over. Meadows and Bryant had been arrested – an inglorious end to a not-so-glorious career – and 365-Television had been put on the open market. Soon, the events of the past few months would be little more than a transitory interlude.

A man stood at the cemetery entrance, nodding to the people as they filed toward the stationary cars. He was medium-sized and slender with receding hair and prominent features. "Who's that?" she asked Bullard.

"Stephen Thirkeld, the General's only surviving son. He works as a lawyer in Los Angeles."

Caroline looked at Stephen with interest. He displayed little resemblance to his pugnacious father. His features were sensitive, and there was a hint of gentleness in his soulful dark eyes.

"Excuse me a moment," she told Bullard. "I'll be right back."

She walked up to the man and held out her hand. "Mr Thirkeld, I'm Caroline Force."

His cheeks were pale, almost pasty, and his gaze carried a curious deadness as if some essential part of him had inexplicably expired. "I know who you are, Miss Force. I've seen you on television."

"I'd like to express my sympathy at the loss of your family. It must have been a terrible shock."

A flicker of pain crossed Stephen Thirkeld's face. "It had to happen sooner or later. He was a crazy old man with crazy ides. I tried telling him a thousand times but nothing in the world would change his mind."

He was not a handsome man, she thought, but there

246

was a certain vitality to his features – or might have been, if they hadn't been locked into that deathly grey mask.

He looked at her curiously. "I'm surprised to see you here after the way my father treated you."

"I did it for Danny. He would have wanted me to come. "Besides . . ." She shrugged. "There'll be no headstone to mark Danny's resting place. Your father's grave is the only thing I've got."

His eyes filled with sympathy. "He wasn't any good, you know."

"That's what Eric Bullard keeps telling me. However, you can't choose the people you fall in love with."

"What will you do now? Go back to England?"

"No. I've been offered a job on the BBC desk in Washington. It'll be a blessed relief to get back to straightforward news reporting again."

"Well, I wish you luck, Miss Force. Take my advice and put the past behind you. Think only of tomorrow."

"Thank you. I certainly intend to try."

She headed back to rejoin Bullard, her cheeks glistening in the rain. Stephen Thirkeld was right, she thought. The past was over. If she remembered it at all, it would be as part of some half-forgotten fantasy she had scarcely been party to. Except that some elements would never die. Like the rapscallion gleam in Danny's eyes or the crooked way his mouth tilted when he smiled his secret smile. You never forgot such things for they were ingrained deep in your psyche until they became an unalienable part of you. And out of them a miracle arose, the miracle of rebirth, of hope for the future. She was going back to rebuild her life because that's what Danny would have wanted. At the moment she'd needed it most, his love hadn't failed her.

She was filled with a sense of new beginnings as Bullard escorted her to the waiting car.

*   *   *

Stephen Thirkeld climbed into the limousine and laid his head against the padded neck-rest. A terrible emptiness had gathered inside him. It was not the simple anguish of grief, which he recognised and knew how to handle, but

247

a chilling, blood-draining sense of desolation that bore no resemblance to rational thought.

The three men seated among the luxurious upholstery examined him with sympathy. One of them, a stately figure with hawkish features said: "We know how you feel, son."

"I don't think you do, Judge," Stephen told him dully.

"We're not machines. There's not a soul here who doesn't recognise the fact that you made the supreme sacrifice."

"It had to be done, Stevie," a second man put in. "Together, your father and Bundy would have destroyed our Movement for good."

The hawk-faced man leaned forward, patting Stephen's knee. "We appreciate how tough it must seem at this particular moment but as time goes by, you'll realise that we were right all along."

"Were you right about Wayne too?" Stephen asked bitterly.

The man's face clouded. "We're sorry about Wayne, truly sorry. He wasn't meant to be part of the equation, but the General had be stopped at all costs, for everyone's good. Now that he's out of the way, you can finally enter the political arena. The years we've spent building up your image as a defender of the weak and a saviour of the poor should allay any suspicions on the FBI's part. Is the girl in position?"

Stephen nodded. "We have a friend at the BBC office in Washington, DC. He's arranged a freelance contract on their diplomatic desk. By the time we need her, she should be firmly established in all the essential areas."

"And she suspects nothing?"

"She thinks the Movement disintegrated with my father's death."

"Good." The hawk-faced man leaned back in his seat, beaming with satisfaction.

"Gentlemen, we are going to do what General Thirkeld could never have achieved in a million years. We are going to put a man in the White House."

Through the cabin window, Yvette Lazaire heard the faint murmur of power boat engines as the Cajuns trawled the bayou for crawfish. It promised to be a good season, her father said; if the catches continued, probably the best ever.

She picked up the food tray and headed into the sunlight, a sturdy girl with strong hips and muscular shoulders. Her black hair was braided into a single pigtail that hung over her back like a length of rope; her cheeks were dark, her eyes lustrous.

She walked toward the woodshed, humming softly under her breath. She was happy at the prospect of seeing the stranger again. For some reason she couldn't explain, she felt irresistibly drawn to the man. He was so elegant, not a bit like the boys who lived on the bayou; where they were rough, with coarse features and calloused fingers, he was sensitive and refined, and his handsome face was as innocent as an angel's.

Yvette remembered the day her father and brother had brought him home; they'd found him floating in the bayou more dead than alive, his sinewy body riddled with bullet holes. He hadn't looked so elegant then. A scarecrow, he'd been, with his ravaged skin and shattered ribcage, but they'd dug out the metal fragments and nursed him carefully back to health. It had never occurred to them to contact the police. People in the bayous minded their own business; the law – and everything connected with it – belonged to a different universe.

Yvette balanced the food tray against her thigh as she opened the woodshed door. The stranger was seated on a pile of straw, playing happily with a piece of string. The wound in his skull had left a ragged scar across his forehead but apart from that he looked almost as good as new. Except for one thing, she thought sadly. His mind was gone. He was like an exquisite doll, beautiful to look at, but empty inside.

She felt a tinge of sadness as she laid the food tray in the straw at his feet and went through the ritual she performed every morning. Pointing to herself, she said

249

in a bright voice: "*Je m'appelle* Yvette. How are *you* called?"

A glimmer of awareness came into the stranger's face and his blue eyes sparkled in the August sunlight. It was the only word he ever spoke, the only one he ever recognised. His teeth shone like pale jewels as he answered happily. "Danny."